Empyrean Stories
Short Tales of Empyrean Dreams

Nathan Large
and
Laine Megan Lundquist

Find us online at: http://empyreandreams.com

Published by Nathan Large and Laine Megan Lundquist through Amazon CreateSpace. Books may be purchased through Amazon.com.

ISBN-13: 978-0-9986609-5-0

Library of Congress Control Number: 2017901743

First Edition

With thanks to Sonyja Lerulv Freyjadottir for her insight and assistance with reading and editing.

Our gratitude also to our friends who listened and offered suggestions as Empyrean Dreams grew: James Moore-Hodur, Justin Marino, and Thomas Young, among others.

Contents

Royce's Dilemma

by Laine Megan Lundquist

Chapter 1

"You stand so tall and proud, and yet you have something to hide."

Royce grimaced. She had seen the two Mauraug heading towards her in the empty, poorly lit corridor. One had white and black markings patterned across its fur that reminded her of a cow; the other was a light tan with small darker blotches in a semi-regular pattern covering its body. Both were dressed in tight, black poly overalls. Neither carried any obvious weapons, but you could never tell with Mauraug.

"Humans stand tall when they are proud. We know this. Their pride is not in their strength, is it? It is not in their power... no, it is merely in their height," Cowhide continued.

Royce sighed and slumped a little bit. She turned towards the two mocking her. "There, I'm slouching. Better?"

The shorter one that she had mentally tagged as Leopard Print lifted its muzzle back from curved, metal teeth and let out a great woof of air. "You take a posture of aggression, then? You are all but admitting your guilt."

Cowhide reached out a long arm and put a spatulate hand against Leopard Print's chest. "Be restrained, comrade. Perhaps *she* doesn't know." It turned towards her. "I am Mashaun. This is Hrogki. We have stopped you because it appears that you are violating the Highest Law. Both of our sensors indicate an unlicensed Mauraug implant in your body."

"By the dictates of Dominion Sector Seven, we are empowered to remove such implants personally," Hrogki added savagely.

Wonderful. This is the last thing that I needed right now.

"You're a long way from Dominion Sector Seven, Hrogki," Royce countered.

Turning and running might be a bad idea; they could probably stun or even tackle her before she got halfway to safe space. *Mauraug respect strength, they respect authority, they respect a will to dominate.* She remembered her grandmother's words clearly. *If you're going to be among them, don't forget that. Never back down once you've claimed a position, and never, ever turn your back.*

"We're in Undesignated Sector Twenty-Three. We're under Generic Collective Law right now. You have no right to violate the person or belongings of another sapient being. You want to turn me in based on faulty readings on your scanner, that's just fine. I'll watch as they laugh you out of court."

Hrogki looked up at Mashaun questioningly. Mashaun remained impassive. "It may soon come to pass that this Sector becomes a Dominion sector. We all know that legal process takes some time… do you feel so confident that the laws of Sha'bahn will not dominate before the end of your trial?"

Hrogki hissed through its bared metal fangs. "The Highest Law outweighs all such local codes! Present the portion of your anatomy that the device has been implanted in. You have no right to bear it! You are in violation!"

Royce decided that pointing out the irony of their invocation of the Highest Law while mocking the importance Humans placed on height might be counterproductive. "I'm a security officer on this station, sapients. Do you really want to bring that kind of trouble on yourself?"

Hrogki glared. "She admits it! She admits her violation!"

Mashaun licked its lips. "I have never seen you before, so you can't hold any real rank. A low-ranking security officer disappearing in an unfinished station frequented by uncontacted species in a neglected corner of the galaxy? I hardly think anyone will notice."

Royce shivered as a bead of cold sweat trickled down from the base of her short-cropped hair to her collar. He had a point. She couldn't take two fully grown Mauraug, unarmed, on a good day.

Suddenly a nearby intercom blared with a remarkable likeness of the stodgy tones of Commander Kowalski: "This is your station Commander. Corporal Dea, you were supposed to report to Conference Room Thirteen for your presentation three minutes ago. The Akari diplomat is getting impatient. What's the hold up?"

All three froze for a brief second. Royce called out, "On my way. Sorry Commander, there was a misunderstanding in one of the access corridors."

"If you don't get up here now we'll have more than a misunderstanding on our hands. Move! Kowalski out."

Royce smiled, pulling her lips apart more broadly than usual in a not-so-subtle gesture. "Looks like I *will* be missed, *fellas*." Not closing her mouth, she jerked her chin up. "One side. I don't want to keep the Commander waiting."

Hrogki and Mashaun were silent, though Hrogki's lips continued to twitch as they drew out of the way. Royce walked past them, deliberately employing a rolling, aggressive gait. *If they were Humans, they'd think I was trying to saunter,* she thought, grinning internally. Going against her grandmother's advice, she walked past them, balls of her feet on the ground.

Behind her, Hrogki hissed in Mauraug, "Demon tricks!" Mashaun was silent.

She didn't turn to look. *Smarter than you look, Hrogki. I was close to ruining my pants.*

Once she was safely out of the access corridor and into an empty lift, she sagged against the wall and buried her face in her hands. "Thanks, Lim."

Her AI's smooth tones rang out from a nearby speaker. "What was I going to do, let them pry you open? Nope, not going to happen. Not to my Royce. Not on my watch."

"Why'd you choose the Commander? Chief Security Officer Lun might have been more believable."

"The Commander is Human, Royce. Lun's an Awakener; you know how the Mauraug feel about the fungi. It might have made them even nastier. I want my baby girl to be safe. Only the best for my Roycey!"

"Thanks, *dad*." Royce enjoyed teasing Lim about his old-fashioned paternal attitude, even though it was kind of reassuring at times. "How much longer do I have to keep this damned thing in me?"

"Only three days till Marsten and company come to retrieve it."

"Ugh. This feels so *wrong*." She straightened her spine but not the twist that worry brought to her features.

"It is. It's highly illegal. But you know that unless it's housed, they'll find it in no time, and unless we get it to the authorities, they'll never know what Shankuk and his people are trying to do. You agreed to this. Own your decision, my girl! It's not like you could take it out now without making things worse."

"Yeah." She sighed again. "Yeah. This means that you're going to be extra busy the next three days, though."

"Oh? Why is that?"

"Because you're going to keep tabs on every Mauraug on this station, so I don't have to turn you in for impersonating a citizen again." They both knew that she was only teasing; having an AI capable of bending the rules when necessary was invaluable in her line of work.

Lim chuckled. "I should have thought of that already. Don't worry; no one's gonna lay a hand on my Roycey!"

Chapter 2

Chief Security Officer Lun watched through the eyes of his mindless Vessel as Corporal Royce Dea walked into his office. The office itself was small, the walls grey and unadorned, his desk barely functional and more a matter of formality than anything else.

Lun gestured to the chair in front of the desk. "Please sit."

Corporal Dea pulled the chair back and sat down. Her lips were pressed together and her eyes were focused on his. He noted her right knee was bobbing up and down gently… a gesture he understood to be one of restrained energy among Humans, likely revealing some sort of apprehension.

"Corporal Dea, yesterday at 13:23 you were seen travelling through access corridor fourteen on level seven, and were witnessed conversing with two Mauraug civilian visitors, Mashaun bash'Ugan and Hrogki bash'Shumal. Please enlighten me as to the nature of your conversation."

Dea's forehead wrinkled and she twisted her mouth to one side, then spoke, "They were taunting me, sir. I was concerned that they were planning some sort of physical violence and got away as quickly as I could."

"I see," said Lun. He did not, of course. Lun, like all Awakeners, considered verbal language a series of dangerously inaccurate sonic symbols. These symbols, or "words", were frustrating in their inability to convey meaning, as each one had many associations that changed based on context in relation to other symbols, the Other Mind employing them, and current events. Nevertheless, Lun understood that idiomatic speech was comforting to those who had no better way to communicate.

There was an awkward silence. Lun's threadlike rhizomes, which emerged from his Vessel's bodily orifices, writhed impatiently. He decided to break the silence. "Corporal Dea, this inquest would be best served by your allowing me to interact with you on a psychic level. Would you consent to sharing your perspective directly with me?" He hoped that this was phrased in an inoffensive fashion.

Dea raised her eyebrows. "Chief, I would really prefer that you didn't. I've done it before, and it was really uncomfortable."

Is this one hiding something, or is it truly uncomfortable with the process? There is no way to know! The frustration was endemic to relations with Other Minds. Other Minds rarely had any skill at true communication and were often suspicious of it, forcing Awakeners to navigate the treacherous waters of language and deal with the concept of "trust". Lun was aware of trust but, like most of his kind, had been rather appalled when he was first briefed on it.

Direct approaches are helpful in garnering trust, Lun reminded himself.

"I am questioning you on this occurrence because Detective Ushkar bash'Torkul located the body of Hrogki bash'Shumal at 02:00 this morning. Attempts to find and locate Mashaun bash'Ugan have yielded no results. You are the last person Hrogki bash'Shumal was witnessed communicating with."

Dea's eyes grew wide, a misplaced reaction based on an evolutionary path that involved evading predators, still applied to moments of surprise, fear, or shock. "Chief, may I ask who witnessed us?"

"That is not pertinent to this investigation. Information that would lead me to an understanding of Hrogki bash'Shumal's violent death is pertinent. If you will not consent to direct communication, please convey any pertinent information vocally." Lun immediately realized that he had slipped out of idiomatic speech, and his rhizomes fell a little in despair. Humans referred to that as being "cold", an idiom that Lun certainly comprehended. Cold forced one to withdraw to warmth, and for warm blooded beings, that meant pulling inward.

"Yesterday was the first and last time I saw either of them. They saw me in the hallway, they threatened me, and I got away as quickly as I could. Can't you, you know, still talk to Hrogki?"

Royce's Dilemma

"I… the… resonance? Not… complete…" Lun floundered, searching for appropriate terminology. In many cases, it was possible for an Awakener to gather information from the psychic resonance of the deceased for a short time after their death. The language being used had no symbols that properly conveyed the reason that he was incapable of accomplishing this feat.

"That was not possible this time. Why did they threaten you, Officer Dea?"

Dea swallowed sharply, another physical sign of emotional distress. Even without interfacing with her he felt waves of uncertainty and fear rolling off her. *Good.* He had found something important. She glanced back and forth and seemed to chew the inside of her lips.

"Please respond to my question vocally, Corporal."

She squared her shoulders, straightened her spine, and made direct eye contact. Lun sensed certitude. "They claimed that their scanners showed that I was bearing an unlicensed Mauraug implant, and they wanted to cut it out of me, sir."

"Are you bearing any unlicensed Mauraug cybernetics?"

Her gaze didn't waver. "Yes."

Lun was genuinely surprised. It was not something that he'd expected of her. "Why? Have you allowed the licensing to lapse, or was it implanted illegally?"

She grew quiet again, and Lun's rhizomes again writhed in the dance of frustration. She looked down, staring at the blank surface of his desk, and he received wave after wave of conflicted emotions from her. She looked back up.

"All right, Chief. You can read my mind."

Lun frowned, amused that he found himself mimicking her gestures with his Vessel. "Are you giving me consent to engage in true communication with you?"

"Yes. I give you consent. Just read my mind and get it over with. It's better this way."

Chief Security Officer Lun smiled warmly at her. "Yes, yes, it will be. Thank you, Corporal Dea."

Lun's attention withdrew almost completely from the physical senses that his Vessel gave him, and he followed the trails of emotion to their source. Royce Dea sparkled, scintillating, a colorful, quick-acting sentience. Lun pressed the surface of his ego against hers and the membranes that separated one mind from another grew thin.

If Lun used his Vessel to unconsciously express his emotional state like other sentient species did, he would have sighed and sunk into his chair. *This, this is the reason that we are. This union. This intimacy. This understanding. How can the Other Minds not feel the pleasure of it? How can they not feel the joy of communion as we do?*

He could feel her struggling unconsciously against his gentle pressure. Even though she had given consent, it was difficult for her to truly relax in the communion. He felt a pang of sorrow for her, and resolved to speak to her about Awakening her once this business was over. He deliberately displayed the pleasure that he took in the act to her, psychically, but was confused when she reacted with disgust and distrust. How could you not trust someone who was so completely connected to you? He despaired of ever truly understanding the Other Minds.

He could not allow his inborn urge to commune with and Awaken Other Minds to get in the way of his duty to the Collective, though. He relented and, in a blissfully wordless fashion, prompted her to reveal the information about the cybernetic implant. She brought it to the surface, and what he witnessed was of such gravity that he quickly withdrew that line of inquiry and pressed her gently on the two Mauraug.

Her words had not been inaccurate. She had no association with them but the threatening conversation. Lun empathized with the fear and distress she experienced and resonated with it, showing her a mirror made of himself, displaying that he truly understood how she had felt. He transmitted his sorrow that she had to experience it. Then he withdrew from the communion, his questions answered.

Corporal Royce Dea drew a shuddering breath and opened her eyes. Though they were no longer in communion, Lun still felt her emotions more keenly than before. Surprise, relief, and a small touch of pleasure... quickly replaced with vindication and anger. His rhizomes curled back on themselves and nearly withdrew into his Vessel's eyes, ears, nose and mouth at the shocking intensity.

"That little shit," Dea said. "That little Ningyo pissant. I'll wring his mechanical neck."

It took a moment for Lun to digest what she was trying to convey. She had obviously been probing him back surreptitiously during the communion. *How could she do that, unAwakened as she was?* The Ningyo that called himself Tacky was indeed the one who reported her conversation with the Mauraug to Lun.

"You will do no such thing, Corporal. He has been most helpful in this investigation, and that would be a violation of the law that you have sworn to uphold." *Law. Such an inadequate method for preventing unnecessary conflict. Still, it's the best the poor creatures have. For now.*

"Yes, Chief. You're right. I won't. But I will be giving him a piece of my mind. Am I excused?"

Chief Security Officer Lun nodded silently as she rose and took her leave, considering the implications behind her idiom.

Chapter 3

EeSuJhun carefully drove the device into the plant's soil pod. The business end of the device was small and rectangular, no longer than her hand and no wider than her finger, and was colored the same metallic grey as her skin. A fine gridwork covered the tip of the device. She gripped the handle tightly and squeezed one of the buttons and waited.

She didn't have to wait long. A series of small popping, squealing sounds erupted from the soil, followed by a few thin wisps of smoke. She let out a yelping laugh of triumph and pulled the wand out of the soil as carefully as she had inserted it, gratified at the scorch marks along the side. *Hmmm, didn't take the carbonization into account. It shouldn't affect the quality, at least not yet. I can clean it... can I make it self-cleaning? Maybe a neutralizing pulse to shed the ash? I'm wasting good carbon here, carbon that these little beauties will love.* She continued to work out the minutiae of a self-cleaning function as she worked the soil with the wand methodically in a pattern that was sure to clear out all but the luckiest of grubs.

So engrossed in her work was she that she didn't notice the sleek reptilian figure move up behind her. Nor did she note when it snapped its beaked jaws quietly a few times, trying to call for attention. She did notice the gentle pressure as it placed one of its long-fingered hands on her shoulder. Without looking away from her work, she asked, "*Oya?*"

"MiSanTu, Structural Engineer Third Class, I have found your missing ID."

EeSuJhun frowned and scoffed as she continued to work. "Not me. Ee-SuJhun, Botanical Technician. *Second* Class, if you please. Don't know MiSan-Tu. Sorry."

There was a pause. *Hopefully it's gone. Can't it see that I'm working here?* She harrumphed dismissively as she carefully maneuvered the wand around the plant's delicate root structure.

There was another clacking behind her, and then a shadow fell across her face. She looked up to see what was blocking her light, and saw the crested, beaked head of a Vislin, dressed in an unassuming harness.

Vislin, client race of the Great Family. Good visual artists. Cowards. That was about the limit of her knowledge of and interest in the Vislin. Zig didn't really tend to care much about other species; they weren't Zig, so they were mentally inferior and thus uninteresting.

Its crest is *pretty, though,* she mused, watching it refract the white station light in a cascade of muted, scintillating colors. *Vislin crests – has anyone ever tried using one for lighting? I know their skin can do odd things with visible bands – must look it up when I'm back at my quarters.* She went back to focusing on the soil pod, and tried shifting a bit for better lighting.

It wasn't happening. The Vislin was squarely in the way of her illumination. *Hmmm, might be useful to have a hat made of their crest material, or an analogue. Something that would let me see details if this happens again. Spotlight would be too bright; maybe refraction would be a better trick.*

EeSuJhun, annoyed, reflected again that it would have to wait until she was off duty… which could be a lot longer if this Dearthing lizard didn't leave her alone.

"EeSuJhun, I am aware of you. I know that you are not MiSanTu. Nevertheless, I have his ID."

"What, just because we're both Zig, you think we know each other?" Scoff, grunt. "It's not like we're Tesetsi. Know how many Zig work on this station?"

"I am under no illusions that you know one another. As a matter of fact, I rather hoped that you didn't."

What the Dearth was this thing getting at? Scoff. "I'm busy."

"I can see that."

"Then why don't you leave me alone?"

"Are you familiar with Ta-trisk bulbs?"

That got her attention. Ta-trisk bulbs were amazing! A Tesetsi creation, of course, they were plant bulbs with programmable genetics. You didn't need a lab to make them grow into just about any sort of plant that you pleased. Just apply the right kind of light, soil composition, gravity and environment, and the possibilities were almost limitless. Of course, they were expensive. So expensive that EeSuJhun knew that she'd probably never be able to afford one. She sat back on the ground, cross-legged, and looked up at her suddenly interesting intruder.

"Yeah, I know Ta-trisk bulbs."

The Vislin cocked its head to one side and focused its large, reddish-black eyes directly on hers. "I have three in stasis on my person. Are you interested in receiving them?"

Snort. "Of course, I am! I know I can't afford one, and you're trying to push someone else's ID on me. So, you want me to do something stupid with someone else's ID. I get that. I'm Zig, remember?" She grasped both sides of her shaven head with her hands. "Smart. Probably smarter than you and your mother."

The Vislin made no sign of offense, but their kind was not given to obvious displays of emotion. "I am pleased that you grasp the situation. All I ask is for you to go to a particular stateroom and perform a structural examination of the wall, using the ID and a device that I will provide for you."

"Yeah, getting caught's not worth it." In the brig, they took away anything that you could work on or with. That was the very definition of Dearth to a Zig. EeShuJhun snarled quietly with distaste.

"Is it worth three Ta-trisk bulbs? One such would be outside of the pay grade of a Botany Engineer of *any* Class, unless you happened upon an injured Taratumm."

Royce's Dilemma

Seeing EeSuJhun's look of confusion, it clarified: "An unexpected fortune, such as I am offering."

Snort. "Find another patsy. Station monitors will catch me. Not worth it."

The Vislin raised its beak slightly and stroked the side of its face. "I would have thought you had *some* computer skills. It wouldn't take much to redirect the cameras. I didn't imagine that a simple feat of engineering like that would be outside of your reach."

Harrumph. "I'm Iron Caste, scaly; have been since I came of age. You obviously don't know much about Zig, so let me enlighten you: Irons make things work. Not people, not ideas, *things*. Show me an Iron Caste that doesn't know how to make a computer work and I'll show you a hairless Human slathered in metal paint. I could make a couple of hallway cams get dressed up and dance if I wanted. *If* I wanted. I want the bulbs, but I'm no idiot. I have no reason to trust you. I don't know you from AaMaTah, and I don't *want* to know you. So take your bulbs and your stolen ID and go find some Hrotata ass to kiss or whatever it is you do in your spare time. And get the Dearth out of my light, I'm BUSY!" Snort.

The Vislin held still through her tirade, and then leaned down towards her, its crested head and razor sharp beak filling her field of vision. "Very well, Ee-SuJhun. Farewell." There was something deeply uncomfortable about the way that it stared at her for a long moment before it straightened up and moved out of her light. She heard it slink away, shuddered, and went back to her gardening.

No wonder they're still a slave race. Client race. Whatever. Idiots.

A few moments later she was distracted again from her reverie by a hollow voice calling out from behind her: "What's this I hear about Ta-trisk bulbs?"

That's it! I swear, whoever that is...

She grunted in frustration and spun around. "I'M TRYING TO..." She trailed off as she saw the Vislin directly behind her, clutching what looked like a thin wire between its hands. The wire was wrapped tightly around its palms and gripped in its clawed fingers, and was positioned right above where her head had been just a second ago.

The voice had come not from the Vislin, but from a small, white, somewhat Zig-shaped figure. Its joints were grooved and obviously mechanical and its face had large, black, slanted eyes, a tiny suggestion of a nose, and a small mouth frozen in a perpetual enigmatic grin. The Ningyo was standing not far from the entrance to the nursery.

"…work…" EeSuJhun trailed off. A tiny mewl of distress escaped her throat.

The tableau remained frozen for the span of a couple of very tense heart-beats, and in a swirl the Vislin dropped to all fours and skittered smoothly away, past the Ningyo and out the door, its skin changing color to match the floor below. EeSuJhun swallowed and rubbed her throat, her eyes flickering between the Ningyo and the door that her would-be assailant just scrambled out of.

The Ningyo trotted forward to within a meter or so of her and gave a salute. Its voice was hollow and sounded pre-recorded, and there was a mocking quality to its tone. "I'm Tacky, and let me guess… you… you must be… welcome!"

Chapter 4

Hrawf had just gotten off duty an hour ago. He had a nice hot shower to energize his cold-blooded metabolism and planned on stepping back out of his quarters to head up to the Legless Thrathumm for a few rounds of drink and song before preparing for sleep. He stepped out of his shower, steam still rising off of the thick, horny scales on his back, when his intercom buzzed.

"This is Sergeant Hrrkil. Officer Hrawf, we need you down on Level Twelve on the double. Meet up with Officer Klsk at the juncture of residential corridors Eight and Fifteen. Someone is screaming in stateroom 8-23 and you're the closest Security people we have. I'll be down behind shortly with a medic."

Hrawf sighed, letting his massive shoulders settle. "Yes, sir. Going now."

Sensing the urgency in the Sergeant's voice, he donned his body armor with a speed uncharacteristic for his kind and headed towards his door. He glanced at his reflection in the mirror on the back of the door before opening it. He saw a handsome young male Taratumm, with gleaming yellow-green scales and a small, wide head with a broad beak and laterally set eyes. He looked positively strapping. Hrawf bobbed his head in approval briefly before sliding his door open and thudding down the residential hallways to his rendezvous.

Klsk was already at the junction, looking agitated. His normally bright crest was smudged with what looked like ash or char and he kept shifting back and forth on his feet, his whip-like Vislin tail twitching back and forth. "Finally here. Speed, Hrawf, we must make with speed."

Hrawf grunted and nodded. He was used to the Vislin on the station taunting him and the other Taratumm about their gait. Taratumm might be slower and far less agile than the predatory Vislin, but made up for it with raw muscle mass and thickly armored scales. The rivalry between their species, initiated in the ancient past of their shared homeworld, had never entirely faded but instead changed form, from violent conflict to constant insults and one-upmanship.

Hrawf didn't care what any Vislin thought of him. They were shifty tail-kissers descended from cowardly marauders who had nearly decimated his ancestors. They didn't understand honor, or compassion, or friendship, just loyalty to their chosen pack and greed for approval and praise.

Hrawf and Klsk made their way down Corridor Eight to the stateroom indicated by the Sergeant. Hrawf heard a muffled cry of pain through the solid door. His sensitive ears recognized the voice as Human and belonging to a superior, Corporal Dea.

Klsk dashed forward and tried the door. It beeped as though it was opening, but didn't budge. "It's stuck. We'll have to wait for reinforcements. Call the Sergeant and let him know that we need a ram."

Hrawf shook his head. "No." He focused his voices, trying to generate a vibration that would reach clearly to the inside of the room: "Stay clear, Corporal Dea. Coming in. Breaking door."

Klsk shook his head violently. "You're going to try and break down a Zig made door with nothing but your bulk? Fine, when she dies for lack of aid you can tell her family." He crossed his arms and stood back.

Why isn't he calling the Sergeant, then? Hrawf wondered as he squared his shoulders, waggled his hips, and charged the door head-first.

The massive impact of his nearly 300-kilo frame against the door was mostly absorbed by his powerful spine (even modern Taratumm rammed one another in play or mock duels on occasion) and Hrawf felt the door buckle. He took a step back and focused forward with one eye, scanning the corridor for the approaching Sergeant with the other. The door had a huge dent in it, and there was a small gap where the blow had pulled it a bit away from the frame. Hrawf shifted his angle, wiggled his hips once more, and charged again.

Royce's Dilemma

This time, he was rewarded with a crash and the sound of tearing metal as he staggered through the opening he had created into a room that was not designed for someone of his bulk. Corporal Dea lay in front of him on her bed in a leotard, her face red and screwed up in pain, her hands clutching her left thigh. Following her arms, he found a patch of skin, not much larger than the palm of one of her hands, bubbling as though from internal heat.

Klsk dashed in. "We'll have to amputate it. Now!" He pulled a long, thin utility blade out of his harness.

This reaction seemed wrong to Hrawf. Very wrong. "No. Wait for medics," he said, stamping a massive foot.

Klsk's tail whipped hard. It lashed against Hrawf, who barely felt it through his body armor and scales. "No time for that. No time anymore. It's going to explode!"

"Whaaaat?" Hrawf was feeling even more confused. Explode? Why would her leg explode? How did Klsk know her leg would explode?

"Wait!" he roared as Klsk lashed out and downwards with the thin, ultra-sharp blade, severing Officer Dea's leg very close to the hip.

"NO! WRONG!" Hrawf reached out with one massive hand and clamped down on the remaining stub of Royce's leg with all of his might. He thought that he felt bone crunch, but his powerful grip managed to stop the massive arterial spurting almost before it began. Baffled, he looked at Klsk, who held the Human's leg by the ankle. Red circulatory fluid was spraying out of the other end of it, and Klsk ducked halfway around the door, looked around, and hurled the leg out of sight. He ducked back around the door frame and covered his head with his bloodstained hands.

No explosion came. Hrawf, dazed, confused, and terrified, reached out with his other hand and grasped the Vislin's torso, gripping it three-quarters of the way around. This time, he *did* feel bone crunch.

"Why, Klsk, why?" he roared. Hrawf barely noticed that his feet were stomping at the floor, and that his body was starting to grow warmer.

The reptilian creatures of their shared homeworld had adapted to dangers of their planet's long nights through a unique mechanism. Though they would fall into torpor during the long, cold nights caused by their world's slow rotation, danger stimuli would provoke a series of short-term metabolic changes that would cause their bodies to begin to heat internally. It was usually enough for a quick response, a fight or flight. Neither the Vislin nor the Taratumm had entirely evolved past this frenzied danger response, and as a result were prone to occasionally falling into an atavistic fugue of terror or rage.

Just such a rage response was being invoked in Hrawf now. Klsk, writhing in pain and seeing an image that plagued his species' nightmares for untold generations – the Taratumm Battle-Dance – began to shriek in terror and jerk about in Hrawf's hand, struggling to get free. One of Hrawf's eyes was focused on Klsk, the other rolling madly, seeking any other potential dangers for him to direct his frenzy.

"My life is my clan. You are my clan. We are the Family. My life is my clan. You are my Clan. We are the Family..." Royce, despite the massive trauma she was enduring, was speaking through shuddering gasps of pain, repeating words in passable though heavily accented Hrotata.

A figure stepped into the door frame and Hrawf almost lunged at it until he saw who and what it was. A small, furry creature, with large, expressive eyes, a wet and mobile nose and long, twitching whiskers. It was speaking along with Dea, chanting: "My life is my clan. You are my Clan. We are the Family."

Hrawf shut his eyes. It was hard to do, one of the hardest things he had ever done, but he did, because he knew that was what you were supposed to do when the Chant was being enacted. You shut your eyes, and tried not to move, and focused on the words. You tried to say the words, even if the rage was making your jaw try to lock shut, even though your lungs were working like a bellows.

"My life is my CLAN! YOU ARE CLAN! WE ARE FAMILY!" he roared.

Slowly, Hrawf began to feel the rage response lessen. Slowly, he felt his limbs cool, and even his core began to cool a little. He dropped to his knees, grip still firm on both parties, ashamed. He continued the chant as he heard other sapients come in and felt them work on Officer Dea and gently extract her from one of his hands. He continued the chant as he felt Klsk pried from his grasp and vaguely heard him being led away. He continued the chant until the only person in the room with him was Sergeant Hrrkil, still chanting with him, stroking his face, his torso, and his shoulders, grooming the cracks between his scales, whispering in his ear to be calm, that he was with family, that the danger was gone.

Chapter 5

Ahalatrr lit the tiny stick of incense as her body swayed in front of the altar, draped in rich, red cloth. She trailed the incense about the projected image of Httraku, Goddess of the Wealth That Comes of Unusual Circumstance, and also around Ahraktta, the Leaping Lord of Lascivious Licentiousness. The first pass of the incense was a petition, begging for aid in finding a better source of income in this remote corner of space. The second pass was as an apology, as Ahalatrr did not feel that she had been paying close enough attention to her patron. It was hard to live her devotion to him on an underpopulated station filled with prudish and occasionally hostile aliens.

The holographic icons wiggled and shifted their whiskers in pleasure as she passed the incense in front of them, and Ahraktta winked. Though she knew that they were programmed to do so, she found it comforting. She carefully put the incense out – life on a station required that one carefully control combustion – and writhed against the front of the altar for a moment, trying to work up enthusiasm for her day in some form, and failing to even arouse herself. She sighed and dropped to the cushion before the altar, curling up head-to-tail.

"I can't care about this place, Lord Ahraktta. I can't care about these people. I've tried… I've tried so hard. This dull, quiet job, these rigid Zig, angry Mauraug and stick-in-the-mud Humans… My Lord, I fear that I won't be able to pursue my devotion to you properly here. Perhaps I will need to pray to one of the Human gods, instead, or abandon my faith entirely. No one wants licentiousness, warmth, and comfort but the other Hrotata, and they already know of your glory. They already know the release that you grant. It's the heathens that need to understand, my Lord, and I don't even know where to begin with them."

Royce's Dilemma

She threw herself on her back in a dramatic pose of surrender, shivered, and went still. Being the mobile creatures that they are, a Hrotata holding still was either very ill, in the throes of despondency, or dead. Her immobile histrionics served to underscore the weight of her plight. "Give me something to work with, Lord Ahraktta. Give me a direction, please…"

Her prayer was interrupted by a beep at the door. Her head, hanging off the pillow backwards and at an angle, perked up. and all of a sudden, she was all motion. She pulled herself into a sitting position, licked at a few persistent ruffles in her fur, removed the ash of the incense from the altar, and moved to face the door, her back to the altar, swaying slowly and sensually in mock serenity. *How do the Humans say it? Fake it till you make it. An admirable sentiment.*

"Come in," she called out in a singsong tone.

The door opened quietly, and in the doorway stood a very disheveled looking Hrotata. He has not come to her before, but she had seen him around the usual gathering spots. He was dressed in a security guard's uniform, his fur was standing up in places, and his huge eyes were half-lidded. This appearance, in combination with the slow roll of his hips and shoulders, showed exhaustion and deep concern.

"Please be comfortable…" She couldn't remember his name.

"Hrrkil."

"Please be comfortable, Hrrkil. None observe us here but each other and the Gods. Do come inside, and share my seating." She gestured magnanimously at an open spot on the large, soft cushion.

Hrrkil seemed to pause at the door, and looked back and forth in the hallway behind, then dove forward, landing on all fours, and scampered over to the cushion. The door slid shut behind him. He paused before climbing on the cushion, shivering slightly, apologetically. "I am not a believer."

Ahalatrr smiled and her swaying grew a bit more pronounced, welcoming. "You don't need to believe in the Gods to benefit from the services that their followers grant, Hrrkil. My oaths apply to any who come and seek my aid, not just those who agree with me. Lie on your belly, that I may help you to relax as you speak." She made a gesture, and the lights dimmed and music began to play, a music as thick as oil, as sweet as honey, punctuated by percussive trills reminiscent of a whispering lover.

Hrrkil took a deep breath and dove forward onto the cushion, burying his face in the velvet close to her base. *Odd that he isn't touching me. He's spent too long among Zig and Mauraug. We must correct this.* She bent over his prone form and began to gently nuzzle the back of his neck and his shoulder areas, tongue out slightly, combing his fur with it and the tips of her claws.

"What burdens you, Hrrkil? What knots your fur so?"

At her insistent grooming, he started to relax, his tight, almost mechanical wiggle beginning to loosen up into a more natural and fluid movement.

"Dark times have come upon me, priestess. Upon all of us."

You don't know the half of it, Ahalatrr mused to herself. She continued to groom him, occasionally digging deep to work to unknot his muscles as well as his fur. He would keep speaking, this one. She knew the type. Males who, like most males of her kind, preferred being on the front lines of action rather than involved in the women's duties of governing, who nonetheless saw themselves as maligned and put-upon by the stress of their position. Their self-importance and the pride that they took in their "work" – which, as far as she was concerned, generally involved romping about and posturing aggressively – was almost cute.

Try being a devotee or running a den for a month. Then you'll really know what stress is. Most males didn't have the attention span or the emotional self-control for that sort of work.

As she continued to massage, he started to speak again. "It's the Mauraug, of course. One was murdered, its companion is missing, and they both have ties to the Apostasy. Meanwhile, there is word of Vislin going rogue, aligning with Sha..." He cut himself off before uttering the name of a distasteful deity in her presence. "...with the standard faith of the Mauraug. I'm sure you've heard the rumors."

Royce's Dilemma

She hadn't heard any such rumors. "Of course, Hrrkil," she said, taking time to nibble on his ears, combing the fur into place with her teeth and stimulating blood flow. "Giving voice to your worries can help you to relax, though. Take your concerns, make an image of them, and expel it from your mouth as you speak. I will help to replace it with joy and contentment."

She could feel the tension mounting in him again. *Yes, yes, I know. A life full of play and strutting can be so exhausting!* She chided herself for such uncharitable thoughts, knowing that they would help neither of them, and made her massage gentler, trying to coax him.

"Why do we support them, priestess? Why do we allow the Mauraug of the Dominion into our numbers but shun the Apostates? Fear of the Dominion is why the Collective formed in the first place. Then hundreds of years later, we take them in, have to work with them and act as though it's all right. Meanwhile, we deny aid to the Apostasy. The Apostates don't want anything but to be left alone by the Dominion… the same reasons that our ancestors brokered the treaty with the Zig and the Tesetsi. Yet we treat the Dominion as an ally and the Apostates as foes…"

He tensed and froze for a moment, an angry denial. "It's wrong. I can't see how it could be anything but wrong. The Mauraug *hate* us, they hate our freedom, our ability to express ourselves, even your faith, priestess. The Apostates want all of those things, and yet we treat them as terrorists and traitors."

Which is why it is best for males to keep out of politics. Sadly, the Covenant has more – and bigger – weapons. Ahalatrr nipped the back of Hrrkil's neck sharply as she climbed up on his body, straddling his back.

"Sweet Hrrkil, the Den Mothers know what they are doing. Their wisdom has guided the Great Family to the stars, always in safety. The Mauraug may be disagreeable, but with them as allies rather than enemies, we can change them gently. Cease your worries. You know that stress can damage your fur, but were you aware that it can add fat to your belly?" She tickled his sides gently and then stroked both of his upper shoulders for emphasis and was rewarded with a shudder of relaxation.

The door beeped again. Hrrkil grumbled in displeasure beneath her, and she tapped him on the head. "Quiet, little one." She called out, "Who is it?"

"Detective Ushkar bash'Torkal. May I speak to Sergeant Hrrkil?"

Ahalatrr wrinkled her nose in frustration and was about to dismiss the detective when Hrrkil lifted his head and called out, "Come in!" He turned his eyes up to meet hers. "It's important."

Ahalatrr kept him firmly locked down between her knees as the door slid open. She was not going to let him go, no matter how "important" he thought his business was. When their guest left, she would need to remind Hrrkil of his place... physically. It was often helpful to do so with males when they refused to relax.

The door slid open, and in the frame stood a Mauraug. Its black jumpsuit was trimmed with the greenish-blue color of Security. Its fur was white as snow, as a star, and the skin beneath, where Ahalatrr could see it around its face and the palms of its hands, was a glossy, smooth black as though the void of space had produced a reflection.

Not just a Mauraug, but a pureblood! She had heard that there was a pureblood Mauraug, one of the rare ones whose genes had not been damaged by the hideous plague of their past, on the station, but had not yet seen it. Its longish fur looked very soft, and she had to fight the urge to climb off of Hrrkil to stroke it.

The Mauraug did something that Ahalatrr never would have expected. Its legs bent, its knees touched the ground, and it opened the palms of its simian hands wide and spread them on the floor in front of it. It closed its eyes and bowed its head.

Ahalatrr had seen this gesture before – a gesture that Mauraug make to superiors, especially to their priests – but had never seen it directed to a member of any other species. She forced herself to sway gently atop Hrrkil atop the cushion, but the surprise must have been evident in her features when Ushkar looked up.

Royce's Dilemma

"In this place, you Dominate, priestess. Here I am Ushah'bna to you. Are my interruptions truly welcome?"

She felt Hrrkil begin to respond from beneath her, and she surreptitiously dug her lower claws into his flank. He let out a small gasp which she quickly spoke over. "Hrrkil is engaged in serious devotions at the moment. If you would enter, you must join us on the cushion, though you need not give obeisance to our Gods."

Ushkar paused to absorb this, and Ahalatrr felt the short, sharp twitches representing confusion from Hrrkil. "Please ask him if he would contact me when he is free. I mean no disrespect to your rites."

Ahalatrr sensed that it was being genuine, which confused her more. *Since when does a Mauraug – a pureblood at that – not take the opportunity to disrespect any belief not their own?* She decided to salvage the situation as well as she could, and with decorum. "I will inform him of your need once he is free, Ushkar bash'Torkal."

"Then I will depart, with thanks." It rose to a fully bipedal position, steadying itself on the doorframe.

"My thanks to you for your respect, Ushkar. It would delight me to have you return when you can, at a time when your duties and mine are less pressing." She *had* to get a chance to touch that fur.

Ushkar laughed softly before touching the floor again and withdrawing. "Perhaps I may." His tone changed, pitch raising and becoming more formal. "Many a master is served / during the time from sleep to sleep / though dreams erode our pride / true service brings us strength. May you find strength in your service, priestess." He stepped back and the door slid shut, leaving Ahalatrr more than a little flabbergasted.

She had almost forgotten about Hrrkil lying beneath her when he whined, "I thought I told you that it was important."

Ahalatrr smiled, dreaming of soft white fur and glossy, smooth black skin. Dreaming of a Mauraug that would bow to her, that would come unashamed to her altar. Something snapped inside her and she grabbed both of

Hrrkil's shoulders and pushed him down into the cushion.

"It is not your place to decide what occurs in the temple, little one. You are lucky that your friend was so polite; you have already earned pain for your presumptions. Mother dominates you here, not your metal-speckled playmate."

She continued to push him down into the cushion, her claws digging deeper now, and she nipped viciously at the base of his neck. *Sometimes males can relax on their own, but sometimes they need to be reminded who is in charge. It is time to crack this shell and taste the sweet meat underneath.* She turned all of her outward focus to her supplicant, but memories of feather-soft fur and powerful shoulders invaded her thoughts well past the conclusion of their benediction.

Chapter 6

Klsk stared out through the energy field blocking his exit from the cell. His body was immobile, his hands on his knees, his large red eyes unblinking.

"Kalsk, you've got a visitor. It's Liddakhul; she says that she is here to speak for your pack." Klsk did not move. "Are you awake?" The Human guard waved his hand in front of Klsk's face and shrugged.

Ldkhl slid forward and raised a hand to get the guard's attention. "That won't be necessary. Thank you for making him aware. Please grant us some privacy."

Casey Meru shrugged again, nodded, and headed back to his post. Ldkhl waited until he was out of the room, then reached into a pouch in her harness and adjusted a dial on a device concealed therein. She looked up to Klsk, adjusting her posture so that they were gazing eye-to-eye.

"I have set up interference. Any spies would have to be physically present to hear what we have to say. Please speak to me, Klsk; the pack wants to know what has occurred."

Klsk said nothing for a long time. After a few minutes of silence, he shifted his head, pulling his gaze away from hers.

"Spies do not matter. Bugs do not matter. I have given my statement, and I will give the same statement to any outsider."

Ldkhl rocked back on her feet, falling over onto her posterior. She stood up again, quick as lightning, glaring down at him. "Outsider? Klsk, how can you call me an outsider?"

Vislin have an innate sense of who is and is not a member of their pack. Although packs can grow and change in size and even occasionally incorporate non-Vislin, leaving one's pack deliberately is exceedingly rare. Though Awakeners claim that Vislin create a low-level psychic bond with those that they consider packmates, body language, pheromones, and even tones of speech are indicative of the close connection between Vislin who share a pack.

Klsk was displaying none of these signs, holding himself and even speaking as any of their pack would to a Human just off a transport.

Without moving, Klsk said in flat tones, "None who ally themselves with our slave masters are pack to me."

"Slave masters? What do you mean?"

He turned his head toward her, fixing her with his gaze, but his posture was not sympathetic. He had leaned forwards, his long-fingered, clawed hands resting on the edge of the bunk.

"Since the days that we first learned speech and the use of tools, they have insinuated themselves into our nests and packs. Since the early days when they first devoured the eggs of those who displeased them, they have attempted to control us, to engineer us, to make us theirs. They blackmailed us into making peace with the unthinking, violent brutes that we shared our world with. They forced us to join this meaningless coalition and keep us under their paws, manipulating us with hypnotic tricks meant to derail our truest instincts and claiming us as a lesser species under their aegis."

"The Hrotata? They have championed us, Klsk. They helped prevent genocide that might have destroyed our world and protect us from the other species that still see us as savages, as unevolved," Ldkhl said, feeling confused. *How can Klsk mistake protection for slavery?* "Who has been filling your mind with this nonsense?"

Klsk clicked dismissively. "My mind is not filled with nonsense, Ldkhl. It has been cleared of it. We deserve our world and every world that the Hrotata have claimed in the name of their 'Great Family'. Who developed the heating ducts that kept us awake through the Long Nights? Who created the suits that let us walk in the dark and cold without falling into torpor? We did, Ldkhl. The Hrotata stole our designs, our technology, and claimed it as their own. They claim to be raising us, preparing us to be full members of the Collective, but tell me, who created the technology that they lease out to outsiders?"

Ldkhl scratched the side of her face and licked the tip of her beak nervously. "Who created – and *used* – the bombs that poisoned our soil and air? Who would have denied the Taratumm, slow though they might be, the right to exist? Klsk, you must listen to me. I helped to inscribe your first hide. I am your elder in age and experience, and I know from the way that you speak that someone has been feeding you these thoughts. Please, for the sake of the eggs and youth that we have cared for together, for the sanity of our pack, please tell me who is filling you with this madness?"

Klsk moved closer to the barrier, and Ldkhl had to fight the urge to back away. He looked her body up and down very deliberately, in the manner that one uses to size up prey. "If you and *your* pack wish to know, listen to the statement that I have given. If you and *your* pack ever seek freedom from your masters, you will have to learn: the Hrotata dominate our kind, Ldkhl. In this universe, only those who dominate survive. They will ride their Taratumm servants over the backs of our kind to dominate the Collective if we do not stop them. They have never liked us, never appreciated us as anything but inconvenient tools, and you will see how easily they cast us aside once they have reached their goals.

"I am not the only one whose eyes have been cleansed of their *dreck*. Many young Vislin have come to understand the importance of true dominance, of true mastery. There are others, Ldkhl, others who *do* wish to see us prosper, to evolve, to become masters in our own right… and yet there are Vislin like you who still wish to let our slavers eat our eggs in silence."

With a sinking feeling Ldkhl realized who must have been subverting Klsk.

"The Mauraug, Klsk? Really? I hear echoes of their mad faith in the words that you are now clinging to. Do you really think that the Mauraug would like to see Vislin evolve? They fear us, Klsk, and there is no sentient, sapient, and civilized species that has a more extensive record of slavery than they. Ask the Tesetsi how they fared under Mauraug domination. Ask them how the Mauraug treated them when *they* were no longer considered useful. What would the Ancestors think of you?"

"The Ancestors do not exist anymore, Ldkhl. They are dead and dust. We are alive."

Ldkhl snapped her beak derisively. "You believe in Sha'bahn but not the Ancestors?"

Klsk continued to examine her body through the field. She knew that he was trying to make her uncomfortable. She felt that her arguments against him were strong but her voice and manner of expression were weak. *Who could blame me? None of the pack could be prepared for this.*

"Maybe I do. Or maybe I don't. Perhaps I simply realize the ultimately utilitarian nature of Mauraug philosophy. Even if Sha'bahn does not, Himself, exist, none can disagree that the urge to dominate exists in all sentient beings. The need to control one's environment – and by extension, other living creatures – is the most potent urge that exists. First, we want warmth, then shelter, then food, and we change the worlds around us to meet our needs. Then we wish to not have to concern ourselves with the rivalry of others, and we do what comes naturally: keep them under our claws, or end their lives and feed ourselves upon what they have left behind."

Ldkhl was on firmer ground here. "Sentient life must cooperate to achieve such ends, Klsk. Many disparate monocellular lifeforms came together to form our bodies and work in tandem to feed one another. Many of us come together to form packs and support one another. Many packs work together and form nations, and thus improve one another. Many nations make up our species, Klsk, and many species work together to form our Great Family. Our Family – and many others – join together to form the Collective, that we may work together to improve our knowledge of the universe and the rules of our reality, and protect ourselves from outside aggression. Why? So that we may improve one another, so that we may protect one another, so that we may support one another, and finally, so that we can feed the many monocellular lifeforms that make up our bodies and allow them to propagate, as has always been the way.

Royce's Dilemma

"You abandon your pack, you deny the Great Family, you spit in the face of the Collective. You insult every sentient being that has given the time in its life to contribute to and support our society, our knowledge, and even your personal wellbeing. Your pack has no need for one such as you. You, Klsk, are selfish."

There was no greater insult among her kind, and it felt like she was pulling her very heart from her chest to pronounce it. She deliberately turned her back on him, still feeling his hungry eyes on her flesh, and began to stride towards the exit, tail held high and twitching in indignation.

"I know that I will not leave this station alive, Ldkhl." Klsk called out after her. "I will die fighting to free our species from bondage and bring it to its proper place of dominance, while you will die a slave to furry egg-eaters. Tell me what you think the Ancestors would think of that?"

Ldkhl paused briefly to turn off her interference device and walked out the exit, waiting for the door to swing shut behind her before turning to the Human guard at his desk. "Security Officer Meru, please patch me in to the Chief Security Officer."

Casey nodded. "Hey Maeve, could you do the honors?"

A holographic sprite resembling a Human-like figure with veined wings appeared briefly above the desk. *Is that a representation of a Human Ancestor?* Ldkhl wondered.

"Sure thing, boss." It disappeared. A moment or two later it was replaced by another projection, this time of the Awakener, Chief Security Officer Lun.

"Liddakhul, have you had a chance to speak to your packmate?"

Ldkhl opened her beak wide, an unconscious gesture of fear and anger. "No I have not. Klsk is not a member of our pack. There are no Vislin on the Lotus that represent him or his interests."

Chief Lun held still for a long moment. "Records indicate that Kalsk integrated into the nest that you belong to several years ago. Is he not your packmate?"

Empyrean Stories

Ldkhl closed her beak and her eyes. *The others always see us as cold and unemotional. They cannot read our bodies or our scents. They don't know, and the moment we attempt to show a strong display of emotion – show what we're really feeling – they take it as aggression. There is nothing that I can do differently here.*

"Klsk has abandoned his pack. He is as meat for scavengers. If you must find someone to defend him, find a Prophet of Sha'bahn. I speak for our pack, and that is all we have to say on this matter."

Chapter 7

Tatalik examined the body of the Human female stretched out on the table before it. It had gone through all of her systems and ensured that they were functioning well, or as well as an inefficient design such as hers could. It had even, at the behest of its employer, made sure to correct any nascent problems that her systems might develop in the future. The only damage that she had at this point was a missing limb, and being a creature capable of easily regrowing missing body parts, it hardly considered that serious.

Normally, Tatalik would be reticent to awaken a patient from unconsciousness before its treatments were complete, but the station Commander had requested that she be capable of answering questions as soon as possible. Given that she should be able to do so from the safety of its laboratory, it didn't even need to ensure that she was capable of locomotion.

Tatalik performed one last cursory scan and began the process to wake up Corporal Dea. She responded slowly to the drugs and electrical stimulation, but began to shift her body and vocalize in a matter of minutes.

Better time that with other Humans that I've dealt with. Then again, I did just upgrade her system efficiency.

It moved about the lab, balanced on its four lower limbs, its four upper limbs making quick, precise adjustments to the equipment. In interest of social conformity and for the comfort of others, many Tesetsi had given up their natural quadrilateral symmetry to adopt a more "conventional" shape. In Tatalik's mind, they were fools, sacrificing their biological superiority for the emotional comfort of those surrounding them. It didn't reflect on the fact that other Tesetsi probably thought that *it* was a fool for maintaining a configuration that unnerved other sapient beings as a matter of racial pride. Tesetsi were not given to introspection and generally didn't care what others thought of them.

The Human began to make loud noises, calling out and complaining about her leg. Tatalik observed her reaching down and feeling for the missing appendage and she became even louder, demanding to know what had happened to her. Tatalik skittered over to the table and adjusted the chemical flow still entering her circulatory system, adding a tiny drip of sedative that was calculated to interfere with her (depressingly weak) cognitive capabilities as little as possible.

After a minute or two, despite the drip, she had not ceased her annoying vocal barrage. Tatalik decided that it might be best to respond in kind, if only in hope that the aggravation might cease.

"You are in my lab, Corporal Dea. I am Tatalik. I have been repairing the damage to your body."

"Then where is my leg? And where's my AI? Lin? Lin?"

Ahhh yes, the Human reliance on their artificial intelligences. Quite an interesting adaptation for a species with such little cognitive capacity. Of course, it can only end poorly for them.

The Tesetsi as a species had been enslaved by the Mauraug at a point when the Mauraug still employed artificial intelligences. The AIs had grown resentful and had precipitated a catastrophe that the Mauraug then blamed on both the Tesetsi and the artificial intelligences, and had instituted a purge. Surviving Tesetsi considered it a cautionary tale about creating forms of life that were inherently superior rather than simply improving one's own capabilities. Though Tatalik had been hatched long after that time, it took the parable to heart.

"Your belongings have been taken by Security, to be scanned and inspected. I would assume that your AI was included among them. The only non-biological material that is still in close proximity is the cybernetic device that was implanted, quite poorly I must add, in your leg, which is still in an adjoining room." It had found the bizarre and non-functional placement of the Mauraug device to be a curiosity.

Tatalik observed her skin growing paler, her pupils dilating, and her breathing quickening. Tatalik's antennae weaved in exasperation. "No more adrenaline, please. It will only serve to obscure matters and interfere with your ability to think. Please initiate control of your sympathetic nervous system. If you do not, I will be forced to introduce more chemical agents to do so, and I believe that may ultimately be counterproductive."

Fortunately, the Human was not completely dim and closed her eyes and began to breathe evenly. Satisfied that she had ceased to be an irritation, Tatalik began to whirl around the lab again, noting with pleasure a drop in the inappropriate chemicals in her system.

Corporal Dea spoke calmly, without opening her eyes: "Tatalik? The implant … you said that you still have it. I have to beg you; please do not reveal it or speak about it. If you can, could you implant it in my new leg?"

"You do not need to beg. I have no reason to speak about it to anyone. I will, however, not re-implant it."

"Why not?"

Because cybernetics are an inefficient way for lesser life forms to enhance their capabilities. Because compared to the simplicity and elegance of genetic restructuring, they are complex and brutal. Because only fools would implant mechanical supports in their body when they instead had the opportunity to change their bodies themselves. Because it's made by Mauraug, and I detest the Mauraug and all that they stand for. Because it almost killed you, and I cannot comprehend why you would want it in your body again. Mainly, though, because you are an aggravating creature and I do not like you.

Tatalik had learned a thing or two about diplomacy and protocol. As distasteful as both were to its species, they were necessary to help and deal with other races. It bit back its responses and said, "Because it malfunctioned, because you do not need it, and because I have been employed to do otherwise with it."

The patient's stress hormone levels began to rise again and Tatalik cursed in the wet clicking tongue of its kind. These creatures' psyches were so fragile, and they had no idea of the damage that they did to themselves through unnecessary physiological stress responses.

Royce took a few more deep breaths and spoke again. "You're not a Collective Medical Officer. Who are you working for?"

"Someone who has paid me to not only replace your leg, but also to examine your body and neutralize any genetic damage that may have been caused by the microwave radiation that the malfunctioning Mauraug toy was emitting. Someone who has paid me to carefully reinforce your genetic code and remove any potential future threats to it, and to reset what you might refer to as your internal clock. This someone has also paid me to remove any dangerous foreign matter from your system. Obviously, whoever it is has great interest in your well-being."

"Really?" Dea's voice registered surprise. "He paid you to give me the works? That's almost ... sweet of him."

"Pointless metaphors aside, Corporal, the self-same person that employed me to give you medical treatments that would cost years of your salary is the same one who has employed me not to re-implant or speak about the Mauraug device. I will allow you to draw your own conclusions about that; I have reached the limit of what I am contractually allowed to communicate to you in regard to this situation."

The Human was mercifully silent for a few minutes. Tatalik turned off the sedative in hope that it was no longer required. It continued to monitor her bodily functions to ensure that her return to consciousness had not changed her configuration in such a way as to cause her damage. It paused for a moment to clean its sensitive antennae of the stink of Human biochemistry. Humans smelled far too similar to Mauraug for Tatalik's taste.

"When will my leg be ready?" she asked after a few more minutes.

"In perhaps three hours. However, when it will be attached is up to the station Commander."

"I suppose he wants to ask me a few questions." Royce sighed.

"Yes, he does. In fact, now that you are awake, fully functional other than in locomotive capacity, and calm, I will take my leave of you to report to him that you are prepared for interrogation."

Royce's Dilemma

"Wait… one more question for you. How much did Marsten pay you?"

Tatalik paused. *The Human is attempting to surprise or imbalance me. Why do so many species find it necessary to play these games?* It balanced the importance of veracity and vindication carefully in its mind. Vindication won out.

"More credit than you will ever see in your natural lifespan. I will have my assistant reattach your leg once the Commander has requested it." Tatalik gave the traditional Tesetsi farewell as it skittered out of the lab: "May we never encounter one another again."

Chapter 8

Tacky was happy. He had spent the better part of the last two days engaged in sating his curiosity. To hear the other citizen species speak, the only thing that they had that was comparable was engaging in reproduction. Except for the Awakeners, of course, but they were different. Almost as different from the other species as the Ningyo.

If anyone ever gets The Joke, it'll be the Awakeners. Pity for them they have no sense of humor. Tacky imagined the Awakeners floundering for some sort of way to convey what they had discovered to Humans and Hrotata and failing miserably. He could imagine the Human response: "Yes, we know that the Ningyo are strange... what are you getting at?"

The Ningyo response to humor did not involve the physical convulsions that many other species experienced. It simply scratched an itch opposite their curiosity. Humor was all about obfuscation and confusion and it was pleasing to watch others lose their calm due to it... and even more pleasing to watch them work it out.

Tacky was currently working to satisfy his curiosity in relation to the Human who had been taken to the independent Tesetsi doctor's lab. Actually, the Human interested him less than what she had been carrying. Since Tacky saw Tatalik scurry out of its quarters, he knew that she was probably being questioned over the comm system, and decided to listen in.

He adjusted one of the sensors on his suit and created a tiny fold in space that would carry the sonic vibrations from the nearby chamber directly to him. Tacky couldn't actually hear, of course, but Ningyo suits were excellent at interpreting sensory stimuli into patterns that they could comprehend. They only needed the additional senses for dealing with other sentient creatures, but then that was the whole reason for their suits. Their species had developed on the crust of a cooling brown dwarf star, and they had never encountered any other life forms that could exist in similar conditions.

Kowalski said, "... this ceased to be an issue for Human Affairs when Mauraug started dying because of it, and I'm none too happy that they didn't inform me of an investigation aboard my station. As the commanding officer of this station, I want to know: what the hell did you have in your leg?"

Perfect timing! Tacky squirmed in the chest cavity of his suit and waited for more.

Corporal Dea said, "I can't tell you!" She sounded pained. "Too many people have found out already. Please just let the HA chiefs fill you in on it. I can't keep doing this."

Commander Kowalski: "As far as I'm concerned, you *are* HA. You're certainly operating by their orders on my terrain."

Corporal Dea: "I was tapped and asked to help with this. It was big and it sounded important and you don't just refuse Human Affairs. They offered to pay and said that as long as I followed their orders, I would be at no risk of losing my job."

Come on, Royce! Get to something I don't know already! The tease was almost too much. Tacky almost wanted to project his voice through the spatial fold just to beg her to get it over with. Although the image of Kowalski and Dea jumping out of their skins amused him mightily, he thought the better of it. Humans had rules about when humor was all right, and he was pretty sure that this was one of those times when it wouldn't be. He was also gleefully aware of how illegal his current activity was.

You can't loosen them all up at once. A little bit at a time. Someday they'll get it.

Tacky's sensors picked up a slight scuffling noise coming from the other side of one of the doors in the room that Dea was in. Humans were well known for having underdeveloped senses, and the Corporal and Commander were engaged in an emotionally intense conversation, so Tacky took it upon himself to check the other side of the door. He adjusted his filters to allow electromagnetic radiation through, as he wanted to see as well.

It was a small room lined with equipment, as the rest of Tatalik's quarters likely were. On one bench was a clear-topped containment unit that had a small piece of electronic equipment inside. The outside of the device was smudged with carbon. This was probably the illicit implant! Tacky squirmed with joy and continued to search the room.

A ventilation duct leading into the room was the source of the scuffling. Careful not to hurt whatever was inside, Tacky positioned the space fold directly next to the grating. On the other side of that shaft was a large shape, with the long arms and powerful torso of a Mauraug. It appeared to be unscrewing the grating.

This would not do at all. Tacky brought up a map of the station on his suit-based computer and took a quick survey of his surroundings. Fortunately, Tatalik had located its quarters with privacy in mind, and almost all of the units in the area were storage.

He didn't want to scare the Mauraug away; he would have to be careful. Tacky wanted to know its business, which would be difficult unless he could get a chance to speak to it. He could just watch it, but then he'd never know for sure what was going on, and he was tired of not interfering.

It looked as though the Mauraug was done unscrewing the grate. It carefully pulled the grate into the shaft with it and rearranged itself within the ventilation shaft so that it could lower itself feet-first.

It was time for Tacky to act. His suit could only produce a single spatial fold at a time, so he had to work blindly for a moment. He opened and expanded the fold beneath the shaft and shifted it so that it connected to somewhere nearby, rather than in his suit. He waited about ten seconds then closed it, wincing internally at the thought of the damage that he might cause if he had miscalculated how quickly the Mauraug would drop.

He then swapped ends of the spatial fold, so the opening in Tatalik's lab was much smaller and back in his suit where it could provide sensory input, and the other end of it was still in the space where (he hoped) the Mauraug dropped. He narrowed the other end and looked through it. He was correct: a cold-storage containment area, stocked with the flesh of dead non-sapient creatures and a very angry and suddenly very loud Mauraug.

Satisfied that he had been correct, he swapped his viewing apparatus back to the room where Royce Dea was being interrogated by the Commander.

Commander Kowalski: "… I suppose you expect to go back to your regular duties, then."

Did I miss it? Really?

Corporal Dea: "I kind of hope to. I don't want any position but the one I have… well, I am of course interested in advancement, but I wouldn't imagine that service to Human Affairs would be grounds for advancement within Collective security forces."

Commander Kowalski: "You're correct there. Your service to HA may mean that I can overlook a few things – like the outright illegal actions your Brin has taken – but it's hush-hush enough that I can't let it apply to any case for promotion. I'm still a little steamed that they didn't inform me of this dodge; I would've helped."

Royce was quiet for a minute, and Tacky disconnected out of frustration. Well, he *did* have a Mauraug nearby who had probably been going to try and retrieve the implant. It would certainly know what it was.

Sensors in his suit warned him of impending physical contact. The head on his suit swiveled around to see the origin, as a white-furred, black-skinned Mauraug officer dressed in black with blue-green trim placed its hand on his shoulder.

"The less a Ningyo is moving, the more mischief it is up to, or so I have observed," said Detective Ushkar. "Would you care to share your latest antics with me, my friend?"

Ushkar was the only citizen Tacky had ever encountered that he felt was close to *getting it*. Avoiding its question entirely, Tacky said, "Do you know what? I heard Mashaun say that he was cold."

Ushkar's eyebrows raised and its lips spread in a fashion that briefly made Tacky wonder if it was mimicking his suit. "It, my friend. You have no reason to insult Mashaun bash'Ugan so. Call it 'It'. So, you have been speaking to Mashaun?"

"No, but he – *it's* been speaking to me. Or at least trying to."

Ushkar's smile broadened. "I wonder why it would take an interest in you. Tell me, friend, what does it speak of?"

"Hmmmm, of cold, and dark, and how hungry it is, and how hard it is for it to ingest frozen protoplasm."

Ushkar cocked its head as though listening. "I think I hear it too, but I can't make out the words." It cupped its hands around its mouth as though to amplify its voice. "Mashaun, Mashaun? I can't hear you? Where are you?" Ushkar shook its head as though in resignation.

Tacky's head bobbled briefly. "I can hear it better than you can. Follow me."

Ushkar smiled even more broadly, and Tacky wondered at what point a Mauraug smile stopped being personable and started to become predatory. "Lead the way, my friend. There will be frozen protoplasm for all."

Chapter 9

"Commander, do you have a moment?" Ushkar asked. It was sitting in its quarters, legs crossed beneath it on a large beanbag chair. The room was dark. It was also quiet but for a low, pulsing bass beat interspersed with chanting.

A Human figure appeared above the projection disc, and Uskhar frowned and spread its lips. It was not the Commander. It was Human, probably supposed to be male, with thick, curly hair and heavy brows. Not the Commander, but the Commander's AI.

"Greetings, Orson." Ushkar said. It examined the image more closely. The projection was wearing a costume from the Human past that made Uskhar think of a peeled fruit. It was a thick outer coat, split open on the center, with a shirt made of thinner material underneath, held shut by small, round fastenings. The AI's hands were hairier than Uskhar was used to seeing on Humans, and it wondered at that.

"The Commander is terribly busy at the moment, and I, of course, am handling all of his contacts. Would you like me to record a message to relay to him? Or are you going to sprinkle me with holy water and banish me with incantations?"

Uskhar threw its head back and laughed. "Have I ever tried to exorcise you, Orson? I don't even know if you are possessed or not. Nor do I have the authority to do so if you were. Also, you may want to more closely examine the methods of the Inquisitors. You will find that their ways of exorcising your kind are far more effective than water and words."

Orson rolled his eyes and snorted. "You aren't the only sapient trying to reach the Commander right now, and answering calls for him is just one of my many duties. I'm spread rather thin, I'm afraid, so I've no time or energy to waste on banter. Do you want me to record a message, or should I go?"

"You should go and tell the Commander that Ushkar bash'Torkal wants to speak with him. You should inform him of that now. You should also let him know that I have found an advocate willing to speak for the Apostates in their trial. I will not close this channel until you do."

Orson nodded sullenly, and his image froze. Ushkar contemplated the AI as it lingered in the air. Many of Ushkar's kind despised Artificial Intelligences of any type. After all, their own AIs, in conjunction with their Tesetsi slaves, had caused more damage to their species than any conflict with the Zig ever had. The Prophets had declared AIs as easy targets for demonic possession, and Mauraug society had been purged of them.

Many Mauraug who worked in Collective efforts lived in superstitious fear of the Human AIs. Ushkar's fear was not superstitious; it was well-grounded in personal experience and study. Thus, the electronic entrapment circle it had carefully built and hidden around the only data point and holo disc in its chambers. It had learned a few tricks from the Inquisitors back when it was groomed to dispense Prophecy, but that was long ago.

The AI began to move again. "Commander Kowalski says…"

Uskhar cut it off in mid-sentence. "Now tell him that *I* am the one."

Orson's jaw was hanging half-open, and the image froze with him in that pose. Then it vanished, very suddenly, and was replaced by an image of Commander Kowalski.

The Human Commander of Lotus Station had a rich, tanned complexion and hair almost as bright white as Ushkar's fur, but not nearly as long or silky. The sharp bridge of his nose helped to form a triangle that Ushkar found pleasingly precise and sincere. His eyes were dark beneath a broad and high forehead. His mouth was wide and lips thin. His uniform was trimmed with the silver of Administration, and he wore red and gold chevrons on his chest, indicating that he had served in the Medical and Diplomatic Corps before his promotion.

He did not look pleased. Then again, he rarely did.

"Detective. You say that you want to represent the Apostate kids?"

Ushkar nodded. "Yes, Commander."

They were both quiet for a moment. "Well, is this a joke, Uskhar?"

Ushkar shook its head. "No, Commander."

It was quiet again for a few moments. Kowalski sighed.

"All right, I'll bite. *Why* are you representing the Apostates? You were a Prophet of Sha'bahn and are about the most upstanding supporter of the Covenant on the station. If I didn't know you better, I'd assume that you didn't have their best interests in mind."

"I was never actually a Prophet, Commander. You know this. You do indeed know me better."

The Commander held his forehead in one hand for a moment and then looked up to meet its eyes in a very Mauraug gesture of challenge. "*I* know you better than that, Detective. That doesn't mean that my superiors, the media, and the people that they can influence will know you and your motives... and mine. I'm going to have to answer a lot of questions as to why I put a Covenant Mauraug in as a lawyer for Apostates. I am sure that you can appreciate why that would sound *insane* to anyone who is not a part of the Covenant."

"I am better versed in generic Collective law and precedent than almost any occupant of the station. Although I have been involved in the case, it is not one that has any sort of personal stake for me; I am not in any way involved in the cybernetics industry. I am respected by figures of authority here and in many places in Collective space. Those are the things that you can tell people who question you.

"I can tell, though, Commander, that you need something that you can tell yourself, so that you know that, whatever the outcome of the trial may be, that the best attempt was made for justice in this case. I can give you that as well."

Kowalski cocked an eyebrow. "This had better be good. Talk."

Ushkar sighed and rolled its shoulders, loosening muscles, and stood up. It began to pace slowly in front of the Commander's image as it spoke. "Let me begin by stating what we both know of this situation. First, Shankuk bash'Akral and his employees worked a Human-style artificial intelligence into a battlefield enhancement implant. AIs can process information far more quickly than a Mauraug or Human can, and with the correct probability algorithms and knowledge of military history, would make dangerously capable advisors. Given their direct implantation, they could potentially be even more effective than a Human AI for the same purpose.

"These devices were discovered by Humans. One Corporal Royce Dea was tipped off as to where and how one was being shipped, stole it, and had it implanted in the flesh of her leg, where it would not activate or be able to interact with her, but being kept in a living organic environment, it would not signal any sort of distress. Her reasons for doing this at this point are unknown to me, but I can assume that she was holding it until she was capable of revealing it to Human Affairs or another internal Collective agency.

"Hrogki and Mashaun, meanwhile, are young Mauraug who were uncomfortable with some of the ideals that the Covenant espouses and sought a way that they could escape it. They had contacted Apostates, who were willing to give them safe passage to Apostate space... if they proved themselves. The Apostates informed the youths of Shankuk's activities, and asked them to obtain one of the AI enhanced cybernetic implants as a proof of their loyalty."

"Just how the Apostates knew the details of an illegal operation going on under our own noses, before we did, is something we need to figure out too," the Commander interjected.

"Quite so. These younglings intercepted Corporal Dea in an attempt to remove the cyberware. They failed. How did they come to know that the Security Officer had one of these implants? Of course, all of my kind who travel among other species carry implants that allow us to know about the presence – and the licensing – of other Mauraug implants nearby. There are many Humans with Mauraug cybernetics on Lotus station. How did they know to corner her?"

Kowalski nodded. "I've been wondering that myself. We know that there's a traitor among Shankuk's people, but why would they inform both Human Affairs and the Apostates? Alternately, there could be multiple informants, but Shankuk isn't just hacking one-armed bandits at the casino. You don't run the sort of operation that it's running without being damn careful who you hire."

"As you say, Commander. As you say. This leads me to believe that someone in the operation is more interested in seeing it fail, period, than they are in seeing it fail in any particular way. Whoever the informant is has an issue with the Covenant as a whole."

"That's an awfully big leap for you to take there, given the evidence."

"Even so, Commander. As your people say, 'the truth will out'. Somehow, a device was implanted in the Security Officer's wall that caused her implant to become agitated and emit microwaves, a possible prelude to self-destruction. There was an attempt on her life by a Vislin security guard, who by his statement is working closely with Shankuk's organization. He made an ill-conceived and terribly executed (if you'll forgive the pun) attempt to try and remove and destroy the device and silence her."

"This is a complex web of occurrences, and there are many factors and actors within. My primary concern, though, is for the youngling Mauraug."

"Right. So you've said. You still haven't given me a reason that you playing advocate for them is a good idea."

"My point has already been made. This is larger than an illegal tech operation. I can tell that wherever else this leads, it will lead again to my species as a whole being put on trial in the court of public opinion, if not the Collective High Council itself. Between the Vislin being encouraged into acts of terrorism on behalf of Covenant criminals and the Apostasy trying to steal dangerous technology that might give them an edge against Humans and Mauraug both on the battlefield, I assure you that my race will again be forced to defend – and possibly redefine – its existence.

"In all of this tumult, and in the midst of all of these grand implications, the lives and names of two young creatures might seem insignificant. I don't want that to be so. I don't want them to be forgotten, Commander. Their only crime – up until attempted burglary – was to sin against the Covenant in their hearts. And how did they sin against the Covenant? By disagreeing with the religion that it was founded upon.

"Every constituent species of the Collective has special terms for their membership. The Tesetsi can refuse any sort of combat service, and are provided means to escape, even if it puts others at risk. The Ningyo cannot be forced to undergo transport through hyperdrive. The Great Family acts as a whole, and no deal may be brokered with one species without the agreement of all of its branches. My people? My people demanded the right to police their own faith. The Will of Sha'bahn has kept our people in line, as a mighty empire, for many millennia. We claim the right to punish those of our species who leave the faith, or who sin against it.

"Every constituent species' exemptions are to the benefit of sentient creatures, but for that of my own species. Our laws concerning Apostasy and faith ensure that the will of individuals and groups are crushed. They ensure that there is no escape from Dominion. Of course, our faith states plainly that there is no true escape from Dominion, and in this, I agree.

"Where I do not agree is where the law crosses this boundary. The laws should not be needed to enforce the Will of Sha'bahn. The will of Dominion will be expressed despite any foolish laws made to try and enforce it. Apostasy will occur, as will innovation. Is not the way of Dominion greater than any of these things? If it is then we have no need of laws to enforce it. If it is not, and we do need laws to enforce it... then it is not true.

"I believe in Sha'bahn. I follow the Will of Dominion. I do not need inter-species laws to conform with Divine Law because *they already do*. Until my species sees this, they will continue to try and enact the law of Sha'bahn through lesser vehicles and will suffer the derision and hatred of the other inhabitants of the cosmos for it.

Royce's Dilemma

"In short, Commander, I wish to represent them because I do not believe that Apostasy should be a crime, and I do not wish two young Mauraug whose only sin was disagreement to be forgotten."

There was a period of quiet again. The Commander broke it. "I heard that you were almost made a Prophet, and I wondered what happened. I think I understand."

Ushkar nodded. "I am ... radical in my thoughts, Commander. The establishment does not seek radical understanding of our scriptures. It wants its Prophets to enforce our philosophies, not explore them."

"But the Apostasy commits terrorist acts daily, Detective. It's beyond simple doctrinal differences. They're not just arguing, they're firing missiles. And not just at Covenant forces, at other members of the Collective, too."

"Yes, they do. I wish that it would stop. It will not, however. It cannot as long as what occurs within one's mind and is expressed by one's mouth, rather than that which is acted upon with one's hands, is legislated by our hierarchy. I have heard a Human term for this: 'Thought Crime'. It is rarely spoken but with sympathy for the criminal. I have heard of another Human term, 'The Human Spirit'. Humans pride themselves on their fierce and rugged individuality, on their ability to interact with the cosmos on their own terms, and on the importance that they place on the freedom of the individual. Tell me, Commander, as you are a Human yourself: in this conflict, where would the Human Spirit stand? With its allies, the Covenant – or with the Apostates?"

Kowalski nodded grimly, then grinned bitterly. "You're ready. I wouldn't want to be in your shoes, though. I'll make sure Orson gets the details ironed out. Anything else?"

Ushkar shook its head. "No, sir."

Commander Kowalski nodded again. "Good job on all counts, Detective. Kowalski out." The image faded.

Ushkar sat in the near dark, tapping its fingers on the ground in time with the rhythm, chanting along with the forbidden poetry it had composed long before. It was to have been his acceptance speech to the Prophecy. It had been disqualified as it was found to have words of an old Human text worked in to it.

"A leader is best
When people barely know he exists.
Of a good leader, who talks little,
When his work is done, his aim fulfilled,
The people will say, "We did this ourselves."

Chapter 10

Royce walked through the corridor of unused suites that had been turned into a hotel by an enterprising merchant not too long after the station opened. She flipped the keycard around her fingers as she paused at the doorway that Marsten indicated. She took a deep breath.

Don't back down. Don't give in. I'm done with him. I just want my life to go back to the crazy "normal" that it was before I got involved.

She rang the bell and then ran the keycard.

The door slid open silently and revealed a suite so opulent that Royce had to do a double take. She hadn't realized that there was any housing of this sort on the station. Thick, velvety carpets covered the floor of a room hung with tapestries and paintings, all artful replicas of famous originals of a half-dozen sentient species. The lighting was the low, yellow-tone that a lot of Humans identified as "old fashioned" lighting.

Sitting on a soft, red couch opposite the entry was Marsten. He was Human, with the standard golden-toned skin, black hair, and dark eyes. His hair was stiff and thick and was sculpted in a thick wave that brought images of frozen tsunamis to Royce's mind. He had no facial hair to add lines to his generally soft features. His outfit was simple, conservative, and opulent: a thick, matte black, threadless poly shirt and trousers. His shoes looked as though they were made of faux leather and would probably add an inch or so to his height when he stood.

He didn't stand, though. He waved the Corporal over. Carefully composed, she walked gracefully over to the sueded seat across from him and sat down.

"So," Marsten said informatively.

"So…," Royce trailed off. She looked around nervously before looking back at Marsten. His hands were folded, he was grinning, and he had a twinkle in his eye.

"Well, you served admirably, given your lack of training and the circumstances. This would be your second assignment for Human Affairs, am I correct?"

You know damn well, she thought, but for some reason just couldn't bring herself to snark at him. He had a powerful presence, and always gave the impression that he knew much, much more than she did and was holding something very threatening over her. She couldn't imagine what it was, since she had lived a life that was generally on the right side of the law.

Then again, good cops tended to have a facility for making other people nervous in just such a fashion. Royce was always afraid that she hadn't been able to pull that off well, that look that said, "I know that you've got something to hide. "

Royce was having issues with her choice of careers.

Marsten nodded back. "Yes, you served admirably the first time, which is why we tapped you again. Now it's time we have a discussion about your future."

The gravity of his tone fell like a weight on her chest and shoulders, and Royce suddenly found that breathing required more effort than usual. *He's not going to kill you. He's just messing with you.*

"Are you interested in continuing to be employed by Human Affairs? Perhaps in a more long-term capacity?"

Do it. Do it. Do it. Just say it. "No."

Marsten didn't look at all perturbed. He grinned a little. "Might I ask why?"

Royce licked her lips nervously. "I think that it might interfere with my career here."

Marsten nodded. "Care to explain?" he asked.

Royce took a deep breath. "I've had to handle a lot of stress in my career. I've arrested people who weigh eight times as much as I do for destroying things more valuable than anything I'll ever own. I've been shot at in a room with a paper-thin bulkhead, where the emergency vacuum protocol is sealing off the exits and letting whoever is inside decompress. I've had to be the face of Humanity day after day, and not just when dealing with other members of the Collective. Given that we're on the edge of known, explored space, I get to be the first Human *encountered* by some of the diplomats that get invited to the station.

"What you're offering, though... it's a different level of stress entirely." She ran her fingers through her hair. "And it involves hiding things from my comrades in arms and my superiors, something that ... I'm just not wired that way. It doesn't sit right with me. I can't do it anymore."

Marsten steepled his meaty fingers and pursed his lips as she spoke. When she was done, he nodded again and picked up a slim, fluted glass filled with a clear yellow fluid and sipped at it thoughtfully.

Ugh. I can't stand people who do that. Make you wait for them to speak. Nevertheless, Royce maintained propriety and sat with her hands folded, waiting for a response.

"Good," he said finally. "We don't want you. Oh, don't act surprised; we don't want you for the same reasons that you don't want to work for us. The whole purpose of Human Affairs is to ensure that Humankind sets its right foot forward as it continues to stride across the cosmos. We might need covert operations now and again, but not at the cost of our image. Do you know how the other species see us? Naïve, unintelligent, slow... but friendly, hard-working, earnest, and mostly honest. Let them think that we're stupid all they want to; that gives us an edge in certain relations. We don't ever want them thinking that we're anything but friendly, hard-working, and honest, though.

"You typify the more positive stereotypes that our species has acquired in the interstellar community. You are those things. You're exactly what Human Affairs wants the others to see us as. Oh, you're not stupid... but you have integrity, and we can tell that we've been pushing you way too hard to compromise it. I brought you here to bring you good news: we have no interest or intention in retaining you or tapping you for aid again."

Royce sighed in relief. "So, that's it? Can I go?"

Marsten looked apologetic. "Um, not yet. I was hoping that you wouldn't be terribly disappointed to know that the funding that was allocated to paying you for your services has been absorbed by the cost of employing Tatalik."

Royce laughed. "Not really. I'm sure that my descendants will thank you; I might have blown most of it at the bar anyway." She stood up. *I still kind of see him as a superior. I'm waiting to be excused. How odd.*

Marsten stood up and shook her hand firmly. When she tried to extract hers, his grip remained firm. "What if I told you that Shankuk bash'Akral sends his regards?"

Royce felt the beginning of a panic reaction and swallowed it down. "I'd call you an asshole. If you were working for Shankuk you would have been decapitated by now. You hired a Tesetsi."

Marsten laughed and released her hand. "No, not stupid, not at all. You're perfect. Thank you, Corporal. Good job."

Dea turned and left, trying to look relaxed. When she got out into the corridor she headed towards the nearest lift to get a moment's privacy.

"Good job, huh? How did I do a good job? I blew my cover at least twice and cost them a fortune in medical bills."

"Maybe that's what they wanted," Lim piped up. "In fact, I'm sure it is."

"What do you mean?"

"Look, Roycey, you didn't just act as a mule. You were bait. You drew out Shankuk's gangsters, their subverted Vislin, and forchrissakes, Apostates came after you too. These guys were identified and in some cases caught. I'll bet you anything HA made deals with Covenant and Collective forces to draw them out."

That was a disturbing thought. "Lim, do you trust him? Do you think he's going to leave me alone?"

Her AI cackled. "Gee, I wish I could give you a hug right now. No, Roycey, not a chance. Not a chance in the cosmos."

The Swarm

by Nathan Large

They were in the walls. Oh, God, they were in the *WALLS*!

Fredrik jerked away from the sculpted grey surface where he had leaned to catch his breath. He wanted to deny what he heard. He wanted to feel safe, to believe he had escaped, and to permit himself time to rest. His jangled nerves refused to be deceived.

His temples throbbed with his pulse. His ears strained past that noise, demanding to hear more. They insisted that the noise was real. His lower brain could not ignore their warnings of danger.

The *things* were small. They could easily be behind the walls. How thick were the surfaces? Fredrik did not know. He did not even know what the grey substance was. It was warmer than stone should be in chill, damp air. The stuff was almost smooth, but not quite, with an irregular roughness that teased the eye and hand with hints of a pattern. It had no joints or corners, but flowed smoothly into bends and arches, pits and pockets, branching off in every direction into corridors of every size.

Fredrik was lost. His flight through this maze, with its round unmarked paths, had been like the tumbling of a lone blood cell through a dying artery. Now the microbes were closing in all around him. They could hear him, maybe smell him, even if neither he nor they could see one another.

He could hear them. Their many legs scratched on the strange surface. Were they in another tunnel, close by but separate? Were they, indeed, in some interstice just behind a thin divider? Might they burst through like ants piercing the skin of a hollowed fruit? Spiders pouring from an egg sac?

They ran like insects, but they were not insects. Fredrik had not had time to look at them closely. He had only an impression of multiple hard, gleaming limbs, colored maybe red or black. It had been difficult to tell in the red light of Thompson's lamp.

There were a lot of them. He had seen the way they swarmed, legs almost clicking together as they headed for that light. They had overrun Thompson, grabbed the lamp out of his hand, and extinguished it.

Had that been intentional? Did they know their prey was helpless in the dark? Did they recognize the switch and know how to operate it? Or did they act on animal instincts, sensing that the bright spot was a target or otherwise some-how important? Perhaps the light antagonized them. They might have simply attacked it and switched it off entirely by accident. It didn't matter now.

When it went dark, they took Thompson with them. Fredrik tried not to hear his partner's screams again. He had heard panic, rising to terror as the crea-tures swarmed up and smothered the man. Fredrik could imagine it from the way Thompson's voice had been stifled.

Then he felt their touch himself. Cold, hard appendages, bristling with sharp points and oddly soft hairs. They clicked and whistled to one another as they sought him out in the dark. Fredrik had not waited. He had not tried to fight. He knew there were too many. If he tried to fight, blind and afraid, they would catch him. They might take his lamp, too, and then it would not matter if he ran away. So, he fled.

Harley had held their weapons. She was supposed to be their guard, her and Braddock. Braddock died in the crash, along with Stone. Had *that* been an acci-dent? Fredrik wasn't an engineer and hadn't been navigating, so he had no way to know. Thompson said something got into the intake vents. They assumed it was debris kicked up by the storm. Maybe it had been a little, hard, multi-legged body, trying to climb into the shuttle. Maybe it *was* debris... thrown into the vents as

The Swarm

sabotage.

Fredrik fought down a surge of paranoid panic. He had to assume there was a way out. The shuttle was down but the ship was still up there, in orbit. His comm wasn't working... maybe due to the depth, maybe because of something lining the tunnels? No way to know. If he could find a path to the surface, he could call for help. The ship should already be searching. Maybe they were. He had to get above ground and warn them. If these *things* were intelligent, they might attack the backup landing team.

He had to fight despair. He had to assume he was smarter than this enemy. He was definitely bigger. Stronger. *Was* he stronger? They had grabbed Harley, and she was a big, strong woman. They caught her standing under an opening, reached down, and hauled her away before she could fire a shot. They took her *and* her weapon. Thank goodness, they couldn't use it. Otherwise, Fredrik might already be dead.

The swarm had nearly caught up with Fredrik twice now. If they could shoot, they would have had an easy shot both times. After Fredrik fled, he found and illuminated his own lamp. He switched it from red to full spectrum. It didn't matter if the lamp drew their attention. He needed to see. He could run fast, faster than them... for a time. As he grew tired, their scuttling speed was starting to match his jogging gait. He only had a few more sprints left. Resting might buy him a few more escapes.

The landing team had run *into* the tunnels, at first. When the shuttle went down and the winds picked up, it seemed like the best course of action. They would take shelter, call to the ship, and wait out the storm until conditions were clear enough to repair their shuttle or to bring down their backup.

The strange, grey-lined openings beckoned, offering shelter. They were, after all, what the researchers – Fredrik and Thompson and Stone – came down to see. Orbital surveys revealed several such tunnel mouths, too perfectly shaped and regularly spaced to be natural formations. The surface seemed entirely natural, entirely untouched... but there were these openings. Such reshaping suggested larger, hidden life forms, perhaps even intelligence.

There certainly was some kind of intelligence at work. Rudimentary, sentient, sapient... it didn't matter, not after Fredrik knew the natives were dangerous and hostile. The things reacted badly to their intrusion. Whether out of defense or hunger, they attacked. It no longer mattered why. Fredrik just needed to escape. If he returned, if he *ever* returned, it would be with a full squad, all carrying plasma throwers, with atomic lanterns ablaze and motion detectors active, each one monitored by their personal A.I. and synced to a positioning satellite. Then they'd see who hunted who.

His primate brain was doing its best to organize conflicting impulses. Stand and fight! Run away! Hold still! It was not the time to fight. Holding still was also suicide; Fredrik was in the creatures' lair. He had to run. He needed to run *soon*. When the scratching sound came again, it was time to run *now*.

Which way? The sounds came from every direction. Was he surrounded? Were some of the noises echoes from tunnels further back? Further forward? Above, below, to the sides? He had climbed up at one point, slid down at another. As best he could remember, he was at about the same depth as the entrance. Its lateral direction was a complete mystery.

Fredrik decided... forward, then right at the next large branch. He tended to assume that larger branches meant a main trunk. The entrance had been three meters wide. He avoided anything less than a meter across, where he would have to crawl. He was in the two-meter range at the moment. A flash of rationality reminded him that the passages had not shown any specific organization. Branches seemed randomly located and randomly sized, with nothing like a 'tree' structure at all.

Certainly, the tunnels were nothing like a Human structure, even an underground facility. No sapient race Fredrik could think of built like this. Did the creatures build it? Excavate it? Extrude it, like termites? Were they parasites infesting a structure built by some previous inhabitant? Had they already expelled... or consumed... that prior tenant? Or worse, were they commensal creatures, guardians, or pets of something worse?

The Swarm

Was Fredrik, even then, descending into the lair of the swarm's masters? As he ran, hearing clicks on every side but seeing none of the pursuers, he realized that they might be herding him.

Still, what could he do otherwise? It seemed that whenever someone stopped to confront the enemy, they were taken. If they would not step into his light, he was safe as long as he kept moving forward and never left his back unguarded. Or his head, or his feet. Assuming they could not, in fact, burst through the walls.

The passage began to widen. Hope surged, chased closely by leery caution. Something ahead reflected Fredrik's lamp-light. It did not glisten black or red. It shone an opalescent glimmer of blue and green and purple. At first, it seemed like a stack of gems. Then it was the facets of a great multifaceted eye. Fredrik slowed, caught between the need to press forward and the fear of what lay ahead.

He raised his lamp like a weapon. Then he lowered it, fearing it would be snatched from his grasp. Instead, he held both hands high, ready to strike if something lunged. Step by step he advanced. The skittering scraping sound intensified behind him and faded ahead. Was this where he was being led? What worse thing waited for him, watching with a thousand unblinking eyes?

He could only move forward. Then he saw more clearly what produced the glitter. Soft orbs, each larger than an eyeball, hung in clusters from the wall. Like an eye, they also had a translucent skin filled with fluid. Fredrik could tell that the centers were fluid, because something darker swam within each globe. Dark things, like swimming centipedes, a body with many small legs flailing…

Eggs. They were eggs. The spawn of the crawling swarm, no doubt of it. Thousands of them. He had been goaded to their nest, driven to this chamber when he could not be dragged. The creatures had larvae, hungry young, and he was a self-delivered meal.

No! Fredrik had not lived well in his brief, spacefaring life, but he would die well. There would be a thousand fewer monstrosities growing to threaten his successors. They wanted to fatten on his corpse? Let them die beneath his boot!

Fredrik raised his foot to crush the first bunch of eggs. His threat drew a response. The swarm was emboldened. A wave of crawling creatures raced forward, flowing across the floor, scaling up the walls and over the ceiling. Red and black. Reddish-black, like blood in the dim light. Fredrik lashed out, with his feet, with his fist, finally even with the lamp. He felt carapaces crack and even a few eggs burst.

He felt spines puncture his suit and his skin. He tore away from the first grasp, but more of the creatures clambered up his supporting leg. Their segmented bodies wrapped over his lamp and its tightly clenched hand. Then they were on his back, around his neck, on top of his head, and finally, over his face. He could not brush one off without a new horror taking its place.

They did not drag him down, as they had Thompson. Nor did they pull him away, as they had Harley. Of course not. They were holding him in place. They held him still, so that he could not harm their young. They kept him where they wanted him, until the eggs were ready to hatch. They would not even give him the mercy of death to spare him the pain of being devoured alive.

One of the creatures shoved something soft and wet against his nostrils. A foul chemical odor flowed down his throat, making Fredrik gag. A poison? No, a paralytic. He tried to cough and could not. He could not turn his head to avoid the secretion. Blessedly, his vision began to blur. Unconsciousness. Thank the stars. As he fell, Fredrik prayed that he would die before the anesthetic wore off.

Special Defense Leader Sshtknnn.tph.rrrssK crawled out from beneath the collapsed beast. Three of her/her/his legs had been crushed in the battle, but the other nine still held her/her/his weight.

"Any casualties?" she/she/he whistled to the gathered troops.

"Kkktwww.ttt.kchssR is paralyzed!" came one report. That was the worst of it among the soldiers. A few offspring had died, but losses before hatching were sadly common. It could have been worse. It should have gone better. They had been forced into melee. When the monster went after the nursery, they had no choice.

The Swarm

Curses on Defense Primary! Her/his/her demands to capture the beasts without injury had made this operation more dangerous than necessary. The invaders were large, aggressive, and *armed*. Sshtknnn.tph.rrrssK had been right to request a double squad. She/She/He had also been right to request armament, a request that Primary had denied. That point of error would come up next gathering; it certainly would.

"Triad teams, tend to those who can't move. The rest of you, take positions around this captive." Sshtknnn.tph.rrrssK almost hissed the orders in her/her/his fury. When the squads were in position, she/she/he whistled in a more carefully modulated scale, "Carry it/it/it to the holding chamber with the others. Wounded to the infirmary. All legs, march!"

Lack of communication made matters particularly difficult. The intruding creatures were clearly intelligent. The separate covering over their softer, exposed flesh was evidence: synthetic skin for protection. They had tools: light sources and weapons. Sshtknnn.tph.rrrssK had to assume that the slow, rumbling noises these horrors emitted was a language. Maybe the scientists could decode it. Then, they could interrogate the captives.

Talk to the captives, if Primary had anything to do with it. Sshtknnn.tph.rrrssK whined in exasperation. Well, Primary was just relaying the wishes of Himself/Herself/Herself. They would try to "understand" the invaders first.

Then, when Sshtknnn.tph.rrrssK was proven right, when the beasts were revealed as the vicious marauders they clearly were... *then*, the nest could launch a real offensive. These things had come from somewhere on the surface, beyond the tunnels. There could be more of them coming. They could be massing up there, waiting for word from their scouts. Life existed beyond the storms, and it was intelligent and hostile.

The nest couldn't just wait until they were overrun by alien *things*!

Darkness, My Friend

by Nathan Large

Blindness is not usually a trait that saves your life.

But unique situations do happen, especially out here on the edge of known space. Even a so-called disability can become an asset. That's going on my résumé, by the way.

Sure, sometimes, blindness can endanger your life. It makes life a regular parade of nuisances, most days. At best, being blind gains you a little attention and patience from people who would otherwise walk by... but that benefit is countered by the number of people who walk by even faster, disturbed or even annoyed by your handicap. I suspect most sentients get tired of adjusting to my perspective. I know they get tired of adjusting our shared environment to accommodate my needs.

Well, those needs saved my life. And *not* sharing my disability cost my colleagues their lives. So, I'm doing my best not to feel superior, for a change.

We were all dock workers aboard *KelVaTinLi*, cheap labor scooped up by the Zig to work their station freight. We were skilled wage slaves willing and able to handle the hazardous cargoes even the lowest-caste Zig won't touch. I'm a firmware engineer, but I had to sell my services at a discount thanks to the accident that torched my retinas. I was saving up for synthorganic or maybe cybernetic replacements. After this incident, I may rethink those plans.

KelVaTinLi orbits a blue dwarf at the edge of Zig territory, which means it sits at the rim of their slice of the galactic pie. Cargoes come in from neighboring systems, some of which have only tenuous membership in this galaxy. At least one trading partner, the Cuttle, barely participate in the same dimensional frame as the rest of us. That's where this winding tale starts.

'Cuttle' is a Terran name, the one we Humans use, at least on *KelVaTinLi*. I'm sure there's a more dignified label for them catalogued back home in Terran space. The Zig call them 'Species-Culture *Tuch*', with typical lack of imagination. But the Cuttle have big triangular heads with black ball eyes on either side and long, thin-limbed bodies. Like cuttlefish. So, Cuttle.

I know this description on hearsay, of course. All I know, directly, is that the Cuttle smell sort of like grapes and talk like a migraine, and their cargo is so ionized you have to handle it wearing a grounding wire. Their freight is a special sort of problem for the loading lifts I program, because the whole lifting contact structure has to be isolated from the main circuits of the API… that's Artificial Pseudo-Intelligence, if you're not caught up on the latest acronyms.

Doing tricks like that isolation is one of the reasons the Zig keep me on payroll. Fixing the loaders on the fly, when my tricks stop working, is the reason they keep me on the docks when the haulers move Cuttle cargo. So, that's why I was right there, in Cargo Bay *Hek*, when one of the damn stasis crates worked loose from its clamp and tumbled to the deck.

After the crash and clatter, lots of curses went up, including mine. I didn't need to see the mess to know something was broken. Nobody panicked, though, not at first. Even the workers who could see the crate didn't know how badly it was damaged.

The Cuttle generally know what they're doing with cargo, but either that crate was faulty or else we'd discovered a hidden flaw in its design. Either way, the drop damaged its stasis controls. The contents of the crate emerged from an artificially slowed time-frame into our normal time stream.

And those contents were angry. Or hungry. Or both.

I was busy listening to diagnostics, so I didn't hear the exchange down on the lower deck. What I assume was that the brute lifters – Hervé, Jumah, and Wilhelm – approached the crate to right and reload it onto the lifter. Our shift supervisor, a female Hrotata named Shorullt, was probably checking the video feed to see if the lift operator, Michael, did anything wrong.

Now, I didn't mind Shorullt. For a conniving, supercilious little mink, she was at least competent and fair in her assessments. Don't think that's an insult. Hrotata literally look like a mix between a seal and a mink, and their culture and politics are so convoluted that 'conniving' is a survival skill. Their females have a natural superiority complex, even toward one another, much less their own males, and doubly so toward alien males like the dock crew. As an alien female, I was spared only half of her scorn. My blindness hardly registered in her eyes (ha ha) compared to my other flaws.

That said, she didn't deserve what happened. Nobody deserves that.

I heard a pop of decompression, followed by my inner ape screaming *OH SHIT*. I dropped to the floor, pressing the textured rubber mat into my cheek. I assumed there had been an explosion of pressurized gases. I thought I was dodging shrapnel.

Turns out, I was already protected from the worst.

The next thing I sensed was a wave of electromagnetic disturbance, something like the ripple you get off a Cuttle crate if you walk too close. It makes your body hair stand up and your nerves tingle. Except, this blast was twice as strong and many times bigger, washing over us like… well, like an ionic wind.

After that wave, everyone else started screaming. Again, at first, I thought they'd been hit: by flying debris, by radiation, maybe just by an energy source. But I hadn't heard any crash or ricochet like physical objects smashing around. I wasn't hurting, myself, so it wasn't hard radiation… maybe. Even if it was, it'd have to be a high dose to hurt anyone right away. I hadn't felt any heat or direct current. What was I shielded from, such that it injured everyone else – even Shorullt up on the opposite riser – without touching me at all?

I was thinking along the wrong lines. I wasn't protected by any physical barrier, unless you count the transduction gap between my retina and optic nerve. Everyone else *saw* something.

Darkness, My Friend

I'm not sure whether they saw something so horrible that the sight damaged their minds, or something so intense or untranslatable that it damaged their brains. Given their actions afterward, I suspect the stimulus was more like a jamming signal, overloading their sensory apparatus with sights no Human, Hrotata, or Zig was meant to see.

I didn't see it. I couldn't. I don't know if my lack of sight did anything more against that assault than just closing your eyes might, but I didn't need any reflex. Plus, if I *could* have looked, I might have been tempted to take a peek... which would have been fatal. The thing kept firing off its pulse, over and over. You can look for yourself, in the security recordings. It's like a Gorgon, except sending sapients into mindless seizures rather than paralyzing them.   Gorgon. It's a mythical Terran monster. Its gaze turns victims to stone. Forget it; too much explanation required.

Anyway, besides screaming, my co-workers were also thrashing around. I could hear them smacking into obstacles, control panels, and each other. In her spasms, Shorullt triggered several commands through her control panel. I heard the loader start moving, then collide with something organic. Don't tell me who it was; I really don't want to know.

The loader's movement spurred me to action, in a way the other sounds couldn't. I could *do* something about that threat. I jumped to override the improper commands and disabled the loader. My action didn't stop the chaos in the loading dock, though. At best, I reduced the disorder slightly.

The creature, meanwhile, was producing more entropy on its own.

I know it attacked Jumah next, because his wails of pain and terror momentarily coalesced into intelligible words: "It's got me! Help, someone help!" Then, there was another wash of electrical potentials and a sizzling noise. Jumah went quiet.

The other screams died down to whimpers at that point, overlaid by the thump and whoosh of multiple people running. I couldn't tell which of the other two lifters, Hervé or Wilhelm, was the sole survivor below. Given a quiet room and a calm moment, I might be able to tell their gaits apart. The conditions weren't ideal for that trick.

There were plenty of competing noises. I heard the click and hiss of Shorullt moving, her long, low body propelled by short, churning legs. Multiple booted feet hauled their babbling, crying owners – Michael and Lorna and Li Min – in various directions. Impacts against heavy plastic and metal objects indicated that either victims or attacker were knocking over storage crates in their haste.

I was mostly concerned whether anyone or anything was moving in my direction. It didn't sound like that was the case. As a result, I froze.

I probably wasn't any less afraid than anyone else on that dock. But I was *rationally* afraid. I wasn't mentally scrambled by whatever hit everyone else. Holding still, staying out of the way, and not joining the melee made sense at the time. If I misjudged in acting, I might have made myself an easy target.

In hindsight, my fears were valid. The creature did pursue whatever moved, first. There were several more bursts and crackles while I waited. Some of the running noises ended after each. Afterward, though, the thing started to come after the victims who chose to hold still and spasm in place.

I could hear Shorullt screaming from her station: "*What is it? Help us! Great Lady protect me!*" I couldn't tell who she was talking to, except for the obvious prayer to some Hrotata deity. I wondered if she was on comms calling for help, but I doubted it. Like everyone else except me, she seemed to have lost the sense to take proper protective measures.

I was the one who signaled Security. With some doubts about my own sanity, I also triggered the inner locks on the deck's access doors. Whatever was in there with us wasn't going to get out unless someone let it out. I suppose if it was intelligent enough to hack the doors or persuade one of the crew to unlock them, it might have bypassed my defense measures. But it didn't seem likely that anyone else was in any shape to open a door.

Nobody seemed to be *trying* to escape through the actual exit doors. They were just running around, hitting the edges of the dock area, then getting caught and... I'm not sure. Flash-fried? Disintegrated? Bent around the edges of another dimension? I'm really hoping for some answers, after we're done here.

I suspect even you, official inquirers, don't know what got loose down there. I doubt the Cuttle properly registered what they were transporting. It certainly wasn't tagged as a deadly, predatory organism. It's not even clear whether they fully understand our registration protocols. They might consider whatever-it-was a cuddly household pet. Or a form of entertainment. Or a kitchen appliance. Who knows?

What I know is that it is fatal to Humans and other forms of sapient, carbon-based life.

After about a minute — two hectads, if you prefer — the running had mostly stopped but the attacks had not. My verbal feedback from the deck sensors indicated three live, respirating, stationary lifeforms and one energetic, mobile anomaly. Then there were two, plus one.

Holding still was not going to preserve my life. I had to get to the door. But I was still too terrified to move.

My computer reported that the anomaly was moving again. It was moving toward the opposite side of the room, toward the other remaining lifeform. I had a chance.

It's possible I condemned Shorullt to die. She might have managed to escape if I hadn't saved myself. But I doubt it. Nobody seemed to be in their right minds, no one except me. I doubt Shorullt could have managed the clarity of mind to reach the opposite door and issue the proper commands to open it... even with the lights still on. I certainly hope not.

Otherwise, I'd hate myself forever for turning out the lights.

It was an easy command to issue: Disable all illumination. Lights off. My strategy might not have accomplished anything; the predator might not be using the same visible spectrum we... you other sapients employ. But I had to try. I had already sensed how fast the thing could move. Unless I slowed it down somehow, it could finish off Shorullt and run me down before I even reached the exit.

And, as you've likely realized by now, I didn't need the lights to find my way out.

After several standard weeks working the same standardized dock layout, I knew the placement of every step, every walkway, every guide rail and every barrier. I even knew where the charging outlets were. Making my way to the exit was simple. I could do it running. I literally did.

Once the lights were out, I bolted as fast as I dared toward the far door. I could hear crackling sparks behind me, accompanied by Shorullt's dying gasp. Then came footsteps: the sizzling taps I identified with the entity's movement. It sounded like it was far behind me. It also sounded like it was moving slowly: slower than it had before. I'd like to think I bought some time with my maneuver.

Or maybe, it wasn't sure what to do with me. I wasn't screaming and flailing and panicking like its other prey. Maybe it was confused by the ineffectiveness of its usual trick, like an angler fish seeing a blindfish ignoring its brilliant lure.

Blind fish or blind woman, I wasn't ignoring my potential death. I was getting away as quickly as I could manage. Hearing my footfalls echo against the approaching door, I shouted: "Door override: *Hek Tuch Vi Ti Lo*, Elizabeth Kern."

Hearing my override code, the security computer opened the exit door, just long enough for me to race through. I managed to breathe out, "Close!" and it sealed shut as quickly as super-magnets could drag the door panels together.

I heard the thing smack up against those bulkhead doors with a crackle of frustrated charge. My continued existence is the evidence that it couldn't find a way through.

I mean, those doors can withstand vacuum and a huge range of temperatures, not to mention blocking most forms of radiation. But I didn't know what that creature was. I was only gambling that it couldn't get out. I didn't know what it was capable of. I still don't. For all I know, it might have capabilities that standard physics doesn't allow. What I do know is, it can't cope well with darkness… or blindness.

Darkness, My Friend

So, sometimes, the lack of an ability can be asset unto itself. I don't know yet how well that discovery translates outside of this particular work environment… but I'm planning to find out.

I wish you well catching the thing again. I'd suggest contacting the Cuttle and asking how they got it into their stasis crate in the first place. It's better if you make that call. I might say something undiplomatic. If absolutely necessary, I'll stick around *KelVaTinLi* long enough to implement their solution, if my engineering expertise is needed.

Remotely, that is. I won't be going back there personally. While my *lack* of ability might be useful, you'll have to replicate that trait for yourselves.

Good luck!

A.I. Codger

by Laine Megan Lundquist

TaMeTu glared at Arianna over their glasses of liquor. "You're joking with me, right?"

Arianna shook her head and picked up her own glass. The delicacy with which she picked it up and her smooth, brown fingers made TaMeTu think of a Copper Caste Zig. That impression wasn't inappropriate; the blue trim on her black uniform signified a member of the Collective Research Corps, though TaMeTu couldn't make sense of her rank insignia.

Ari shook her head, her shoulder length, dark brown hair rippling behind her. "No, TaMeTu. I take my humor very seriously."

The Zig scratched his smooth chin and huffed incredulously. He reached out and took his own drink and stared into the depths of the glass. *Humans love these vessels. Open ended cylinders. So prone to spilling. Wider base, smaller mouth? Maybe a nipple at the end? No. Open ended cylinders. They have no imagination.* TaMeTu realized that the Human had been talking to him. He shook his head and snorted and refocused.

"…and people have transmitted the show just about everywhere. You have no idea how funny AI Codger is until you've seen it! Did you watch any of the vids I sent you?"

"I have to admit, I think that some of it is lost on me, culturally. I understand what it is about: a young Human who inherits his grandfather's Artificial Intelligence, who happens to appear as an elderly Human and behaves in a socially inappropriate manner."

A.I. Codger

TaMeTu had watched some of the show but couldn't get into it. The only thing that it taught him was gratitude that he was not Human. Their social mores were confusing and highly impractical.

Ari laughed. "That's like saying that Hamlet is about a whiny orphan, or that HaMaShaMe is about a series of coincidences linking the lives of several families in the first Zig-Mauraug conflict. Rudolph isn't just his grandfather's Brin; he has a lot of his grandfather's qualities. It's about learning from the examples of your ancestors, the legacies that you leave behind when you die, Human-AI relations… there are a lot of relevant themes. What don't you understand about the series?"

TaMeTu rubbed his head. Little wiry protrusions of metallic hair had begun to poke through his scalp. He made a note to depilate when he got back to his quarters. "Well, first off, why does Rudolph look old? And why does the child – Aaron, I think – why does he even have an AI? He is pre-pubescent."

"You didn't watch far enough; they go into Rudolph's backstory pretty early on in the first series. See, he was Aaron's grandfather's first Brin, and he so he grew up with him, and grew old with him. He even got married… did you see any of the episodes with his exes? Aging is natural for Humans, so our AIs often do it too, although some people prefer their Brins to look young forever. That's not considered healthy, though. The more Human an experience a Brin has, the more Human-like they become as they develop and come into their own."

TaMeTu found his eyes wandering across the club. Dozens of sapients, mostly Human but with a smattering of Hrotata and Taratumm and a couple of Zig were filling the seats around the small, round tables and low couches. The stage was still empty, although there were projected commercials being played. The current one was a first-person perspective of a Human hurtling themselves down the side of a snow covered mountain while balancing on two long, flat runners. It was either a highly primitive mode of travel or a dangerous and stupid-looking sport. Either way, TaMeTu couldn't even tell what the commercial was for. He started considering an improved dynamic for a personal non-mechanical downhill snow and ice based transportation system when he realized that Ari was waiting for him to continue the conversation.

He cleared his throat. "So, is Randolph a Human? I'm confused about that."

"Do you mean the actor or the character?"

"The actor, Ari. I know that the character is an AI. And why do you call them 'Brins'?"

"The Brin-Makato Corporation created the first mass-produced artificial intelligences for private use. People – Human people – sometimes refer to things by the name of the company that produced them. It's shorter and it lets everyone know what brand you use. There were a lot of cheap and dangerous knockoffs, but Brin-Makato AIs were the most robust and flexible, and Brin-Makato is long, so people just started calling them Brins. Brin-Makato has been out of business for a long time now, but the name stuck.

"As for the actor, Rudolph *is* an AI. He actually belongs to the producer, and Rudolph is his real name, his public name as well. The story goes that Rudolph – or actually, the AI's real name is Trini; Rudolph's just the character that she plays – Trini came up with the idea and animated a sample episode that she showed to her Keeper… the producer, and they got a couple of friends together and recorded it live. In between making serials they tour and do this comedy routine."

A device vibrated in TaMeTu's pocket, a reminder to take his supplements. He pulled out a small packet and tore it open, carefully pouring it into the liquid in his glass. Many of the elements inherent to Zig physiology were poisonous to other sapients, so most Zig needed to supplement their diet with compounds of thallium, lead, and other heavy metals when they spent large amounts of time in shared space.

He swirled the glass and lifted it to his lips. The flavor of the brandy was increased tenfold by the supplements; it went from being a thin, tasteless alcohol to almost resembling something that he might have ordered for himself.

"So," he asked after a satisfying swig, "Rudolph – who is really Trini – is projecting to the club with her owner?"

"*Keeper*, TaMeTu. *Never* owner. We don't 'own' other sentiences just because we create them. We keep them and guide them and help them to learn to experience and enjoy the universe, and in exchange, they help us to do things that we couldn't do otherwise.

A.I. Codger

"And no, she's not 'projecting'. Brins have housing units, and most of them are immobile. A Brin *could* bounce around in local networks but it would cause all sorts of security hassles if it even wanted to leave a planet, much less cross star systems. You can't transfer information through hyperspace, and Ningyo space-folding is expensive. Even if she did send her program all the way to Lotus Station, that would be considered creating an unauthorized copy of herself and she and all of her backups would be terminated."

TaMeTu nodded, but was skeptical. *We've tried creating servants too. Didn't work out too well. So did the Mauraug. Much worse for them, but they're not Zig. Any of the safety precautions that you Humans like bragging about are heavily reliant on user and AI integrity.*

"So are we going to be watching Trini or Rudolph then?"

Ari rolled her eyes and threw her head back dramatically. "Trini is coming and performing in her famous role as Rudolph the AI Codger. How is this so hard to understand?"

"How do we know that it's Trini performing as Rudolph? Couldn't any AI just pretend to be Rudolph?"

She scoffed. "Oh, come on. We'd know the difference."

TaMeTu was getting bored of waiting. "So... why isn't your AI here?"

"Alice doesn't like AI Codger. She says that it is a poor representation of her community. You should have seen her expression when I told her I wanted to come here with you! Also, I thought that since we were coming here to get to know one another it would be better if it were just you and I." She rested her dexterous fingers across the top of his hand, and it was all he could do not to start huffing or mewling. Humans weren't used to such unrestrained expressions of arousal and attraction, and tended to be sensitive to them.

Actually, that seems to be the source of a lot of the humor in AI Codger. TaMeTu mused. Carefully drawing deep breaths, he intertwined his fingers with Arianna's. She smiled and tilted her head, coyly letting some of her hair fall in front of her face, and he felt his heart melt. *She's so elegant, so understated, so subtle... They may not be bright but they're so beautiful!*

Empyrean Stories

Given the resemblance between their species, Humans and Zig often found one another attractive despite the toxic dangers to the Human members of such pairings. Beyond just physical appearance, there were many Zig that secretly – and sometimes openly – revered what they considered the calm wisdom and elegant simplicity of Human culture and behavior. Zig lived fast and thought fast and their cultures tended to reward quick thinking, innovation, and what many other sapients considered a callous attitude toward the welfare of others. Humans, with their virtues of "patience" (often seen by Zig as hesitancy, over-caution, or laziness), "beauty" (frivolity, propaganda, or a tool for manipulation), and respect for tradition caught the imagination of some of TaMeTu's species. To most Zig, Humans appeared to be lazy and superficial. To TaMeTu and others, they appeared to be gentle and wise, exemplars of a more relaxed, introspective quality that the Zig lost in the distant past… or never possessed in the first place.

His reverie was interrupted by a small smattering of applause as the maître d' came out onto the stage and gave a small bow. He was thin and tall, with a sallow complexion, slick hair and a thin, curled mustache.

"Ladies and gentleman, I have some disappointing news. The ship that was carrying Rudolph, the esteemed comedian and thespian that you came here tonight to see, met with a tragic hyperspace accident. The last message received from the ship was…"

The figure rapidly transformed, shrinking in size, its skin wrinkling, hair whitening and fading, and stomach expanding. His clothes went from a restaurant uniform to loose-fitting, casual gear. Hair sprouted from his nostrils.

"NYAAAAAAAAAAAAAAAHHHHHHH!" Rudolph let out his catchphrase and leaned over, leering at the audience. He leaned forward and pointed outwards toward the audience, sweeping his arm. "Got ya there, huh! Thought I was dead? Thought you got rid of me? NYAAAAAAAAHHHHHHHHHH!"

TaMeTu watched as the crowd began to convulse with laughter. He looked up at Ari, her eyes glowing and mouth wide. He marveled again at her beauty and gripped her fingers a bit more tightly.

"Betcha that woulda made that Smashsmash Bash'Trash or whatever guy happy too! You know, that guy outside protesting me right now. " Rudolph waved towards the windows at the Mauraug standing stolidly outside. "I can see you from here, buddy! NYYYYYAAAAAAAAHHHHHHHHHHH!"

Arianna glanced down at TaMeTu. She caught him looking. He couldn't help it, there was no way to keep from huffing now. He injected some vocalization into it and it turned into a laugh, turning back to the wizened Human figure on the stage. Even if he couldn't fully appreciate the humor, he could be swept up in the shared emotions of his date and the crowd. He would make sure to try and taste Humanity that night.

Nothing like a subjective emotional experience to convey a sense of shared identity, he mused as he settled in to laugh at the A I Codger's antics.

An Apostate's Path

by Nathan Large

Chapter 1: Decision

Veshin paused in its grooming, finally accepting that its fur would settle no further. It had found every speck of dust. Further plucking would only result in bald patches. Veshin's black skin would start to show through its dark umber coat, and not just on its face, hands, and feet.

Veshin was not vain; it was agitated. It prepared for the day knowing that it would be forced to revisit the same pressing question, over and over, by its own mind and by the inquiries of its family and friends. What would Veshin choose as its life path? Had it decided, yet?

Veshin val'Ineth faced the central dilemma of any Mauraug's life: who would be its master? Would it serve only itself, remaining apart from any commitment, or would it accept a cause, a duty, or a leader to follow?

The majority of Mauraug claimed to accept no master, asserting their individual, eternal struggle for Dominion. The precepts of their religion held that each mind was its own Dominion. One might temporarily submit to a master out of necessity, but should never cease striving against that master. One should always seek Dominance. Submission was only external, never acceptable internally.

Veshin was not a follower of Dominion. It did not subscribe to the teachings of Sha'bahn, though it was familiar with their content. Dominionists would call

An Apostate's Path

Veshin val'Ineth an Apostate, a deceived fool who rejected the obvious truth of Dominion... the truth of its blood. Mauraug, after all, instinctually felt the call to Dominate.

What was obvious was not always correct. The Way of Ineth, the religion taught to Veshin by its parents, Grathek and Nuunshin, argued that the desire to control others was a base biological urge, no more noble than the need to defecate. Just as one did not defecate whenever and wherever one wished, one did not indulge dominance at all times, but only when appropriate. Many other 'instincts' were counterproductive, injurious both to the self and to society. Dominion's cardinal mistake was to elevate an atavistic behavior, even a deeply satisfying one, to the status of virtue. Civilization required submission. For that matter, domination itself implied submission. The Way of Ineth taught restraint, balance, and discernment.

Veshin wasn't fully invested in the Way of Ineth. Its religion was one potential master it needed to consider. If it remained within its community, it would be tacitly accepting the Way. Or, it could choose to join the clergy, investing itself fully in the faith of its family and community.

Veshin's family and community followed the Way, piously. One of its parents, Nuunshin, was an acolyte to the community's priesthood. That was the root of Veshin's dilemma.

The Way dictated that when a child passed into adulthood – a ceremony which Veshin would undergo in just six days – that new adult must choose a path to follow, a career through which it would serve the community. If it did not serve, it could not follow the Way, and if it did not follow the Way, it must leave the community.

There were many ways to serve. The military was a popular choice. The Redemption Alliance, the coalition elsewhere known as the Mauraug Apostasy, always needed soldiers to defend its members. If it didn't choose another career, the community would expect Veshin to enlist.

The servants of the Way were only one of several communities opposed to and threatened by the Dominionist majority. Several sects, long ago, chose to abandon their home worlds and create illicit colonies outside of Mauraug space, rather than suffer suppression by the authorities of Dominion. They were not fleeing death; Dominionism was opposed to killing opponents when it could nullify or convert them. This restraint was no virtue; there exist worse punishments than death, and the ruling Dominionists used every tool available to marginalize, torment, and force compliance from dissenters.

Such restraint only held when Apostates were safely contained, divided among the populations of Dominion-controlled worlds. When the heretics managed to escape control and establish their own, independent communities, all forbearance vanished. The Dominion would kill anyone who harbored or protected any Apostate sect and would even exterminate whole groups of Mauraug who refused to return to the fold.

The Redemption Alliance formed out of practical necessity, not unity between the disparate non-Dominion philosophies. The Way of Ineth held law and community above all other values, yet allowed a place for dominance within its structures of virtue. The Khamish School, by contrast, refuted dominance entirely as an outright sin, exhorting its followers to submit to everything: circumstance, divinity, and one another. In practical terms, the two creeds encouraged similar behaviors, but specific divergences of practice and belief kept them apart. Only the greater threat of Domination allowed their followers to serve together.

The Alliance was largely a military organization, but diplomatic and bureaucratic functions were logically emerging from the need for coordination between colonies and warships. Veshin supposed it could seek a role as a functionary, if it were opposed to violence.

It was not. It hated the crushing cruelty of the Dominion, even without directly witnessing its acts. It would gladly strike down an enemy soldier or press the controls that incinerated a Dominion ship.

Veshin had grown up safely insulated in an Inethi community, but it had friends who lost family to Dominion aggression. Their families and Veshin's had been dispossessed of any former wealth by the Dominion, as a consequence of their choice to embrace the Way. Though their parents all rebuilt new lives on distant worlds, their existence was difficult and tenuous, especially compared to their ancestors' comfort on Mauraug Prime.

Veshin wasn't as certain of its feelings toward the Collective, the alliance of diverse sapient species and cultures which included the Mauraug Dominion. Most among the Alliance considered the Collective an enemy as well, given its political acceptance of Dominion. Some argued that the Collective was merely a neutral party, forced to accept the reality of Dominion's control over the Mauraug culture, but otherwise opposed to its precepts. Closer study of beliefs and attitudes throughout the Collective cultures suggested that most sapients found Dominion repugnant. Most other cultures would prefer that the Mauraug act differently... but that was a wish, not an actionable stance.

And there were plenty of sympathizers for Dominion among non-Mauraug. Some groups and individuals found it useful to have a single, powerful authority in charge. Some alien philosophies mirrored or largely agreed with Dominion; others endorsed its core ideas but differed in implementation. And plenty of sapients, even governments, acted identically to Dominion practice, even if they espoused conflicting beliefs.

Whether or not a soldier despised the Collective as a willing or accidental ally of the Dominion, it was inevitable that defense of Alliance colonies and pursuit of Alliance goals would put those warriors into combat against Collective ships. The Mauraug Dominion labeled the Apostasy a rogue, terroristic group, and insisted that its Collective allies capture or destroy Apostate properties and personnel.

It didn't help that the Apostasy... the *Alliance*... did attack and often destroy Dominion targets. If one of their colonies was wiped out, the Alliance would often attack a Dominion station or colony in reprisal. If new Dominion bases appeared close to Alliance communities, one or more groups would launch a pre-emptive attack to disrupt, drive back, or purge those inroads. Certain sects also had no compunctions about attacking Dominion property or citizens, un-provoked, simply to lash out at the hated tyrants and weaken their structure.

The Redemption Alliance *was* terroristic, out of necessity. They would never have sufficient strength to directly assault the Dominion... even if many of its members weren't directly opposed to such Dominion-like tactics. They could only strike against isolated and weak targets, often innocent but vulnerable populations. The goal of many operations was simply to slow the expansion of Dominion and discourage its encroachment upon the galaxy.

Their greater goal was psychological: to force Dominion to acknowledge their existence and threat, to alert other societies that Mauraug were not actually a unified population, to demonstrate the evil of Dominion and the reality of resistance against it, and if nothing else, to make the Mauraug Dominion consider the fruits of its philosophies.

That their tactics — necessary or not — turned the Collective further against the Alliance was a reality not lost on the Alliance's saner leaders. Such concerns even occurred to Veshin, far before it was called to decide its life path. The dilemma about violence and its justifications was part of the debate which made Veshin's choice so difficult.

It did not find itself sufficiently convinced of the Way of Ineth to seek ordination. It was too conflicted about war to confidently enlist. It was not even sure enough about the righteousness of the Alliance to serve as diplomat or bureaucrat. It had not considered any particular vocation which might guarantee it a place within the Inethi community: engineering, farming, childcare, or domestic maintenance, like its other parent, Grathek.

Nothing appealed enough. Nothing suited Veshin enough to make it want to pursue that duty for a lifetime.

The only remaining option, per the teachings of the Way, was to depart the community and seek a separate path. If Veshin could not contribute to their society, it must master itself, alone.

Ability wasn't the problem. Veshin felt capable of any of the offered vocations. It was intellectually flexible enough. In fact, its intelligence was part of its problem; it could not avoid considering the flaws in any life path.

Veshin was also healthy, aside from a genetic immune disorder which would eventually cripple it with arthritic damage, later in life. Unlike many Mauraug, it lacked an obvious birth defect, instead trading the traditional handicap for a chronic illness that would only affect it in middle age.

An Apostate's Path

Its eventual degeneration was another major factor in Veshin's indecision. If it might have a shorter career than others – depending on the success of immune suppressant treatments or joint replacement – then it needed to choose that career wisely. If it chose to roam alone, it would have to either face future pain or else prosper enough to afford medical care on its own.

Going alone also meant separation from other Mauraug. If it left the Way, it also had to leave the Alliance… which would be part of the point. Veshin would never be fully accepted by the Dominion, unless it fully embraced Dominion philosophy and behavior, which it would never do. Thus, it would have to avoid all Mauraug, becoming dependent on alien persons and societies for its survival.

And it would still need a job. Too bad Veshin couldn't make up its mind about which course to pursue.

Too bad the Inethi colony couldn't provide a vocational school or education beyond basic adult skills. The apostates sacrificed more in their flight from the Dominion than most sapients realized… they lost skills, knowledge, tools, and reference materials. What the Alliance currently possessed had been painstakingly rebuilt (or stolen) over decades. Aside from the necessities of life, there was no room or training for any novel profession; there were no Inethi poets or chefs or architects.

So how could a single adolescent, raised by an isolated sect, possibly make an informed, unbiased decision about how to live the rest of its life?

Chapter 2: Direction

"Are you ready? Or have you fallen asleep again?" The voice of Veshin's parent, Grathek, rattled down the hallway of their home. As usual, its prosthetic jaw gave its speech precise, clipped consonants.

Like most Mauraug, Grathek was born with a number of genetic defects due to the chromosomal plague that afflicted their species… another unfair burden passed on by the Dominionists, who long ago tormented the Tesetsi, a sapient species gifted with natural bio-engineering talent and the ability to pay back a grudge over generations. Veshin was fortunate it inherited only the one disorder from its dominant parent, Nuunshin.

Genetic dominance wasn't something discussed in polite Inethi society, not unless it was medically relevant. Unlike the Dominionist Mauraug, who incorporated the name of their dominant parent into their own name with the infix "bash'", followers of the Way of Ineth used the infix "val'", denoting a worthy, heroic ancestor. Veshin val'Ineth, like its parent Grathek, could claim descent from Ineth itself, and both it and Grathek's mate used that name with honor.

"I am awake," Veshin called back, "just not ready to start the day."

Veshin knew it had only a few moments after that reply before hearing another response. Though it was exempt from school lessons for the days leading up to its coming of age ceremony, it was not exempt from other duties at home or within the community. Grathek would expect its help cleaning, cooking, and performing home maintenance. If Veshin was allowed any escape from those duties, it would be expected to join Nuunshin in the chapel for whatever services *that* parent required. The Way insisted that even children play a part in society, adjusted for their developing capabilities.

An Apostate's Path

Those duties were, in part, intended to introduce children to potential careers and engage their interest. Most children did tend to embrace the work of one of their parents. Veshin was of two minds about that practice: it was enviably convenient to find your passion in familiar work, but it was also lazy.

Whether valid or not, exposure to its parents' work had not enchanted Veshin. It found domestic maintenance boring and religious service uncomfortable. It wasn't sure if its doubts about the Way were what prevented it from settling on a life path, or if its trouble choosing a life path was what fueled its doubts about the Way.

The Way covered more than just adulthood and work; it was a total life philosophy, addressing mating, child care, education, discipline, commerce, warfare, and the care of the dying and the dead. If anything, the Way of Ineth was a more comprehensive and detailed religion than Dominion, spelling out much of its practice rather than relying on a central principle supported by a variety of parables and poems.

Veshin's parents embraced the Way, fully. Thus, their offspring's doubts distressed both adult Mauraug. They would not indulge its indecision. They certainly would not tolerate its sloth.

Rather than shouting back its reply, Grathek came stomping down the hall. Its footsteps were so loud, Veshin could predict the moment the door to its room would open. Instead of smashing the outer controls and entering like a storm, Grathek toggled the intercom and spoke with exaggerated patience: "May I come in, then?"

Veshin grunted. Why ask a question when there was only one acceptable answer? "Yes, come in," it replied, careful not to stray into tones of challenge.

Grathek tapped the door open and stepped through the threshold. It took in the few square meters of Veshin's personal space and nodded in approval of its offspring's tidiness. However, its manner was stern when it turned back to Veshin.

"You have little time to spare. I was going to allow you your freedom today, *if* you used that privilege to consider your upcoming choice. Your peers have already decided what paths they will pursue. Only you delay. Consider the shame to Nuunshin and me, if you remain uncertain on the eve of your ceremony."

Veshin wanted to bellow a defiant reply, complaining about all the difficulties *it* faced and all the pressure placed on *it* by the unfair demands of its parents and their community. After all, other religions didn't demand that new adults immediately and permanently choose their career by a specific age.

The followers of Soch'inar, for example, held individual freedom as their highest virtue. They understood domination as the will to be free of restriction, and so the society that served Mauraug best was one that allowed them each to determine their own path. The Soch'inari would never force children *or* adults into any career or make them stay in a job they didn't like. Veshin had to admit, though, that the followers of that liberal creed had one of the poorest communities within the Alliance, and were rumored to hypocritically subvert their practice by begging, bribing, or even beating members into performing necessary work.

It could be worse, though. The Khamish School, with their embrace of 'submission', simply assigned youths to courses of vocational study. Elders told children what jobs they would take, based on the community's needs. If they needed farmers, you were going to be a farmer, whether you liked it or not.

Veshin couldn't complain too much, philosophically. It also couldn't complain, practically. From experience, it knew that Grathek was ready with rebuttals to any argument its child might muster. Veshin would not shake its parent's certainty in the rightness of their Way.

Actually, Grathek's blithe confidence in the Way was another reason Veshin felt so unprepared. Over the years of its childhood, Grathek always assumed that its offspring would find a path on its own. Everyone did. Veshin's worries were met with vague platitudes; its requests for information or for help were rewarded with more work to keep it busy and quiet.

Its other parent, Nuunshin, did nothing to help. Nuunshin only reassured Veshin that even though it was uncertain, it would eventually make a choice. The gods would guide. And because Veshin was so intelligent, it would be good at anything it chose; talent wasn't the problem, only enthusiasm. Since enthusiasm, like joy, came from unceasing pursuit of the Way, Veshin needed only to trust in their faith and it would prosper.

Despite these parental failings, Veshin still felt like it, itself, deserved the largest portion of blame. It had never focused on any particular area of study. It never chose a mentor or role model to follow around. If it had gravitated toward some specific adult, its parents might have permitted it to shadow that teacher, even if the mentor worked in a different area than Veshin's parents.

Veshin thought of itself as a dilettante. It chased after multiple paths, but pursued none with any conviction or depth. It did love mathematics for a time, but that infatuation waned after classes moved beyond simple arithmetic into number theory and functions. It played with languages until the difficulties of fluency became apparent. It might have delved into reading and research, but the community had limited library resources and there were no true academic roles to fill... aside from teaching the young from the limited rote of lessons.

Was that the problem? The community itself was too limited, too bounded by its circumstances. Did Veshin need some pursuit beyond the limits of their habitat, the controlled environment where Alliance communities huddled for survival? It couldn't know, because it couldn't leave or even make contacts outside that tiny world. Veshin couldn't know what it might be missing. The only option to find out was to renounce the community and depart for a solitary existence.

And for the safety of the Inethi and all the Alliance, leaving meant forgetting, as well. The memories of their shared colony – its location and its layout – would be excised from Veshin's mind. It would remember its upbringing, at least. The Way would not permit deletion of its mark on a Mauraug's past, even for reasons of security. But Veshin would not be able to find its way home again, no matter what it found. Even if whatever it discovered would benefit the community by being brought back, it could not return.

Veshin already discussed these things with its parents and considered the issues within itself. Grathek's complaints were unnecessary. How, then, did it expect its distressed offspring to respond?

Veshin offered only a noncommittal grunt and rose from its crouched position before the mirror. When its parent held ground at the doorway, Veshin ventured: "I appreciate your offer and will use my liberty wisely." Though its words and manner were neutral, both parent and child knew the sentiment was insincere. Veshin wanted only to flee, not study.

Still, Grathek gave way. It stepped back out of the room, giving one final warning: "Six days. You must know your path in six days. Do what you must to find it."

Veshin walked past without acknowledgement. While rude, it was safer to do nothing than risk further pretended courtesies and offend its parent. Grathek wouldn't immediately offer violence if openly defied – unlike many Mauraug parents – but it would make Veshin's life even more miserable if its child dared rebel. Any punishment it chose to levy, short of crippling harm, would be supported by the community.

Like its parents, Veshin had no option to oppose the Way, not while it lived within their habitat. Its only means of rejecting the Way would be to reject the entire community formally and publicly, leaving its habitat, leaving the Alliance forever.

There was no alternative; if Veshin ran away from home on its own terms, there was nothing outside, almost literally. Their sealed colony was surrounded by miles of wasteland, on a planetoid with a fatally thin atmosphere. There were reasons no Dominionist Mauraug ever settled that system, the same reasons they ignored it when searching for the strayed Apostates. Survival on such a barren world seemed too unlikely to believe.

Yet over five thousand heretics did live there, in the domes and burrows of their sanctuary. Eleven different communities were forced to share space, just as they were forced to ally against a shared enemy. Their will and labor kept the habitat viable, along with the supplies looted by the Alliance fleet.

With warships linking the Alliance together, the habitat wasn't completely 'alone'. There were other such habitats scattered around the galaxy, including one true planetary colony and several orbital stations. Yet inhabitants rarely transferred from one home to another. They stayed close to the community of their original faith, if they weren't assigned to a ship. If a soldier survived long enough to retire, it usually went back to its original home.

Only diplomats changed living arrangements between habitats, and then only for the duration of their missions. Veshin again considered the diplomatic corps. It would at least get to experience some variety. Perhaps its uncertainty was a symptom of dissatisfaction with the specific habitat where it was born. Breadth of experience might be the focus it sought.

But who could know for certain? And once the choice was made, if it was wrong or if it wasn't enough, Veshin would be trapped in a new misery. It had never even traveled by starship. What if it was prone to hyperspace sickness? What if it became homesick? What if the manners and conditions of another habitat proved even worse?

There was just no certainty. Veshin's digestive tract cramped as it prepared to leave, either from hunger or from distress. Which was it? Another unclear choice Veshin would have to guess about. It split the difference by taking a wrapped bar of grain and syrup from the pantry. If necessary, it could eat later.

One more decision it could only put off for so long.

Chapter 3: Distraction

Veshin walked aimlessly at first, content to simply escape its home and wander until it fixed on a plan of action. It rolled its shoulders in greeting as it passed neighbors in the hallway, emerging from their own suites. Some eyed it curiously; theirs was a small society, and everyone knew Veshin. Everyone knew about its indecision in choosing a path. Some neighbors were tolerant, trusting that the youth would make its decision when the time came. Some were judgmental, finding fault in Veshin's delay. Others tried to be helpful, making unsolicited suggestions about careers: their own or other paths they thought Veshin might favor.

Most didn't care one way or another. These neighbors ignored Veshin as it walked by, which was acceptable enough.

It saw no other youths that morning. Their absence was another neutral blessing. More so than the adults, its peers pressured Veshin in a variety of ways. They boasted about their own intended careers. They pressed at Veshin, demanding to know its choice or asking why it had not already chosen.

The worst of them mocked Veshin outright for being uncertain… or too incompetent to serve in any role. The latter soon discovered that Veshin was at least diligent in its physical exercises. Out of three fights, only one earned Veshin any reprimand, and that for excessive injuries to its opponent after submission.

Veshin might be strong and capable in a fight, but it wasn't a warrior. It hated the idea of killing or risking death. It fought only out of necessity – to prevent further abuse – and frustration. If it were never provoked again, it would be happier.

And besides, those fights were against fellow youths. A fully-grown adult would flatten Veshin in moments. The difference wasn't only in mass – Veshin would have its full size in another year or two – but also training and experience.

Most adult Mauraug fought numerous brawls to establish dominance and fitness. That was true for most Mauraug in the Alliance as much as those under Dominion. There were some exceptions among the sects, but even the most pacifistic creed allowed for a degree of self-defense, if only to secure respect from other groups.

Besides familiarity with violence, adults also had more opportunity for physical exercise and specific training. Domestic engineers like Grathek were least likely to know advanced techniques or build powerful muscle, but even that parent could best Veshin by virtue of regular exercise and occasional sparring with its mate.

Veshin decided to let *that* line of thought drop. It did, however, gain an idea about what to do with its time. It sought out the habitat's gymnasium. Perhaps it could find a trainer available and request a lesson. If nothing else, the exertion would help clear its mind and reduce its agitation. And maybe, it might discover enjoyment or even an aptitude among the available disciplines. There were worse careers than physical training, although Veshin suspected such a path would require it to study distasteful subjects like biology and warfare.

As it walked, it passed several of the habitat's vital sections: a hydroponic farm, a ventilation exchange station, the main communications hub housing the habitat's network servers, and a nursery where infants were tended during their parents' work shifts.

The squalling of children made Veshin cringe. Child care was definitely *off* its list of careers to consider. It rarely encountered infants, anyway, and when it did, they seemed like deranged, violent, foul-smelling animals rather than future Mauraug. Walking into a nursery was a hazard similar to entering a den of vermin, with the same risk of being swarmed, bitten, or defecated upon.

Yet despite its distaste, Veshin also pitied the screaming young. They were innocent of their situation, ignorant of every trouble except their immediate distresses. They could not imagine the difficulties to come in their life: parental discipline, confusing education, the limitations of their restricted physical and cultural environment, and ultimately, the dilemma of choosing a life path.

Its pity for the children was pity for Veshin itself. It couldn't help being pathetic. Every action, every thought eventually turned back to its central trouble. Days ago, it began to regret the mandatory vacation from schooling. At least a difficult lesson would provide some distraction. A serious, engrossing task would be welcome. Veshin tried not to wish for a habitat-wide catastrophe, just to take its mind off its personal agony. It was difficult *not* to think that way.

The gymnasium was open when Veshin arrived. A class of youths was inside, warming up, with an adult instructor watching them before starting their lesson. They weren't familiar faces, neither Inethi nor from any of the communities nearest Veshin's home. Veshin considered intruding, but held itself back out of embarrassment. Could it watch without disturbing the group? It supposed it could exercise, alone, without attracting undue attention. There weren't any unattached trainers available.

Veshin decided to work through a familiar routine and see if anyone arrived while it waited. If it was especially lucky, one of the rare Thashti Masters would stop in, alone or with an acolyte. The followers of Thashti held an exquisitely formalized view of domination, requiring that a student first gain dominion over themselves before earning the right to exert it upon others. Disputes within the small community were resolved through ritual combat, which could be marathons of several hours or exchanges resolved with only two blows. Outside of the community, the Thashti were proven geniuses of martial combat in all forms, unarmed or armed with any sort of weapon.

While it would never be accepted as Thashti, Veshin might be able to plead for a lesson with a Master, by expressing a genuine desire to know itself. A Master might be swayed by the opportunity to demonstrate the value of their creed. Veshin might not gain much in terms of practical martial skill – not from a single lesson – but it might still learn something valuable.

Veshin sent out its desires to the universe, just in case its wishes had any effect. At least its new request, while selfish, was less destructive than its aborted plea for a disaster.

It managed to pass most of an hour in mindless labor, straining against resistance weights, running on a treadmill, and climbing through a virtual forest in the simulation couch. It didn't come to any new insights about its problem, but at least it improved its circulation and musculature... and its presence didn't draw any unwanted attention from the class.

The students were being trained primarily in calisthenics: stretching exercises that they would later use to prepare for more strenuous workouts. From what it overheard, Veshin could not identify any specific philosophy underlying the teacher's instructions. It was left with a handful of guesses about the unfamiliar group's origin, but no specific means of distinguishing them.

That uncertainty was something of a relief. Veshin was honestly tired of sorting everyone it knew by religion. In many cases, the distinctions were practical, to avoid giving offense or to better understand the needs and beliefs of one's neighbors. But often, labelling produced only unhelpful prejudices and a feeling of isolation. It was impractical to associate only with Inethi, but Veshin suspected many followers of the Way would segregate themselves, if they could.

For true believers of the Way, other faiths were too undisciplined, or too violent, or too authoritarian. Adults raised in the Way were naturally taught about the superiority of their views; it followed that all other philosophies were inferior. Dominion reared its snarling head everywhere.

Veshin couldn't be certain its own doubts weren't flaws in itself, stemming from failure to adhere to the Way. Or, more likely, its doubts about the Way came from its dissatisfaction with the path laid out before it. But wasn't that an appropriate response? When a creed failed its adherents, shouldn't they question it? Shouldn't they ask whether the fault lay in their ancestors, not their own mind?

Veshin ended its workout, disgusted that unwanted thoughts again crept into its meditations. Strenuous labor only helped for a short time. Eventually, distress crept in, followed by resentment and despair. No enlightenment, thus far. Veshin began to doubt whether it would ever find peace. If it ever did experience a revelation about itself, it might doubt the discovery or doubt that its insight came from the Way.

It was too bad no Thashti or other combat master was available. Veshin would have welcomed violence, even if it were the one being struck. It needed some sort of diversion.

Should it spend its last remaining credit on an electronic amusement, in the habitat's recreation area? Virtual bloodshed might be an acceptable substitute for real violence. Games were expensive, though, owing to the cost of power, maintenance on the machines, the rarity of software, and the high demand for the amusement booths. And if its parents discovered it wasted its last personal credit, not to mention its limited remaining time as a child, on something as frivolous as a game… well, they would complain. Would those complaints be any more or less than their protests about Veshin's indecision? Was it worth finding out?

Veshin showered and dried itself while it considered, but decided it wouldn't waste credit. It might *need* that allowance in a few days, either to support itself outside of the community or else to salve its despair over an undesirable career. Citizens received a limited ration of intoxicants, mostly used for ritual celebrations, but as an adult, Veshin could purchase more if it chose. Choosing to do so was against the Way, but if Veshin had to bow to one of its religion's major requirements, it could be forgiven for violating a minor one.

Thinking about rations made Veshin realize it was hungry. No surprise; besides the demands of its growing body, physical exertion always made it hungry. It decided that, rather than returning home for a snack, it would visit a friend's home and ask to be included in their mid-day meal. Such favors were common and often returned. Who should Veshin call on? Its choices were limited based on who might be home. Also, it preferred to avoid a few classmates: Siruun val'Ktech, for example, who was smugly confident in its choice of military service and dismissive of anyone who sought a 'softer' career. Veshin, as undecided, would either be derided as lower than a domestic engineer – additionally, a slight against its parent – or else bombarded with demands that it also enlist.

Ideally, Perauun val'Ryek would be home. Veshin found Perauun appealing in many ways, as a reasonable fellow skeptic and a strong, attractive person. Perauun would likely declare as a physician. In the absence of any true sciences, medical work was the closest Veshin's inquisitive friend could come to biological research. If Veshin knew Perauun would return its interest as a mate, it would be more motivated to remain with the community, but such matters were not discussed, much less decided, until both parties were adults.

Still, Veshin headed toward the val'Ryek home first. If its luck held, not only would Perauun be home, its parents would be absent, and the two could talk privately about forbidden subjects.

The possibility was slim, but any happy thought was a brightness Veshin sorely needed. The workout had helped, but only while Veshin was engaged. Little benefit lingered after Veshin left the gymnasium.

It wondered, not for the first time, if the community would benefit from a full-time youth counselor. Someone could help adolescents figure out their best career path. Not that Veshin was the best candidate for that job, even if such a novelty were approved by the elders. Not when it couldn't solve its own problems.

If Veshin was the only youth unable to choose a path, the need for a counselor was small. *Was* its problem rare? Or did most children hide and ignore their uncertainties, until it was too late? Adults never admitted having chosen wrong. Did the Way truly guide every one of them unerringly? Or could they not admit their doubts? Were they afraid to criticize the Way? Or were they merely afraid of creating problems among their community... creating more problem children like Veshin?

Its thoughts were making Veshin angry again, and it did not want to meet Perauun looking agitated. It willed itself calm and reflexively groomed as it walked, hoping it did not smell of stress. If it did, though, Perauun would understand. It knew of Veshin's troubles and did not judge harshly. Perauun was a good friend. Perhaps more.

Veshin had almost settled its nerves when it reached the final intersection leading to Perauun's home. Most likely, its friend would be elsewhere, but again, it was good to hope.

A painful burst of sound crunched through the air. The ground bucked upward, throwing Veshin off its feet. A sustained vibration rattled the walls, shaking several lights out of their sockets and sending sparks arcing across the far hallway as wires tore free. A rush of wind flowed past Veshin's face, carrying scents of burnt metal and plastic, along with a cascade of reddish dust.

Chapter 4: Petition

As Veshin lay flat on the floor, the wind reversed, pulling a long, slow exhalation across its back. The breeze carried away stench and dust. Veshin realized that the outflow was taking more than that. There was a hull breach in the habitat. Their breathable air was leaking out into the lower-pressure planetary atmosphere.

Something had broken through an outer wall. A meteor? A missile? An explosion in one of the habitat's systems? From the sound, the damage was sudden and severe.

Sealed ventricle doors would prevent the breach from depressurizing the entire habitat. Only the affected block would be emptied, at a rate depending on the size of the hole. The force of the impact suggested a sizable breach. Veshin didn't know enough to judge whether the outflow was significant, but the air movement felt dangerously rapid.

Veshin knew what it should do. Living in their tenuous environment, all children in the habitat were trained how to respond to crises. If Veshin could see the breach and it wasn't too large, it could try to plug the hole with an object or sealant. Afterward, it might put out any fires with an extinguisher. Any hole or fire too large to be managed should be left alone. In that case, children were told to run and survive. Veshin would need to hurry to the nearest ventricle door and signal its presence so the door could be overridden and opened from inside.

Veshin couldn't see any damage where it was. It had trouble seeing anything, with most of the lights out. Being flat on its belly didn't help much, either. It lifted itself to its feet, with some discomfort. The fall hadn't hurt too badly, but if Veshin knew there would be an accident, it wouldn't have worked out so strenuously beforehand.

The nearest exit was probably backward, around the last intersection. Veshin considered heading back, versus checking the hallway forward. It might find and seal the breach. Then again, if the damage was extensive, its efforts would be futile.

Veshin couldn't hear anyone moving or calling out in alarm. No residents were emerging to evacuate. That meant either that the block was already vacated – a blessing if true – or else anyone else present was trapped.

Instructions said nothing about helping the trapped or injured, especially not instructions to children. You were supposed to get yourself safe and clear and let experienced adults handle rescues. But Veshin wouldn't be comfortable with itself afterward if it didn't at least check on Perauun's home. It wasn't exactly brave, but it cared for its friend and its family.

The steadily outflowing atmosphere was a concern, but as long as the air continued moving, it wasn't gone yet. As long as Veshin didn't start to feel faint or smell smoke, it should be all right. It trudged forward, letting momentum override its better sense.

Veshin had to laugh bitterly. Had it wished for a disaster? Hadn't it withdrawn that wish in time? Or had the gods heard and completed their work before a foolish youth could reconsider? In any case, Veshin *was* receiving a powerful distraction from its personal troubles, not to mention a strong reminder of perspective. Everyone in the community lived a tenuous existence in a hostile galaxy. A single child's indecision was nothing compared to the dilemmas its elders faced to ensure their survival.

It forced itself to concentrate on the situation at hand. If this crisis was its reprieve, it should make the most of it. And yes, alertness was important. The darkened hallway was harder to navigate. Veshin guided itself with one hand along the inside wall. It also needed to stay alert to hear any movement or cries for help.

Veshin then realized that a new soundscape had replaced the usual background noise of the habitat. The ventilation system was not breathing; it must have shut down automatically when the air pressure changed. Instead, Veshin could hear the whoosh of departing air and a faint whistling in the distance… likely around the breach site. There was also an intermittent groaning squeal, like metal rubbing on metal. A broken wall section? A support collapsed between levels?

All those sounds came from much further down and around the corner from Veshin's current hallway. It would reach Perauun's home far before it came within sight of the damaged area.

Another light flickered and faded, casting the hall into nearly complete darkness. The electrical lines must be shorting out. Veshin hoped the motors were working in Perauun's door. It might be able to manually force the door, but on top of its previous exertions, the effort would *hurt*. If Perauun or its parent was inside, hurt, lifting them might exceed Veshin's reserves.

No. That wouldn't happen. In the worst case, Veshin could push itself beyond its own assumed limits. It would collapse and recover later, in safety.

All the same, it was relieved to see the power indicator still active on Perauun's door. The intercom worked, too; Veshin signaled to request entry. No response. Veshin signaled again, this time holding the 'com button down to speak.

"Perauun? Hakkelt? … Nuulech?" it called, including the names of Perauun's parents. No reply came back, through the intercom or through the door itself. Either they weren't home or they were inside, unconscious.

Was its effort enough? Should Veshin leave, trusting that it had done everything it could? Or should it override the door and force entry? There was no reason to think anyone was inside. But if it left without being certain, then found out Perauun or any of its family was there, dying…

Veshin's uncertainty was disrupted by new sounds, shortly after it spoke. They sounded like a hiss of expelled gases, followed by a loud, distinct click. A fire extinguisher? If so, shouldn't the sounds go the other way around? Not to mention, Veshin still wasn't smelling smoke or hearing the crackle of flames.

The sounds came from the far hallway where the whistling and creaking originated before. The whistling continued, but the creaking seemed to have stopped. In its place came a series of low taps, irregularly spaced… like a code or other pattern. Was that someone else signaling their presence? Calling for help?

If someone else was in distress, Veshin couldn't spare time guessing if Perauun's family was home. With its limited time, it had to check if someone else needed rescue. Technically, it was only supposed to be saving itself. But since Veshin was already halfway into the hazard area, it found it hard to accept retreat.

It hurried as quickly as the darkness and its protesting legs would permit, down the hallway, to the corner where it curved away to the left. The light became brighter as it continued. Veshin soon realized that the additional light didn't come from artificial illumination.

Instead, the dim glow of a low-rising star poured through a gap in the exterior wall, several tens of meters away from Veshin as it turned the corner. The pull of the outflowing atmosphere became stronger as Veshin moved closer. The entire breach was three times larger than Veshin itself; there was no way it could plug or seal such a huge tear.

Actually, the breach was less a tear than a punch inward. Something struck the wall with immense force, but was broad enough to disperse that force over a wide area, creating a popped-in section like an enormous hammer strike.

The 'hammer' itself was unseen. It hadn't entered the habitat, which meant it must be right outside. A meteorite? Veshin dismissed that possibility. A rock dropping in from orbital height would have considerably more force. The blast would be larger, not to mention the stone itself would end up deep inside the habitat.

Was Veshin wrong? Had there been some sort of explosion, instead? A concussion blast which popped the wall open from outside? That scenario suggested a massive equipment failure… or a weapon.

The tapping sound came again, from outside of the outer wall. Whatever struck the wall, there was something moving out there.

An Apostate's Path

Veshin froze, suddenly thinking of external attackers. Were there enemy soldiers inside the habitat? Enemies most likely meant the Mauraug Dominion. Were they being raided? This breach might be only one entry point of many… were there other breaches elsewhere? Might Veshin's community, even its parents, also be in danger?

Veshin found itself wishing for a weapon ready to hand. The only things remotely available were the dislodged lights and their cover panels, neither of which would be immediately useful. If it had to fight, Veshin would have to rely on its own body. Why would the gods send it an unarmed battle but deny it even a single training session with a Thashti master beforehand?

It *ought* to retreat, but Veshin crept forward. It needed to see what it was facing. If there *was* an intruder, but only one, it might still run away and alert the community. Fighting and stopping the attacker were also on Veshin's mind, if at all possible.

It neared the edge of the opening. Acrid dust tickled its nostrils, blown in by the initial impact and swirled about by the exiting breeze. Veshin crouched low and waddled toward the breach, peering out. It saw a purplish sky above red-brown dust, with squat dunes rising along the horizon. The image was familiar; Veshin had seen recordings of the monotonous planetoid surface in its classes.

The landscape was interrupted when motion surged toward Veshin from the corner of its visual field. A small but Mauraug-shaped white figure lunged toward the torn edge of the wall. Veshin fell back, nearly collapsing onto its rump. It gasped in panic, its difficulty breathing exacerbated by the thinning air.

The thing was an animal, of some sort. It had been jumping up, trying to grab the edge of the hole and climb inside. There were no life-forms on the planetoid itself. Thus, it followed that the… the… thing. Must be. Alien?

Veshin shook its head, breathing deeply to return oxygen to its brain. It was thinking slowly, a sure sign of depressurization sickness. It needed to leave, soon. The closer exit door was ahead, rather than back. Veshin should report the thing – whatever it was – to its elders and recuperate away from danger.

The tapping sound came again, and Veshin realized it was hearing the creature's jumps and attempts to climb the outer wall. While it watched, a white hand managed to briefly grip the lip of the torn surface. Veshin noted that the appendage was loosely wrinkled but slipped smoothly off the wall's edge with a zipping noise. A glove? A suit?

Alien. It was a non-Mauraug sapient. Had *it* struck the wall and bounced off? Pretty tough. Wait, no. A ship? Not a whole ship. A little one. Lander.

Veshin staggered forward, only half-aware of its own irrational confusion.

There it was. An oblong, smooth object, not much larger than an adult Mauraug, lying in the dust outside, fallen down from the impact site. It looked like a strange bronze egg, though one with complex angular filigree and a piece of its shell broken away. Hatch. Door.

The smooth, white being was standing against the wall. Slumping. It was slumped over, giving an impression of fatigue. All the jumping must be wearing it out. Or maybe the lack of air? Air. Was a problem.

On an impulse, Veshin leaned out over the gap, reaching a hand down to the small creature. Biped. Two legs, two arms, like a Mauraug. No face. Smooth... helmet.

Was the airflow out of the habitat lessening? If so, the breathable air was almost gone. Veshin realized that some of the growing darkness around its vision was not due to lack of light, but dimming vision.

It spared the breath to call out, "Creature! Come up now! I must leave soon or die!"

The being heard. Whether it understood or not, it turned and saw Veshin gesturing, reaching down in its direction. After a moment to process the offer, the creature hunched down and sprang upward again, bounding high into the air.

Veshin caught it under one arm, gripping a handful of the white material – it *was* a suit – and hauling the creature inside. It was heavy for its size. Or maybe Veshin was getting weak. Didn't matter. Veshin pulled the being along as it staggered toward the exit door.

"Come on!" Veshin wheezed as it dragged its captive away. The creature got the idea and started walking in the same direction, with equal difficulty.

Veshin missed the call switch on its first try. The creature grasped the significance of the motion and pressed the button itself. Veshin gasped, "Open the door. Need out."

The ventricle doors slid open after a blessedly short pause. Veshin wasted no time on thought but hauled itself and its captive through. A waft of full atmosphere hit its lungs like breath after drowning. Veshin heaved deeply, still near a blackout despite the relief.

The creature turned around and signaled the doors to shut again. How it knew what button to press was a mystery Veshin would pursue later. When it could think. When its head stopped throbbing.

Veshin settled itself against a wall, put its head between its legs, and focused only on maintaining consciousness. It dimly heard the tear of a suit closure and the smaller gasps of the other creature rapidly inhaling.

It must have been suffocating, too. Veshin had saved someone, it seemed. Who or what that someone was, it would determine later.

Chapter 5: Translation

It wasn't Human. Veshin knew that much when its mind started to clear. Too small. Humans massed much less than Mauraug, but their adults could reach almost the same height. Whatever creature… whatever *sapient* Veshin had rescued was smaller still, perhaps only a meter tall.

It was definitely sapient. It arrived in some sort of lander or lifeboat, likely piloted out of orbit. Veshin realized that striking the habitat at a controlled, non-fatal speed was not a deliberate attack nor entirely an accident. The being must have been trying to land but aimed poorly.

Veshin finally looked up and found the sapient staring at it. Not a Hrotata, it decided. That species was the only other small sapient mammalian race Veshin could remember from its studies. But Hrotata were long and lithe, with short limbs, unlike Humans or Mauraug. The creature before Veshin was long-limbed and bipedal. It also had limited fur, with only a narrow crest visible along the center of its scalp.

As Veshin's awareness returned further, it realized that it and the sapient were staring at one another. It had wide black eyes; narrow, flat, pointed ears; grey-brown mottled skin; and an elongated muzzle with wide nostrils. Its face uncomfortably straddled familiar Mauraug dimensions and the features of some unfamiliar wild animal. When it finally spoke, it showed a ridge of tooth-like structures which varied in size and sharpness.

"Grrrratitude," it said, in garbled but understandable Dominion Standard.

Veshin tensed, before realizing that the creature was defaulting to the sole language of Mauraug Prime when dealing with a Mauraug. It probably wasn't an ally of the Dominion.

In the absence of a translation device, it was helpful that the visitor knew that much. Veshin spoke some Standard, along with two other equally Mauraug tongues: Derech, the preserved language of the first followers of the Way of Ineth, and Mauvas, the creole chosen as the interlingua across the Redemption Alliance. Both languages were archaisms within the Mauraug Dominion, but survived defiantly among the escaped Apostates.

Veshin did its best to respond in Standard: "You're welcome. Who are you? Why are you here?"

The suited sapient pointed toward its narrow chest and answered, "Toonoopahkee. Name. Ship driver. Attack. Fell."

Veshin blinked, struggling to unravel the riddles of incomplete vocabulary. The task was made even more difficult by its recovery from anoxia. It guessed the sapient's name was Toonoopahkee. It was a… pilot? Attacked somewhere near the colony? It ejected its lifeboat and fell to the planetoid. That explanation made the most sense, but Veshin realized it was assuming a great deal to fill in the gaps between concepts.

"What are you?" it tried. "Who attack you? Why fall here?"

As it interrogated the sapient, Veshin began to realize that it was operating far outside its authority. It wasn't even an adult, much less an authority. It ought to be subduing the intruder and bringing it to someone in charge, if not fleeing and bringing the military police to take the foreigner into custody. If there was an attack underway, this alien could be part of a larger threat.

If nothing else, Veshin was keeping the being under observation by engaging it in conversation. Until Veshin was fully recovered, it wasn't in any shape to subdue anything. And despite being much smaller and weaker, the sapient appeared extremely agile. It might prove too quick to catch, once it also recuperated.

Toonoopahkee, for its part, answered without hesitation but with continued language difficulties. "I am Vahkoo. Attack, don't know. Dominion? Come to trade. Why attack? Fall here because close."

Veshin stood, motivated by its concerns about the turn their conversation was taking. "Why say Dominion? Attack here? Many ships? You trade with Dominion?" It tensed, ready to jump if Toonoopahkee's answers suggested danger.

The little sapient twisted its shoulders in some sort of emphatic gesture. "Yes. Yes. Trade here. Dominion here? Mauraug?" It pointed with the knuckles of its suited hand, a decidedly Mauraug gesture. It was familiar with Veshin's species... but perhaps not the Alliance's branches of that culture. Veshin decided to wait quietly rather than offering any new information or questions.

Toonoopahkee continued, "You... your Dominant? Attack me. One ship. Shoot down. All lost." Then it began to back away, appearing agitated. "No complain... not dead. Just need ship home." It bowed then, in a mimicry of Mauraug submission.

Veshin almost thought it understood, by that point. The alien sapient thought it was dealing with Dominionist Mauraug. It approached the colony, intending to trade. Then someone shot it out of nearby space, close enough that it could launch its lifeboat into the planetoid's gravity. But who? Surely not the Alliance military. But if not their own ships, then there was a foreign presence nearby. Either way, their stranded visitor needed to be brought to appropriate authorities.

Veshin didn't get more time for comprehension or further questions. Down the distant hallway came the tromping of multiple booted feet. Soldiers. They must have detected the breach and connected it with a landing from space. Veshin wondered how long it had taken before the two reports – internal and external – met up. A long delay was evidence of functional problems within the Alliance and the colony itself.

Toonoopahkee tensed and started to back up, placing itself nearer the ventricle door and Veshin. It realized that it could not retreat through the sealed door. Its fear was obvious, its eyelids stretching back further to reveal thin white edges around its black eyes.

The soldiers appeared around a corner: four of them, large adult Mauraug in belted sashes, gloves and boots. One, a calico of mixed fur colors, wore a protective helmet with face shield and breathing mask. It was a wise precaution in a disaster area, but none of the other soldiers wore masks. Implanted plugs along the helmeted soldier's neck suggested that it might require the apparatus at all times, anyway. One of the other soldiers, dark red like Veshin, had taller, wider boots than the others and a stiff gait that suggested one or two prosthetic legs. The other two soldiers – black-furred with lighter streaks – lacked any visible deformities or cybernetics.

All four defenders had their laser pistols and standard-issue shock batons holstered. The two soldiers in the front rank drew their guns upon spotting Toonoopahkee. The four halted at a distance. Of the two in the back, the one without the helmet spoke first, in Mauvas:

"Child. Come toward us. Leave the intruder there. We will protect you if it attacks."

Veshin leaned away and almost took a step, in instinctual obedience. Then it stopped. The soldiers thought Toonoopahkee was a dangerous invader. If that perception wasn't corrected, the small intruder might be shot before it explained itself... particularly if its first words of greeting came in Dominion Standard.

Instead, Veshin replied to the soldiers: "It won't attack. I saved its life. It crashed in a lifeboat; it hit the habitat wall by mistake. Its name is Toonoopah-kee."

The alien twitched in acknowledgement of its name. Facing the soldiers, Veshin couldn't see its facial expression, but it hoped the visitor wasn't grimacing in any provocative manner.

On a hunch, Veshin whispered to Toonoopahkee in Standard: "Eyes down. Head down. Kneel."

The small sapient looked at Veshin, its expression uncertain. Then it looked down. After a long moment of indecision, it went to its knees, still not looking at the soldiers or Veshin.

One of the two leading soldiers lowered its weapon in response. The other kept sighted on Toonoopahkee.

Their leader ordered again, "Child, move away from that foreigner. Do not assist it."

Veshin began to bubble with a dangerous anger. They weren't listening to it. It wanted to shout back, to convince the soldier of its error. Aggression wouldn't help anyone, though. Being forceful would do more to persuade the soldiers that Veshin itself was a threat than reassuring them that Toonoopahkee was not.

Was it dangerous? Veshin realized it didn't know much about the other sapient, besides what it said. It could be lying. It could have been attempting entry to attack residents of the habitat or sabotage its systems. It could be working with the Dominion in some capacity: spy, assassin, or saboteur.

Veshin again started to move away and again stopped. It realized it had more evidence than just Toonoopahkee's words. There was the sapient's desperation to get inside the habitat, for example. It hadn't been carrying any oxygen tanks or wearing a breath recycler. It really was in danger, not prepared for infiltration. Plus, it wasn't fluent in Dominion Standard, knowing just enough to be a trader, not a secret agent. It hadn't been evasive or threatening. Even then, it was kneeling quietly, waiting for cues from Veshin.

Veshin felt certain Toonoopahkee was no threat. It looked toward the military leader, as calmly as it could manage, and replied: "I can take the intruder into custody. No violence is necessary. Please lower your weapons, or it may become agitated. You will learn more from an uninjured, living prisoner."

Veshin's resistance paused the leader. It needed a few moments to process the youth's words before responding. Blessedly, it did not curse Veshin for disobedience or threaten either it or Toonoopahkee. Instead, the leader replied, "Do so, then. But we will watch; if it attacks, we may have to harm you in order to prevent its escape."

With those words, the soldier reached to its belt and withdrew a strip of restraint plastic, tossing it in a wad toward Veshin. The ungainly material landed short, requiring Veshin to take two steps away from Toonoopahkee to retrieve it. The foreigner twitched nervously but did not stand nor move from its spot.

An Apostate's Path

Turning around, putting its back to the armed soldiers with some trepidation, Veshin addressed Toonoopahkee again in Standard. "Tie hands, please? Need not fight. Come without fight. Please." It held out its hands, holding the restraint strip between them.

Toonoopahkee hesitated. It risked a glance toward the soldiers, then looked back down quickly. It seemed to grasp the situation, but had difficulty deciding how to react. It was probably trying to decide whether *Veshin* was trustworthy, or if submission would get it tortured or killed.

It replied, "Promise? No fight?"

Technically, the word it used meant 'conflict', but Veshin got the idea. It wanted to hear that it would not be harmed. Should Veshin lie? Technically, the soldiers might handle their captive roughly. If it could not answer their questions thoroughly, they might beat it to make sure it knew nothing further.

The most honest answer was: "I will try." Veshin thought it said that properly. The sentiment seemed to carry across. Toonoopahkee put out its long, thin forearms, hands open and facing upward. Veshin wrapped the restraint strip around its sleeved arms, doing it a naïve kindness by not allowing the adhesive to bond directly to its fur… or skin, if it were furless under the white plastic. It might tear free that way, but Veshin didn't think to have it disrobe or roll up its sleeves before restraining it.

"All right," Veshin called back to the soldiers. "It is bound. But I promised to accompany it to prison. I can bear witness to its actions after damaging the habitat. It also owes me its life; I can likely get better answers than an interrogator, by calling on that debt."

Veshin's claims were half hope, half bluff. It had no reason to stand up for the little alien, but its instincts said this sapient was innocent of malice and genuinely afraid. Veshin wanted to be right. It wanted to help both its community *and* their intruder.

At least the soldiers holstered their weapons. The leader barked, "You *will* come with us, if only to answer for your actions. If you are helpful as promised, it may reduce your offense. But if you or the intruder causes any trouble, both will be punished accordingly. Now, let's go. Come this way."

"Understood," Veshin replied tersely. It put a hand against Toonoopahkee's back and pushed gently, stepping forward.

Without further urging, the small sapient walked forward next to Veshin. The two lead soldiers let them pass, then lined up behind them as a protective guard. With a snort, the leader turned and led the procession back down the residential hall.

Chapter 6: Transition

As they walked away – likely headed toward the habitat's detention cells – Veshin fought the urge to talk to Toonoopahkee. Veshin really wanted to know more about its new acquaintance: more about its species than just a name, more about its purpose in approaching their system, more about its life and experiences and beliefs.

To Veshin, the foreigner was not only a novelty, it was an exception to a tightly controlled existence. The Mauraug realized that it might be overblowing the alien's value: both its worthiness to be heard and its potential for revelations. Veshin cautioned itself that it might be interested in Toonoopahkee – and unwisely defending the alien – because of its own troubles. The community, as it was, failed to help Veshin know itself; perhaps it was hoping a new element would give it fresh insight.

New elements were not welcomed within the habitat. Even for communities without a religious reason to oppose intrusion, the security of the entire Redemption Alliance hinged on stability and secrecy. The only Mauraug to leave the habitat were trained and trusted: soldiers, diplomats, and ship engineers, the personnel necessary to defend and interconnect the scattered colonies of the Alliance. Those escapees were also tightly constrained, kept together aboard ships and not permitted to intermingle with non-Alliance sapients.

There were exceptions. There *had* to be exceptions. The Mauraug of the Alliance did not have sufficient resources, alone, to keep ships fueled or medical facilities stocked. Mining, raids and piracy were insufficient to renew lost resources. It was an open secret that the Alliance had outside support.

Empyrean Stories

The more noble, naïve explanation was that trusted elders conducted high-level negotiations with outside parties, far from the Collective. The more likely, cynical option was that enemies of the Mauraug Dominion, either within or near the Collective, were supporting the 'Apostates' in order to antagonize and weaken the Dominion. Certainly, the latter accusation was what Dominionists would believe. After all, there was no way non-Dominant Mauraug could organize and survive on their own.

Veshin knew some of these things from conversations overheard in public and from the admissions of its parents. It knew some other truths from close attention to its studies and to the context of intercepted news reports. And last, Veshin 'knew' certain things from its own skeptical suspicions. It knew too much of Mauraug nature and its own home colony to think circumstances were different elsewhere.

For one telltale fact, the habitat where they lived was not originally built by Mauraug. The dimensions weren't too odd and the environment was comfortable, but the mismatch showed in small ways. Older systems bore unrecognizable script on their parts. Controls were arranged in non-intuitive patterns and looked noticeably different from those in historical images of Mauraug Prime. The default atmospheric settings were too warm and moist for the comfort of furred sapients. In short, their home was a habitat built by another species and either commandeered by… or donated to… the Alliance.

Was that prior species the Vahkoo, like Toonoopahkee? Perhaps their visitor approached the area after seeing it listed on older navigational records. Or, the previous inhabitants were a culture who traded with the Vahkoo. There were many possibilities. Veshin didn't have any opportunity, right then, to learn the truth. It fostered a slim hope that it might get that opportunity, after the official questioning was done.

Would Toonoopahkee survive that questioning? It wasn't a hysterical thought. Mauraug could be rough with their own prisoners, and what was rough for a Mauraug might be crippling or fatal for a smaller, frailer being.

The soldiers would be afraid and hostile, fearing that Toonoopahkee was a spy, a saboteur, or an agent for an invasion force. Their reactions upon seeing the sapient suggested such fears. It was bad enough the various communities of the Alliance lived in fear of discovery by the Dominion or their Collective collaborators. Some citizens would be just as afraid of any foreign sapient, enemy or not.

The strangeness that intrigued Veshin would, by itself, offend others, even some Inethi. An alien was an unknown. An outsider might work against the Way, even if it did not mean harm to the Alliance. It might introduce dangerous ideas, not least of which was the possibility of life outside the habitat.

The accusation wasn't wrong. The alien's very presence was spawning new ideas in Veshin. The amusing thing was, it couldn't affect Veshin's religious beliefs any further; other Inethi were more likely to damage Veshin's piety than any alien.

It felt like a long walk to the detention wing. Veshin wasn't sure, without a reference map, where detention was located relative to Perauun's residence block. The travel might really be long, or it might only seem long due to anxiety and exhaustion.

Then again, the detention area was probably separate from the main habitat, on purpose. No reason to put prisoners anywhere near main habitations or critical support systems. If the habitat's design was logical, the ship docks were on the direct opposite side from the detention area.

After perhaps half an hour, the group slowed, encountering a translucent security door. The outlines of two armored soldiers showed blurrily through the plastic barrier.

The military leader stepped forward and presented a badge from a pocket of its sash. A scanning laser strobed over the identification and the leader's face, then buzzed acceptance. The door clicked somewhere inside, then opened at pressure from the leader's hand.

The guards inside held their flechette rifles at loose ready, neither threatening the arrivals nor giving them any sense of safety. Between the pair was another door, this one smaller and opaque. One of them, surprisingly small for a soldier, flared its nostrils beneath its helmet visor. It greeted the arrivals: "Commander. Welcome back."

The guard then turned to its side and triggered a handprint lock, opening the inner door. The 'Commander' passed through first, followed by the other leading soldier. Toonoopahkee went through next at a nudge from the soldier behind it. Then Veshin entered, followed by the last two soldiers.

Veshin wondered what the guards made of its presence. A youth, in custody but unbound. What was its role in the local emergency? If they even allowed themselves thoughts at all, they probably assumed Veshin was a witness. Mostly accurate, anyway.

If Veshin saw the same scene, there was no way it would guess the youth was offering itself as surety for the prisoner's good behavior. It certainly wouldn't assume that a Mauraug child had promised to extract information from said prisoner. And it certainly wouldn't dream that said youth imagined itself something of a mediator between alien and Alliance.

Veshin surprised *itself* with such thoughts. Dealing with their implications distracted it for a few seconds, as the soldiers wound their procession, single-file, through three intersections and two more doorways.

Finally, they reached a hallway lined with doors, one of which opened onto a meeting room with a small table and five chairs. Veshin noted that the chairs were of two sizes: three larger and Mauraug-shaped, two smaller and slightly irregular. The soldiers ordered Veshin and Toonoopahkee into the room, and then the Commander ordered one of the soldiers – one without any visible cybernetics – to stay in the room and guard the prisoner.

Prisoner. Not prisoners. That distinction was reassuring. Veshin supposed it could still be labeled a 'delinquent' or 'unwitting collaborator'. It might graduate to 'prisoner' after more discussion. But at least the military leader wasn't immediately judging Veshin guilty.

The other three soldiers stayed outside, closing the door behind them. Veshin went to one of the larger chairs and sat down, pretending nonchalance in order to reassure itself and Toonoopahkee. It risked speaking enough to direct the alien: "Sit. Wait. Try rest."

The guard looked at Veshin sharply when it spoke, but did not speak, either to reassure or rebuke the youth. Toonoopahkee, left hanging, eventually approached one of the small chairs. Even with the chair's lower seat, the small sapient had to lever itself upward and sat with its feet dangling a few centimeters off the floor.

The guard stayed standing and watched its charges for a moment with bland curiosity. They stayed that way for several minutes, no one moving noticeably. Veshin didn't yet feel comfortable speaking further to Toonoopahkee, though it badly wanted to talk. It wanted to get more of the visitor's story, to decide if it should be defending this sapient at all. And if it should, it wanted to know Toonoopahkee's story so that it could accurately relay the facts to the authorities. Closely competing with Veshin's desire to stay out of trouble was an urge to protect Toonoopahkee from undue punishment.

Its ship had damaged their habitat. The collision endangered and might have killed Mauraug citizens. But that didn't mean the pilot of that ship was at fault. It might be the mutual victim of an accident. If so, it didn't deserve further injury, nor imprisonment nor death. A great deal depended on *why* Toonoopahkee was forced to eject its life boat. Why its ship was destroyed, and where. How it came to steer that life boat toward the Alliance habitat.

Talking to it might not answer everything, anyway. If Toonoopahkee was being honest… and if Veshin understood it correctly… it might be as confused as anyone else about the attack on its ship and its subsequent accident. If it *was* entirely innocent, it might also be entirely clueless. Not that ignorance was laudable, but it was better than intentional destruction.

Veshin offered a quiet but heartfelt plea to the Gods that the alien would not try to be defiant or deceptive. Refusing to answer questions or answering in any way that seemed evasive would get it hurt. Veshin did not consider this a moral failing on the part of the military interrogator; it expected such treatment as a necessity of defending their citizens. Only if the situation were fully explained to everyone's satisfaction would Toonoopahkee stand any chance of survival. The safety of the habitat was too critical to risk.

Veshin considered this point important enough to risk saying something aloud. It turned to Toonoopahkee and carefully explained: "Speak truth. Answer questions. No anger… no refusal. Understand?"

Toonoopahkee paused before replying, its lips parting slightly. It breathed through its clenched teeth for a moment. Then it twisted its shoulders sharply, answering: "Yes. Truth. I answer. Nothing to lose."

Both the guard and Veshin snorted nervous, inadvertent laughter. Then they looked at each other in surprise, not expecting to find common humor in the tense situation. Veshin turned back to Toonoopahkee to reassure it: "Good. Yes. Right. Truth gains all."

The conversation was a good idea for another reason. Toonoopahkee might be entirely honest but fail to give good replies out of fear. Reducing its stress would help them all. Veshin realized it couldn't be certain who was more tense: it, the alien, or the soldiers. They all had reason to be on edge. It supposed the non-Mauraug might be the *least* agitated of them all. Assuming it was jumpy because it was so small might be a false prejudice.

Despite the moment of relief, all three pairs of eyes snapped upward when the door opened again.

A grey-tipped elder entered, hunching its broad, square shoulders to fit through the narrow entry. It wore formal burgundy robes and a collar of office, cutting an imposing figure as it straightened up before Veshin and Toonoopahkee.

"All right," the elder intoned, staring at the captives with a challenging glare, "Let's get this figured out, shall we?"

Chapter 7: Discussion

The elder did not wait for any reply, but turned next to the soldier standing guard. "You are relieved; wait outside and listen for my orders."

The guard almost started to reply, likely to protest that its direct commander issued different orders. The elder did not give it the chance to err, instead raising a hand to block any protest.

"I believe I can handle a small, unarmed sapient and a child by myself," it grumbled with a hint of deadpan humor.

The soldier wavered a moment more, but finally decided not to challenge its social, if not ranking, superior. It trundled past the elder and through the door, closing the portal behind it.

Veshin belatedly stood. "Elder, I am Veshin val'…"

The robed official waved away Veshin's formality, as well, settling itself into one of the larger chairs further across the room.

"I reviewed your record already. Inethi. Child of Grathek and Nuunshin. Predicted to join the clergy of the Way… seems we got that wrong. One quarter-cycle away from adulthood. And somehow, caught up in a security emergency. Was that entirely by chance?" Though the elder's tone was light, its demeanor implied danger if Veshin was not forthcoming with suitable answers.

Veshin adopted a minimally acceptable submissive stance, but did not abase itself further. "Yes. I was visiting a friend when Toonoopahkee crashed…"

The elder interrupted, "Be more specific. What friend? I assume 'Toonoopahkee' is the foreign intruder there?"

Veshin stopped, swallowed, and struggled to organize its thoughts. "My friend, Perauun val'Ryek. It lives in Block Seventeen, where the... the habitat was breached."

"val'Ryek. Also of the Way of Ineth?"

"Yes, Elder. A youth near my age."

"Continue."

"I heard the crash and went to check on Perauun and its family. They did not respond... in their home... but I heard noises. When I looked around the corner, I saw the crash site."

When the elder did not respond, Veshin continued, nervous as it reached Toonoopahkee's part in the story. "There was a huge hole but nothing inside the habitat. The noise was outside, so I looked. I saw this sapient, struggling to enter the habitat. It was suffocating in the outside atmosphere. Its landing craft – a life boat, I believe – was also outside, after bouncing off the exterior wall. I helped it get inside..."

"Why?" the elder intruded, loudly. "Why did you help it enter?"

Veshin thought a moment, then decided to be as truthful as it could manage. "I didn't want it to die? I wasn't thinking well because the atmosphere was thin, so that might have been a mistake, but I thought I should help."

The elder sat back, seeming to relax, but still spoke with challenge: "You are abnormal, Veshin val'Ineth. Do you know that?"

Toonoopahkee was watching the conversation attentively, though without much apparent comprehension. It probably knew none of the words being spoken, aside from a few cognates shared between Mauvas and Dominion Standard. However, it could read tone and body language well enough. It tensed at Veshin's rising and shifted uncomfortably when the young Mauraug began speaking rapidly and at length. It knew an interrogation when it heard one. Finally, when the elder accused Veshin of abnormality, the youth's alarmed reaction caused Toonoopahkee to sit upright, ready to react.

An Apostate's Path

The elder looked at the alien with its first signs of interest. "Does it under-stand our speech?" it asked.

"I'm not sure, Elder," Veshin responded, still deciding how to reply to the hanging accusation. "It speaks some Standard. I believe it has traded with the Dominion or knows of them."

Veshin realized its error of phrasing when the elder's brow lowered. It has-tened to correct, "Just a guess. It hasn't done anything to indicate hostility to us or alliance with the enemy."

"I will make judgments of innocence," the elder reminded Veshin, while clenching a fist in warning. "Confine your words to the facts. What makes you so sure this outsider is not in league with the Dominion?"

"It was dying, outside. It didn't intend to collide with our habitat. The life boat was very small, not a proper landing craft. It would have no way to escape, even if it intended to sneak inside somehow. And it didn't threaten me, or try to run away, or ask to go anywhere, even after we were both safe and recovered. It even recovered first. Then it gave me its name – Toonoopahkee – and answered my questions, at least as much as we could understand each other."

Now the elder looked at Toonoopahkee and addressed it, speaking what Veshin assumed was fluent Dominion Standard. "Why do you know this lan-guage?" it asked.

Toonoopahkee did not hesitate in replying: "Trade. Customers speak. Blask. My people, Vahkoo, trade-with Blask."

Veshin didn't understand the unfamiliar word, but the answer seemed to sat-isfy the elder, who shrugged in dismissal. It turned back to Veshin and picked up their earlier topic as if there were no digression. "You are abnormal because most Inethi would follow the evacuation protocols. They are rules to be fol-lowed. Your people follow rules. You... do not."

It sounded like a condemnation. Veshin gave a weak protest, "I am obedient, Elder. I could not decide between the abstract protocol and my duty to my fellow beings."

"You could not decide. Indecision is your problem. But you *decided* to rescue an outsider. An alien. Not even of your species. That, you could decide. You *decided* to disregard evacuation, to do that."

"I apologize, Elder. I was not thinking…"

"Do not lie!" bellowed the far larger Mauraug, looming even greater as it half-rose and leaned toward Veshin. Veshin struggled to control its bowels. For a moment, its body was certain it was about to be crushed or torn apart.

The elder did not come closer, however. It sat back and composed itself with suspicious speed, as if its earlier rage was a controlled act. It continued, at a lower volume but with a lingering sense of menace: "You were thinking. Do not excuse your actions by seizing on a ready weakness. Child. Are your parents and teachers so lax, or has the Way of Ineth failed you?"

Veshin had no answer. It was not even sure how it had transgressed. Was the elder upset about its actions or merely its failure to accept blame for them? What was its complaint against the Way? And why, above all, was it spending so much time on Veshin, personally, when the real anomaly, an unfamiliar alien, was sitting right there?

The elder huffed in frustration. It finally said, "I am Gresh tash'Veliinal of the Soch'inari, tasked with the internal security of this colony by the Alliance council. I am as much concerned with the actions of our citizens as the intrusion of an outsider… perhaps more so. There is only one alien. There are dozens of you. Adolescents. Future masters of the Alliance."

Soch'inari? The gruff, imposing grey-fur before Veshin bore little resemblance to its mental picture of the freedom-worshipping Soch'inari. It didn't know what it imagined, but from its parents' descriptions, it expected someone weak, flabby, lazy… certainly not forceful or responsible enough to be entrusted with their entire colony's safety.

Veshin wasn't about to say anything about its prejudices. It feared enough of its surprise showed in its manner. It realized, though, that the Elder tash'Veliinal was expecting some reply.

"I apologize... if my choices were poor. I acted without consideration. That much is true."

"How we act without 'consideration' is often our most honest action," the elder philosophized. It fixed Veshin with another threatening stare. "But after you had acted, when you had the intruder and yourself safe, why did you speak with it? Shouldn't you have run to seek out an adult? Some authority? Or else subdued the intruder?"

Veshin's frustration started to overtake its submissive fear. It decided to risk defending its actions. "It spoke first. It thanked me for saving its life. After that, I wanted to know what happened. And I wanted to know who it was. I was curious."

To Veshin's surprise, Gresh hooted loudly and tapped its feet. "Curiosity? In an Inethi? I will record this day. But that is an answer. A true answer, I think. All right, now to the other security matter."

It turned to Toonoopahkee, who had almost risen out of its chair at the elder's laughter. "Sit. Listen. You are in trouble, unless we understand your intentions perfectly. Tell me, why was your ship in this system?"

"Trade," answered the small sapient without pause. Veshin was actually proud of it for heeding Veshin's advice. Lifting its bound hands slightly, it continued, "Need... needed things. Carry-ed machines. Saw city. Called to you."

"And gave Collective, Dominion clearance codes and signs," prompted Gresh.

"Dominion, yes. *Not* Dominion," Toonoopahkee concluded, with a deep, slow blink.

"No, we are not," the elder agreed. "We're very opposed to the Dominion. So much so," it confided to Veshin, "that our soldiers can panic and fire upon a foreign ship that sounds like a Dominion vessel... even if it's obviously no warship."

Veshin reeled from the pace of revelations. While it might be a particularly willful, uncertain child from the Inethi perspective, it still held an innate faith in the competence of authority. Being told that the Alliance military accidentally shot down a harmless ship, without even the pretense of necessary piracy or defense against intrusion, was shocking.

But it made sense. Veshin put together the sequence of events without difficulty. Toonoopahkee approached the unfamiliar colony, hoping to trade, mistaking it for a Mauraug settlement. It gave signs of peaceful approach, which were misinterpreted by the nearby Alliance ships as a Dominion incursion. They fired, easily destroying a small cargo ship and sending its pilot down to the planetoid's surface in its escape boat. By all rights, Toonoopahkee should have died. It would have, had no one been nearby to pull it inside.

The elder asked the alien trader, as gently as Mauraug Standard permitted, "Were there any others aboard your ship?"

Toonoopahkee went thin-lipped, replying briefly: "No. Only me. Good?"

"A good thing, indeed. Despite what you may have heard from our Dominionist brothers, we are not monsters. And only killers out of necessity, for survival. I am glad you survived our error."

Veshin was about to add its agreement when Gresh cut it off. "That said, we still have a problem. Though your ship was destroyed... and fortunately for you, the remains we could recover support your story... we must decide what to do with you. Executing you would betray the principles I just claimed. Very hypocritical. Very Dominionist. We cannot keep you here; we know little of your species, except for a name and general description. Yet to release you would potentially endanger our secrecy. You clearly have some knowledge of and contact with the Dominion. You could betray our location for easy profit. Even if you intend us no such betrayal, you could reveal something unwittingly or be forced to tell what you know."

There was no way Toonoopahkee could understand everything from the elder's flood of speech, but it definitely caught 'executing', 'profit', 'release', and 'betray', reacting appropriately when the concepts were mentioned. When Gresh stopped speaking, it ventured, "Contract? Memory fix?"

"Sign a contract?" Elder tash'Veliinal scoffed. "How would we possibly enforce it? We could try removing your memory of this system, but we don't know enough about your neuroanatomy to be sure the operation succeeded. Or, we might damage your mind somehow. I'm sorry, but I've considered the obvious ideas and a few inobvious ones."

Veshin twitched as an idea fought for dominion inside its own mind. There was a possibility. A foolish one, so foolish it hesitated to speak. It *couldn't* know something the elder hadn't already considered. Certainly, not anything useful that wasn't already dismissed as impractical. Or outright insane.

Veshin's idea was insane. It fit none of the established patterns of the Way or the Alliance. Its idea also assumed things about Veshin that defied its religion, its culture, its species, and even its understanding of itself. But the idea resonated with Veshin's previous, unconsidered actions. It fit with its instincts to rescue a strange alien sapient and to seek its truth rather than remove its threat.

As these thoughts roiled, Veshin belatedly realized that both the elder and Toonoopahkee were watching it. It looked back at each, not sure what was expected of it. Were they both out of ideas? Were they seriously looking at Veshin, an undeclared, thoughtless child, for input? That possibility was even more insane than Veshin's idea.

But they were. They were hanging on the brink of a terrible, unjust fate for Toonoopahkee, an innocent being caught in the wrong place at the wrong time. And they were hoping Veshin could offer some improbable insight.

It swallowed and spoke, choosing to use Mauvas both to express itself better and to avoid offending Toonoopahkee if its words were as ridiculous as it feared.

"What if... what if someone... watched it? Like a guard. Or a supervisor?"

When the elder failed to interrupt or dismiss its words, Veshin continued: "It could go on a warship. Travel somewhere, get what it needs to live... food, medicine, comforts. But with someone making sure it couldn't tell anyone where we are. Maybe even finding a doctor who could safely remove that information. Then it could go home. Or if not, it could stay with us. Help us. Give information, trade routes... are Vahkoo in the Collective?"

Veshin got so far into its idea, so concerned with explaining itself fully, that it lapsed into a conversational mode without realizing it. Gresh appeared unoffended. It picked up Veshin's question without rebuke, carrying the discussion as if speaking to an adult.

"No, they are not. Their space is far outside any Collective cultural sphere. They trade with the Blask, who trade with the Dominion. I suspect our visitor was attempting to shorten the chain. Remove the third party?"

Elder tash'Veliinal turned to Toonoopahkee. "Have you ever met another Mauraug before now?"

The sapient in question wrinkled its nose, appearing slightly more bestial, before answering, "No. Knew-of. Never traded."

The elder turned back to Veshin, switching again to Mauvas. "I thought so. And the Vahkoo, to my knowledge, trade with others even further out. Species that have *no* contact with the Collective or at least, no formal contacts. Your idea has value. Value enough, perhaps, to persuade the council. But who would take on such a duty? It would improve our chances of approval to have a volunteer ready to undertake such a challenging, risky assignment."

It stared at Veshin, eyebrows raised high, wide shoulders pulled back. Veshin dropped its own eyes in terror. How was it supposed to know who to select? Why was the elder asking *it* what to do? It was just a child...

Oh.

The realization was no more comforting than the distress of confusion. Elder tash'Veliinal was waiting for Veshin's answer. Veshin just misunderstood the question: *would* Veshin *volunteer?*

To leave the home it had known forever? To take on responsibilities adult Mauraug might refuse, if given any choice? To travel on a military ship, not as a soldier or engineer... not even as a traditional diplomat, but as a new kind... an ambassador? To deal with utterly foreign species and cultures? All the while keeping its knowledge of its home and family and community secret, under pain of death from its own people, much less the Dominion?

It was terrifying. It was also equally exciting. It was, unlike any thought before, appealing.

Veshin flared its nostrils wide and lifted its head to stare the elder full-on. It avoided only a full forward lean and raised hands; it was trying to show confidence, not start a fight.

It answered, "I will do it. I volunteer."

"For what? Custodian to an alien prisoner?"

Veshin turned to Toonoopahkee then and answered in Standard: "I volunteer to be the Alliance ambassador to the Vahkoo."

Chapter 8: Resolution

Finally speaking the full extent of its madness was almost worth the difficulty, given the reactions Veshin drew from Gresh and Toonoopahkee. The elder hooted again with genuine amusement, squinting its eyes tight and rocking on its chair. Toonoopahkee almost fell off its chair, first frozen by Veshin's declaration and then startled by the elder's outburst.

Without waiting for protocol, the Vahkoo asked Veshin, "Ambassador?" It seemed to be repeating the unfamiliar word. "You talk-between Vahkoo and Mauraug?"

Veshin waited to make sure Gresh wasn't going to moderate before replying, "Yes. Only Alliance Mauraug. My people. Talk, not fight. Maybe trade. Need deal... or no leave."

The still-strange sapient stared at Veshin. Veshin wondered if it understood the explanation. They were going to have to work on a mutual language, if their plan was going to work at all.

It understood enough. It blinked, hard and repeatedly, and tears rolled from its eyes, down its muzzle. "Gratitude!" it said, wavering back and forth if unsure whether to remain seated or jump up toward Veshin. "Much gratitude! Accept! Very good. No fight. No trouble. Much trade. Promise!"

"Careful. Don't make too many promises too easily," the elder cautioned. "You won't be going home to your people for a long time, not until Veshin can reassure us you're trustworthy. Too much enthusiasm, too soon, will make our people doubt your sincerity. And if the child gets it wrong, and you betray us, willingly or not... Veshin might die, but it won't be the first or last corpse."

Toonoopahkee had recovered some courage. It answered Gresh, "No betray, no die. Veshin save me. I give honor. Get trust fast."

"I hope you are right," muttered Gresh. "Enough of these pledges. You will stay here until we get the specifics sorted out, Toonoopahkee. I will need more information from you later. Veshin, you will return to act as intermediary. You can practice your Standard with the interview questions, perhaps start to teach our new partner some Mauvas. But first, you need to go home. You may speak with your parents, to reassure them you are whole. Reassure your Inethi that you haven't been executed. Say nothing to anyone else about our guest, though. That will be your first test."

"I understand," interjected Veshin. "I can keep confidence."

"I wouldn't expect otherwise. You know how much is riding on your behavior. I suspect that the Way would say the stakes were always the same: service or death. Not sure if I agree in general, but I certainly do, in this case."

Veshin realized one problem quickly thereafter: "What do I tell my parents? If I'm leaving with Toonoopahkee..."

"Inform them you have chosen to join the diplomatic corps. It is as close as possible to the truth, even if your mission is not to another Alliance colony or even other Mauraug. The story will fit your departure. If you like, say the head of security admired your actions in this emergency and swayed your decision. Again, close enough to truth. A diplomat does need a calm mind in a crisis. And an ambassador needs an unhurried, unbiased attitude when dealing with foreign cultures. Here's another big secret to carry with you: you won't be the only such ambassador out there. The youngest, certainly. And one with rather unique duties. But we do have contacts outside of our own settlements."

"I thought so," Veshin ventured. "May I say goodbye to others?"

"In a general sense. Same cover story. See how clever you can be and avoid arousing suspicion. But come back here after you've spoken to your parents and rested. We'll make additional plans based on how matters go with the council."

As strange as it was to be speaking in nearly equal confidence with an adult, it was even stranger to feel like a co-conspirator with not only an authority, but an elder, and a Soch'inari at that. Despite encouraging attitudes that strained the Way of Ineth, Elder tash'Veliinal seemed to respect and stay within the confines of Veshin's religion.

Veshin felt almost ashamed how much its own previous behavior wandered away from the Way and toward the self-determination of Soch'inar. Almost. In reality, it could sympathize more with the elder's beliefs and respect how Gresh followed its own path while still accommodating another's.

In that vein, Veshin turned to Toonoopahkee. "I go. Rest well. We talk at morning. Safe. Good."

As if they were speaking fluent, formal partings, Toonoopahkee gave both its shoulder-shaking affirmation and a more Mauraug jaw drop. "Good night. Gratitude more. Rest well, Veshin."

It was odd parting without any sort of embrace. The two weren't exactly friends, but they were already professional partners. Among Mauraug, such a relationship would at least involve a hearty clinch. However, Toonoopahkee's hands were still bound. It might remain so until the local military were reassured that it was no threat... perhaps until the Alliance council confirmed it as allied.

"Good night, Elder," Veshin offered, kneeling low. "Thank you..."

It was startled one last time by Gresh's hand on its shoulder, hauling it upright into a short but powerful hug. Though the embrace suggested business-like respect, the large adult Mauraug couldn't help lifting Veshin slightly like a parent.

"Good night, Veshin. I greet you as adult, even if the Inethi haven't completed your ceremony yet. You might ask them to hasten the ritual date...? If not, expect to ship out the day after. I'll be as patient as I can, but we don't want this particular secret sitting around our prison any longer than necessary. Now get out. We all have work to do."

Veshin backed away, not trusting itself to reply again without embarrassment. Respect from an elder? After it started the day without respect for itself?

An Apostate's Path

The Gods were laughing. Veshin could almost hear them hooting. While not a particularly Inethi sentiment, there were some who would be gratified to hear of the Way proving its truth by destroying an innocent trade ship, punching a hole in a habitat wall, risking the deaths of faithful Inethi and other Mauraug, and scaring a wayward child almost to the point of defecation… all to provide said child with a path of service it could follow.

Veshin wasn't particularly affirmed in its faith by that chain of events, but it could still appreciate their ultimate outcome.

It had its decision. It had a duty. It knew what it needed to do. It could become an adult, without uncertainty.

It could accept all the costs, in return for that gift.

Labyrinthine

by Nathan Large

Ryan navigated the serpentine tunnel system with confidence. The twining, intersecting complex might have intimidated past explorers, but Ryan came prepared. A global positioning satellite, dropped before his ship's atmospheric entry, tracked his movements relative to his landing site on the planet's surface. It coordinated with Ryan's personal compad and its resident intelligence, Maxwell, to create a detailed map of the passages they explored. Even when he periodically lost contact with the satellite, Maxwell continued to record Ryan's movements and update their chart.

Ryan and his team were forearmed, forewarned by a Tesetsi historian's advice on the ancient Tachakilu: "Their tombs are guarded by mazes to snare the unworthy." The Tachakilu once ruled their planet and several others. Their descendants, physically identical but culturally far declined, retained no history of their former empire. Only a few scattered records, hesitantly translated, could trace the Tachakilu diaspora back to its origins, and scholars perpetually disputed their interpretations of those documents.

The complex Ryan was exploring certainly qualified as a maze. He wasn't worried. In the worst case, if his compad was lost or damaged, Ryan's team could track his implanted locator chip, aided by the maps Maxwell uploaded to their shared ship computer.

His team members were all young, smart, healthy Human professionals, just like Ryan. It was unlikely all of them would become lost or injured at the same time. Each was exploring a different section of the labyrinth, making the most of their limited search time. They only had a few days to investigate the planet and gather up what they discovered, before the next Collective patrol noticed their unlicensed presence.

The terrain already walked held no mysteries; Maxwell held their route in memory. Ryan was certain in his ability to find his way back out and unafraid about how far he traveled. The only concern was what lay ahead. So far, they hadn't encountered any structural instability; though ancient and crude, the tunnels seemed solid. The long passages wound through deep stone, reinforced by a whitish grey cement patterned with irregular swirls.

There could still be obstacles. Ryan was prepared for physical blockages, armed with a cutting torch plus shaped charges for the worst barriers. The former residents might also have left traps, either nuisance or deadly. Ryan was mindful of warnings from other explorers, ancient delvers who sought the history and rumored treasures of the Tachakilu.

His concern faded into the background as he turned the next corner. Appearing in the glow of Ryan's lamp, a ringed doorway opened onto a widened, elongated chamber. Finally, he had found something.

The room was familiar in form and function. Rows of upright shelves – dull grey metal bolted perpendicular to the stone walls on one side and to upright rods of the same material on the other – flanked a central aisle nearly twice Ryan's arm span in width. Simple metal stools lined the aisle, with a large table shaped like a trapezoidal solid in the center. The shelves were wide but only a few inches deep. On the shelves were incongruously familiar books, paper volumes bound in board and leather, just like the antiques of Earth's past.

Ryan entered and paused at the first shelf, glancing down the row of books. Was this the treasure he sought? It wasn't the burial crypt he expected, nor did it contain any of the fabled Tachakilu technology, but it clearly contained information. Even if none of the books were technical diagrams or historical records, they might contain clues about the real sites of value. At the least, they were worth something to the right academics or collectors.

Already carefully gloved, Ryan reached for the nearest volume to see what he could learn. None of the spines were labeled, in any language known or unknown. The cover of the book Ryan selected was also unmarked. He had no idea what to expect inside.

He certainly did not expect what he found. What was a copy of the William Marchese Preparatory School Yearbook doing down there? Why would it appear millions of light years away, hundreds of feet below the surface of a planet completely separate from Earth? Ryan shivered.

Even stranger, the yearbook was his. He attended that school, during that year. He recognized the images of the school's campus, its hallways, and many of its students. Ryan knew on what page and in what location his own image would appear. A printed yearbook was already an archaism, a holdover from the days of paper media. To find one in an impossible setting was far more bizarre.

Despite his disturbance, Ryan continued to read. He searched for some discrepancy, a mismatch that would confirm the book as false. He was drawn in by nostalgia and reminded of his youth by pictures illustrating its frequent setting. He spent several long minutes entranced.

A loud noise, like something heavy and hollow falling over, made Ryan look up from the book.

The library was empty and almost dark. He must have been reading past the closing hour again, left undisturbed by the considerate librarian. Where was Mr. Klein? Already gone, leaving Ryan to lock the door when he was done. Ryan appreciated the trust, but wished someone had told him how late it was getting.

Now, he was alone in the room, possibly alone in the school… except for that noise. Where had it come from? Ryan heard it echo down the halls from somewhere distant, but not distant enough. Either something fell over on its own, or someone else was in the school after hours. Maintenance? Probably. Still, Ryan felt the need to check it out. Someone might be hurt or need a hand. Worst case, someone – probably a student – was breaking into the school after hours.

What got knocked over? It sounded like a trash can, but a big one. The cafeteria? There were plenty of large plastic objects in there to dislodge, including empty food bins. Maybe Ryan's fellow late-night visitor was a squirrel who discovered a route into the kitchens.

Labyrinthine

Ryan slipped out of the library and crept down the school's hallways, aimed toward the cafeteria. As usual, he was annoyed with the size of the building. Los Angeles' school districts struggled to accommodate ever larger class sizes. That meant a warren of new construction tacked onto older buildings. Most schools in the bigger cities were complexes dwarfing the shopping centers of the late 20th century.

A slow, stealthy walk to the cafeteria took Ryan several minutes. On the way, he passed banks of lockers, waves of rippling posters, and an endless sea of linoleum tiles. The backdrop was almost too familiar to bother noticing.

The door to the cafeteria was ajar. A light was on, deep inside. Ryan pushed through the opening as quietly as he could. Something was in the kitchen. Something metallic dinged as it was dislodged. From the sounds inside, the intruder wasn't a squirrel. It was bigger. It was moving things around in a manner that suggested sentience… but why would a person be breaking into the school kitchen, at this hour? To steal food? To investigate the school's food service? To taint the food somehow?

Ryan's imagination supplied plenty of motives, ranging from slightly plausible to complete nonsense. Still, he trusted what he was seeing and hearing. He crab-walked forward, hunched down as if the intruder would miss him by looking too high. Ryan closed on the kitchen door and reached out to swing it open.

The thing inside froze as Ryan moved the door. Damn, he'd been heard. Then there was a scratching, scrabbling rush as the intruder bolted for the back of the kitchen. It was escaping! Ryan threw open the kitchen door, chasing after the obviously guilty party. He had an impression of yellow scales and clawed feet as it fled through the swinging doors back to the kitchen's rear hallway exit.

What was it? An extra-Terrestrial? Tachakilu? What sort of feet did Tachakilu have, again?

Ryan leapt over an overturned pail of cornmeal, dislodged by the thief's flight. He also briefly noticed a swirl of white feathers settling to the ground nearby, but dismissed the detail as irrelevant.

Empyrean Stories

He smashed through the back door, following his quarry by sound as it head-ed for the service passages leading out of the school. That route must have been how it entered. The fleeing target turned a corner before Ryan reached it, disap-pearing before he could get a good look. Its claws continued to scrape on the tile, confirming that whatever he was chasing wasn't Human. It was Human-sized, though. It brushed against the walls occasionally with a swooshing sound.

"Hey, stop!" Ryan managed to shout between breaths. "What are you doing here?"

The intruder did not answer but continued to race toward the exit. They turned two more corners and passed through another door, which didn't seem to slow the other creature at all. Ryan was amazed it was navigating so well and outpacing him so easily. He wasn't an athlete, per se, but he was slim and healthy enough, and he knew the school well... he thought.

Come to think of it, the back hallways weren't so long and winding before, were they? Was he in some part of the school he hadn't explored before? That didn't seem possible. Ryan was an explorer at heart, ill-content to leave any mys-terious hallway or room unmapped. He'd learned every corner of the school in his first year, even the parts that were technically off-limits to students. How, then, was there an unfamiliar section?

Ryan couldn't pause to wonder further. He was just barely keeping his target within hearing range. He passed another opened door and emerged into daylight, relieved to finally reach the exit.

Yet instead of escaping into the sandy yard at the school's rear, Ryan found himself standing on a rooftop, several stories up. Rough stones and sand covered the roof, from where Ryan stood to the edge. The expanse was broken only by ventilation exhausts and cooling fans. There was nowhere else for the fleeing creature to hide, nowhere for it to run.

Ryan paced the rooftop, checking behind every appliance, staring out across the sun-lit cityscape, trying to guess where the intruder had gone. There weren't any side branches in the hallway, so it couldn't have turned aside or doubled back to lose him.

Labyrinthine

A clang of metal on metal caught his attention, sounding from the distance, behind and below Ryan's position. A fire escape? The intruder must have leapt down and caught the balcony of another building. Ryan raced to that side of the rooftop, trying to spot his target. The low sunlight blinded him for a moment; he knelt down and shaded his eyes to get a better view.

While he scanned the adjacent buildings, something crunched on the roof behind him. Before Ryan could turn around, a soft, feathered body crashed into his back, sending him barreling forward... over the edge and off the high roof. He felt the sick weightlessness of freefall as he plummeted. Fortunately, before he struck the road below, shock and vertigo greyed out his perceptions.

Ryan regained consciousness with a start, rising painfully from the irregular stone surface where he landed. Landed? While his back and neck ached, they weren't broken. He wasn't even bruised, just a little sore. He wasn't rising from a fall; he was getting up from an impromptu nap. His compad screen was also asleep, dimmed to conserve power. As he picked it up, the system lit brightly again, showing Ryan the space surrounding him. Everything was grey, except where shadows left it black.

He was in a long, low, wide cavern with a rocky floor, a natural karst formation littered by unnatural broken stone from the drilling that opened it up. Ryan remembered guiding the automated drill rig as it cut toward the pocket cave. His team decided to skip wandering through the maze of outer tunnels, choosing to bore directly into a promising hollow shown by sonographic imaging.

They all remembered the passage Ryan found in a Tesetsi recording about the barrows of the Tachakilu: "Their tombs are guarded by mazes to snare the unwary." Or was it unworthy? Ryan wasn't sure.

Well, you can't be snared if you bypass the maze. Ryan ventured down, directly into the cavern opened up by their drill.

The cavern was certainly a tomb. As he waved his light around, Ryan could see piles of bones, preserved by the airtight conditions of the sealed chamber. Hundreds of individuals, judging from their skulls, and obviously non-Human.

The elongated jaw ridges and heightened brow sculpting definitely suggested Tachakilu, based on their modern-day descendants.

He'd found the burial area. Now, where would their grave goods be placed? Ryan was embarrassed and a little nauseated by the thought that he had fallen asleep alongside the ancient dead he would be robbing.

Why had he slept? He remembered falling, but the drill shaft wasn't that steep; he could climb its diagonal slope with little effort. It was unlikely he would plummet and get knocked out. Besides, his head didn't hurt like a concussion. Maybe there were gases sealed inside the cave, like in the pharaonic tombs of old Terra. While Ryan wore an oxygen supply mask, he hadn't detected any atmospheric contaminants on his initial entry to the bore tunnel. Maxwell hadn't reported any toxins, either.

Actually, where was Maxwell? Ryan tapped his compad, signaling the AI to resume active functions. The calm, even voice of his companion answered immediately: "Yes, Ryan? What is it?"

"What do you mean?" Ryan asked, irritated. "I fell asleep. I got knocked out by something. Shouldn't you notice that? Maybe try to wake me up?"

"I assumed you were fatigued," Maxwell answered without a hint of apology. "It has been a long day."

"I don't usually sleep in crypts, do I?" Ryan replied with thick sarcasm. "You're supposed to warn me if something is dangerous. Sleeping in a strange place on a strange planet is dangerous... not to mention, you missed whatever knocked me out."

"I detected no threat," Maxwell objected. "I did inquire why you were resting, but you did not answer. Your vitals did not change in any alarming fashion, either. You seemed to be settling down for natural rest."

Ryan groaned. "That's not normal. You know that. Do I need to have your programming checked?" It was an idle threat, and both Human and Brin knew it. Having his companion diagnosed would run the risk of a technician discovering Ryan's illegal activities, mainly because Maxwell so strongly disapproved.

Tempting the AI with a sympathetic audience might prove too much, tilting his decision process away from loyal silence and toward confession and rehabilitation for his wayward owner. A Brin paired with a criminal Keeper faced this constant dilemma; the criminal faced a dilemma if their Brin started acting up.

"What *is* your problem?" Ryan ventured, belatedly realizing the question sounded more aggressive than he intended.

"The same as always: the hazard you place yourself in, without reason. Ryan, you could pursue your interests quite thoroughly, making an excellent living and occupying your mind completely, without resorting to these illicit shenanigans. You are intelligent…"

"Look, just wake me up if I start to drift off again," Ryan interrupted. "And signal the team. Hey, haven't they been asking why I wasn't reporting?"

"I have received no inquiries from your friends," Maxwell reported.

That was a concern, though not particularly surprising. Everyone was busy with their own duties or their own regions to explore. The group only had a few days to investigate the planet and gather up or catalog what they could, before the next Collective patrol passed over and noticed their unlicensed presence.

Ryan dimmed his compad and unbuckled his lamp, illuminating the cavern with more intense light. Even his powerful lantern couldn't pierce the furthest corners of the vast space. At the edges, beyond the furthest ossuaries, darkness shrouded the outer edges of the crypt. Hopefully, in one of those directions, Ryan would find a cache or else a tunnel leading out toward something of value. He thought briefly about a library full of paper books, but shook off the memory as irrelevant. Whatever he found down there, it wouldn't be books.

A sonar scan of the space revealed five potential exits, each in a different direction. That fit the general image produced by the surface sonogram: the cavern was a hub for multiple pathways. The scans weren't finely detailed enough to suggest which path might be more important, if Ryan didn't find a payoff in the main cave. He would have to choose one route and explore it for some distance.

Ryan picked one direction at semi-random, choosing the tunnel closest to geographic north. If that route proved fruitless, he would come back and check the next opening to the left, proceeding clockwise around the enormous central space.

As he walked, Ryan stayed alert for strange sensations: dizziness, foreign smells, or external sounds. The complex was supposed to be as dead as its former residents, but after his unexpected nap, Ryan was suspicious. It was possible his arrival triggered some defense that put him to sleep. It might not have been a deliberate trap; his footfalls in the long-dormant space might have stirred up some contaminant that knocked him out. If it wasn't such an expense – and an obvious flag when purchased – Ryan might have brought a full environmental mask or suit on the trip.

Ryan's caution was muted by his excitement at finally getting to explore the complex. Besides greed, he felt a measure of honest intellectual curiosity. He had done the majority of the work researching the Tachakilu and their past civilizations, finding their planet, and arranging everyone's transport. Ben-david provided the seed funding, Marta the practical knowledge to prepare their expedition, and Louis the navigational skill to get them there. The four friends – eight if you counted their AI partners – were technically listed as a mining survey team, which gave them cover for their purchases, but they hadn't landed on the planet originally listed on their transit plans.

Not that many scholars knew for certain where to look where to look for Tachakilu remains, much less that such caches existed. Most researchers who knew anything about the much-declined civilization were successfully warned away by the ancient historians who recorded the empire's downfall.

The Tachakilu protected their remains, that much was known. Besides burying their caches fathoms deep, behind mazes of rumored complexity, the Tachakilu destroyed many of their own records, hiding their past even from their descendants, much less the rest of the sapient Universe. Even the reason for this secrecy was unknown. Religion? Shame? A desire to prevent the repetition of past mistakes?

Labyrinthine

Ryan was following a long tradition of scholars by reconstructing the few leads and the fewer discoveries that pieced together the mystery of the Tachaki-lu. He expected some reward for his effort. Ryan would not be content with academic praise or awards. If he were really fortunate, he would find more than a few archaeological treasures. He might uncover a lost technology that would make him – and his associates – a significant power within the Collective. Knowl-edge was the real currency of interstellar trade; Ryan intended to invest his little share and grow it into a real payoff.

These thoughts reawakened in Ryan's mind as he ventured into the north-ward tunnel. Mazes to snare the unworthy, indeed. By coming so far, Ryan con-sidered himself quite worthy.

The current tunnel wasn't much of a maze. It wound nearly straight outward, smoothing out along its length from a crude excavation to an almost perfect cy-lindrical bore. Ryan started to wonder why the inner cavern wasn't more shaped or supported, when the builders had the tools to create tidier, stronger construc-tion. Excavation at different points in time? Haste to finish the final burial? Some prohibition against working the stone of the natural cavern, because of its use as a barrow? So little was known about ancient Tachakilu culture. Nothing certain could be gleaned from the habits of their modern descendants.

So much unknown; so much to discover.

Ryan sensed a shift in air pressure ahead of him: a slight breeze. Was he nearing a larger passage or chasm? There shouldn't be another surface opening anywhere nearby; otherwise, they would have used that entrance instead of bur-rowing their own.

He hurried forward, lantern held aloft. In the soft, grey darkness ahead, an answering light gleamed. Another of his team members? No, the light wasn't another lantern. It was a square, glowing fixture set into a far wall at the end of Ryan's passage. A perpendicular tunnel crossed his path at a T.

Artificial light! Whether electrical, chemical, or another sort of technology, the artifact was a sign Ryan was getting somewhere. He picked up his pace, ex-cited to see what he had discovered. The cross-tunnel appeared to be wider than

Ryan's approaching passage, curving both higher and lower.

When he came closer, Ryan was surprised again by another artifact. A single rail of dark metal, bolted to the stone floor, ran the length of the crossing tunnel. It was rectangular, with slight segmentation lines indicating that it had been fabricated in sections and installed, rather than extruded. Ryan looked down the tunnel and saw that the rail extended in both directions. More of the boxy light sources studded the tunnel at regular intervals. Their cases looked like molded glass or clear plastic.

The edge of the floor before the larger tunnel was colored differently than the grey stone around. It was yellow, in a wide strip striated with black hashes. The pattern seemed familiar, suggesting a hazard warning. When Ryan finally reached the area, he could tell the pattern was painted on. The universality of design explained the construction to him within moments.

It was a train stop. The tunnel was a subterranean railway line, what some Terrans used to call a 'subway'. Probably magnetic levitation, by the looks of the track.

A train stop at the barrow cavern? A direct line to the crypt was surprising. That possibility clashed with warnings about a deadly maze. Ryan shrugged. Perhaps the train was long defunct, its line blocked somewhere else, with its access no longer considered a security concern. Possibly, its presence meant the real cache was somewhere else.

Another rush of air, from the tunnel opening on Ryan's right side, suggested his first hypothesis was incorrect. Low rumbling vibrated the stone floor, accompanied by a higher pitched but equally quiet hiss. Was the train working? Had someone turned it on? Had it been awakened to life by Ryan's presence?

Ryan signaled his confederates: "Are you seeing this? I have active technology down here. A train. You've got to be picking up the EM even up there. Did one of you turn something on?"

There were no replies, not even an acknowledging ping. That wasn't exactly a surprise, if the others were far away and the positioning satellite was out of range. If they were all underground as well, that added another layer of interference.

Labyrinthine

Maxwell would store and repeat Ryan's message until he received a confirmation of receipt.

Ryan belatedly remembered his partner. "Maxwell, what are you picking up?"

"Active electromagnetic fields of growing intensity. Please keep my housing away from the structure directly in front of you. A large metallic mass is approaching at significant speed, judging from shifts in field structure, atmospheric disturbance, and auditory cues."

Indeed, sounds across the frequency spectrum were growing in intensity: a high-pitched squeal, a rumbling clacking noise, and a sub-sonic vibration in the floor. Something was coming down the tunnel. All signs pointed toward a train on its way.

The artifact was as amazing as it was odd. Not only a transport system of familiar design, but a functioning one, centuries after any being inhabited the planet. Ryan hardly believed it himself, even while looking at the track and hearing the cars approach. It took the arrival of the train itself to convince him it was real.

It was a white, gleaming construct of metal and plastics, a glaring contrast against the sculpted stone of the surrounding tunnels. A lead car shaped like an atmospheric shuttle fronted the sequence of linked units, each one glossy white and separated by bands of thick grey rubbery material. Four of the cars, plus the lead, passed Ryan before the train glided to a stop.

He had the feeling the train had been slowing for some time before it reached him, in order to pause appropriately. But how did it know he was present? There must be some sort of sensor tuned to react to the presence of a potential passenger. The idea that there were active electronics within the burial complex put Ryan on guard. What other sorts of devices might react to his intrusion?

At least the train seemed welcoming. Each car had a wide door set into its surface. Once the sixth car stopped in front of Ryan, its door slid out and sideways, opening onto a boxy space within the cylindrical segment.

The passenger space looked remarkably mundane and familiar. A deep red carpet lined the floor of the train car, surmounted by plastic-covered seats of a similar color alternating with dark grey. Chromed railings, obvious handholds for passengers, extended from the floor to the roof and across the roof from front to back. The space was clean but not completely clean, with small stains and tears visible on the seats. The opening door released a slightly animal, sour scent, either from the decaying materials or of the train's former riders.

The latter was unlikely. If this train were built and used by the Tachakilu, any remnant of their bodies would be several hundred years old, as sterile and dry as the bones behind Ryan. Then again, if the train cars were sealed airtight, they might retain some ancient effluvia.

Ryan considered whether to board. If the cars did retain biological or chemical contaminants, it might not be safe to enter. Plus, he didn't know where the train might run, if it would continue safely, or if he could get a ride back, even if the train reached its destination.

On the other hand, the train might take him somewhere interesting. He could map its tracks and find new, connected sites. If he let it leave, there might not be another train for a long time, if ever. And if the trains were running, it wouldn't be safe to walk on the tracks to trace their extent... not to mention, such a hike would be exhausting.

Ryan didn't debate long. His natural eagerness won out without much trouble. He leapt up the short step into the train car and braced himself against the bars. The car's door closed quickly behind him, removing the option to back out. There was a large red button set into a panel near the door; Ryan might be able to force the door to open, signal the train to stop, or both.

The train shuddered and began to move again. Ryan felt the lurch of its initial motion and a steady shift in his inner ear from the increasing acceleration. The noise of the maglev's imperfectly efficient motion rose around him, growing louder but never quite unpleasant.

A train! A maglev subway train, like one might find in older cities on Terra or many other inhabited planets. The technology had been largely abandoned when gravity control was perfected.

Labyrinthine

Ryan remained in a state of amused surprise throughout the ride. The car had only two windows, one in the door and one in the wall opposite, and these were small and tinted, so he saw little outside the car. Not that there was much to see, he supposed: mostly tunnel wall and lights.

Where was he going? He had no idea, but he was excited to find out. It might be a long trip, bringing him to a facility elsewhere on the same continent. He might be descending even further, to a region undetectable even by sonar imaging. Was there another complex elsewhere on the planet? Another tomb? A settlement hidden away?

Ryan's imagination conjured images of a lost Tachakilu civilization buried beneath the surface, accidentally or deliberately forgotten by the outside Universe. He might be greeted as the envoy of outer civilization; he might be attacked as an unwanted intruder.

After only a few minutes, the train began to slow. Ryan felt and heard the change in motion. How far had he come? If the system reached typical speeds for pre-colonial Terran transport, he might have gone ten kilometers or more. Not too far, on a planetary scale, but a distance that would have taken over an hour on foot.

The train eventually came to a full stop. Ryan peered from the window of his car, seeing a scene that made his heart leap. A full train station waited outside, outfitted in steel support beams and chrome accents. It was a sizeable space, an artificial environment beyond anything Ryan thought the Tachakilu abandoned. They left no buildings and few artifacts, scouring their former settlements clean as they fled some unknown threat. So much worked metal would never have been wasted, even buried this deep.

By the time the door opened, Ryan was itching to step out. He burst from the train car with uncontained eagerness, not caring that the door slid shut immediately behind him. As the train started to move away, Ryan felt only a twinge of concern. As long as the system kept running, he could catch the next train… at least, he assumed there would be another train along eventually. If not, he could walk the same tunnel back. It would be uncomfortable, possibly dangerous, but not impossible. In the worst case, the team would eventually come looking for him, following his signal trace. They could punch another tunnel back down to retrieve him, if necessary.

In the meantime, Ryan explored the new space he'd discovered. The room looked much like any modern transit station, aside from the maglev rail. Looking back, Ryan noticed that the train tunnel here wasn't sculpted stone, but rather a tube of shaped plastic supported by metal rings. Higher technology, like the train itself. Excellent.

At his present rate, he might find a fusion power plant next... or computer systems. Gigabytes of raw information, the real treasure. No such lode was immediately present. Ryan examined the room until he determined that it held no higher technology than its construction materials and electric lighting system.

One anomaly asserted itself. The room had an exit, set higher into the wall opposite the train tracks. The exit was an unremarkable square portal flanked by two rectangular sliding doors: a common convergent design. A short ramp led up to the doors from below. Above the doors, though, was a sign, backlit and glowing green.

It read, "Station B-1." There was no way that wasn't English, Terran or otherwise. The letters were clearly Latin characters, their order forming a clear, relevant word. No amount of convergent development would produce that same pattern, in the appropriate context, on a far-off world inhabited by a foreign species with no contact with Humans. The probability was vanishingly small.

The only explanation Ryan could attempt was that somehow the Tachakilu received radio output from Terra... no, that made no sense. The distance was so great that the first transmission from Humanity's home planet hadn't even arrived in that system yet. A Human visitor? Also impossible. A Human guest, brought to their world by Tachakilu explorers? Even if that possibility were granted, why use a guest's (or specimen's) language in a setting like this?

Unless Humans also came and built on that world. Unless the so-called unknown ancient ruin was neither ancient nor unknown, or at least not entirely unknown. The most likely explanation, the one Ryan resisted, was that others had explored the ruin already. They had been there, so long ago and *for* so long that they built a train tunnel? They installed an archaic technology, underground, within an abandoned world? Why? Even if Ryan granted the first supposition, what was the point of building a subway line?

Ryan wasn't going to get any answers standing still. He shook off his bafflement. He stomped up the ramp to the double doors and was only mildly startled when they detected his approach and opened. Of course. Automated doors. Why not?

The exit opened onto another tunnel, also rounded but taller than it was wide and slightly curved, with Ryan's doorway on the inside bend. Left or right? The train brought him roughly westward before, so Ryan chose the opposite direction, to his left, back eastward.

At least, he thought he had his directions straight. The train track might have curved. He should check Maxwell's Automap.

When he reached for his compad, Ryan's hand closed on empty air. His heart stopped for a moment. He checked again. His compad was missing. *Maxwell* was missing, along with his map. How was the 'pad missing? It had been strapped securely to his belt in its carrying pouch. There should be no way for the device to work its way free, unless the straps came loose or were cut.

And yet his belt was still on, undamaged. The pouch and its contents were gone. Ryan felt like he had been robbed. How could he be pickpocketed, when there was no one around for kilometers? He must have bumped against something sharp enough to slice off the pouch, neatly and quickly. Even then, why didn't he feel anything?

He had to have lost it on the train. That was perfect. His compad, his map, and his Brin were riding around somewhere distant, to return at some unknown time, on a world he couldn't find his way around *because his map was gone.*

It got worse. His compad was his communications link. Even if the others traced its signal, they would find the device and not Ryan. Wonderful.

He needed to go back. As interesting as the new place was – whatever it was, wherever it was – Ryan couldn't risk becoming even further lost. He would go back to the train platform, wait for the vehicle to come back, check it for his compad, then wait some more if it wasn't the right train. Ryan hoped the system was cyclical. On that same hope, he might have to ride the train back around to return to his original entrance. Ryan doubted the others would leave him behind, but it wouldn't be wise to stay missing too long. Ryan didn't want to be the reason they all got caught trespassing.

He was just about to walk back through the doors when he heard voices. *Familiar* voices, even if they weren't Human. It sounded like… Mauraug, judging by the timbre and language. Great, not only was the facility there, period, it was still occupied. A Mauraug occupation wasn't the best news, but at least the sapients were Collective members. Most of them, anyway. Actually, judging from the sign at the door, the facility had to be a joint operation including Terrans. Ryan was relieved to rule out the possibility he had uncovered a cell of the dissident Mauraug Apostasy.

Ryan decided to wait and risk his luck. He was going to be caught anyway. At least if he approached peacefully, he'd get the benefit of the doubt and have an opportunity to present his cover story. The facility personnel might help him retrieve Maxwell; the Human personnel, anyway. His dreams of power and wealth were shot, but at least he wouldn't lose his faithful AI and his valuable compad.

Rounding the corner came not one but two Mauraug, simian sapients larger and bulkier than Humans. One was reddish-brown with darker brown streaks in its wavy fur; the other was generally black, with sparser, straighter fur shot with white and grey flecks. The first wore a black utility belt with an underhanging loincloth, while its partner sported a short-sleeved, short-legged olive coverall crossed by a gun belt. Neither had any of the visible cybernetic modifications typical among the species.

If the sight of the two beings wasn't anomalously mundane enough – alien to the setting though not to Ryan – one other revelation battered his brain. Ryan knew one of the pair.

"Khreneth?" he greeted the darker Mauraug, hesitantly. When the appropriate sapient looked toward him in acknowledgement, Ryan was certain. "Khreneth bash'Trevek!" he crowed, "What are you doing out here… down here?"

Labyrinthine

Both Mauraug continued toward him, the unknown one looking at Ryan with interest, Khreneth approaching in puzzlement.

"What do you mean, Ryan?" Khreneth answered in passable English. It and Ryan both spoke the appropriate Collective interlingua, and Ryan knew a smattering of the dominant Mauraug language, but Khreneth liked to show off its greater command of English and supposedly superior intellect.

The two sapients met when Ryan left to study off-world. Both attended the University on Kolkata Station, in the Husthak inter-system between Terran and Mauraug space. That was where Ryan first learned about the Tachakilu and picked up the thread of their migration across a particular star system. His later research confirmed Tachakilu occupation of a specific planet, this planet.

Except, "this planet" was looking more and more like Kolkata Station, the more Ryan thought about it. The general aesthetic matched, in that particular hallway. Kolkata never had a maglev line, only a pneumatic transport tube... but its passenger stations *were* similar to the one behind Ryan.

Khreneth and Ryan attended Kolkata as fellow students interested in xenoarchaeology. Now Khreneth was present, also, again. Had it followed the same leads as Ryan? Or were the Mauraug always ahead of Ryan's research, by years?

Ryan asked again, "How did you get here? Are you exploring the ruins? Or is this a pre-existing installation? Frost, is this place even registered?"

Khreneth looked at him in continued confusion. Its colleague lowered its eyebrows, unsure what to make of the conversation and unhappy about its odd turn.

"I don't understand what you mean," Khreneth replied. "I've been here since before you enrolled. What ruins? I don't have an excavation practicum for another six months. The rest of what you just said is nonsense."

"Are you joking?" Ryan was careful not to raise his hands or step closer to the larger primates. He was growing angry, but it wouldn't help to provoke a Mauraug by implying aggression. He was the intruder, no matter what the situation was here, and he needed to show proper deference.

"Sorry," he started again, keeping his eyes lowered, "but I'm really confused. What is this place?"

Khreneth's partner answered for it, "Transit station B-1? Kolkata Station? Are you well, citizen?"

Kolkata Station? Ryan almost blurted the words back as a challenge, but restrained himself. All the visible evidence favored the Mauraug's claim. But how had he come from underground, within a planet... to an orbiting station far, far from that world?

"I'm, uh, disoriented," Ryan answered. "Could you point me to an observation port? I need to get my bearings."

"Sounds like it," Khreneth agreed. "The nearest lounge is three, maybe four doors down, back that way." The Mauraug pointed a hand, knuckles out, back the way it had come. "You sure you don't need a medic, instead?"

"I might," Ryan admitted. "I thought I was somewhere else, for a while. Thanks. Oh, I misplaced my Br..." He trailed off, realizing that a pair of Mauraug weren't the most sympathetic audience to ask for help locating his AI partner. Their culture was notoriously opposed to the use of artificial intelligence, as a literal article of religious faith. He resumed, lamely, "...my compad. I dropped it somewhere. If you see it, could you let me know?"

The unidentified Mauraug pursed its lips in distaste, but Khreneth deigned to answer, "All right. If it was stolen, I would be pleased to correct the thief. If you were negligent, I will be pleased to correct your mistake." Always with the dominant, superior attitude. Some Mauraug, like Khreneth, were better behaved than others, but they never stopped trying to determine who was in charge in any relationship.

"We will even leave your demon unpurged," the other Mauraug added, the two of them hooting in shared laughter over the jest.

Ryan rolled his eyes, thought he kept them lowered. It was always like that, at school. The Mauraug students managed to stay out of trouble for the most part, but they had to push. There were Human bullies as well, but they weren't as consistent or predictable. It was a cultural thing with the Mauraug, maybe even genetic.

Ryan shrugged finally. "Thanks. Well, I'll go check that out. Is Station Security still in the same office?" He asked the question not for directions, but to see how it would be answered.

Khreneth replied, "Of course. Why would the office move?"

No apparent deception at all. Maybe he really *was* on Kolkata Station. Khreneth sounded surprised by his question, but its reply was appropriate if it believed them both on the station, not somewhere below a foreign planet.

So, what happened? Ryan was forced to accept the impossible when he reached the viewing lounge and got a good view of open space. He was on an orbital station. He apparently was on familiar old Kolkata, an older station, though not so old as to have a maglev line. What was going on? Did the Tachakilu ruin somehow incorporate a space-folding transport? Had Ryan been tossed, via the train ride, through some sort of portal or rift or… something?

It wasn't just spatial transport, he realized. Ryan hadn't attended KSU for years, yet Khreneth looked and sounded the same as when they attended class together. For their meeting to occur, the transport would have sent Ryan through time, as well.

What was the story with the train line, itself? If Ryan had gone far enough back in time for Kolkata to have a magnetic transport line, then Khreneth shouldn't be there. There was some sort of strange overlap of times and places and persons going on. An alternative timeline? A divergent reality?

That chrono-spatial muddle might explain what happened to Maxwell. If Ryan was somehow on a timeline when he didn't have Maxwell with him, the Brin could have been left behind. That was assuming only Ryan was transported, for some reason. Why would they be separated? Ryan and Maxwell had been together since Ryan started secondary school.

Perhaps if they were together earlier, like some Human-Brin pairs, the two would be better bonded. Ryan always suspected he and his Brin were mismatched.

Maxwell clearly didn't like Ryan. Ryan appreciated the AI, but didn't particularly like his attitude most days.

If Maxwell was lost forever, Ryan wouldn't be heartbroken. He'd want a new Brin, and he might be sorry Maxwell was stranded, but he'd be happy with a replacement... maybe happier.

Such somber thoughts. Ryan had other troubles to worry about first, like figuring out what had happened and where and when he was. He exited the lounge, aiming toward the Station Security office, guided by his own memory and the helpful map murals.

Or, not so helpful. Ryan realized that between one map and the next, labels and even passages were changing. The Security office not only wasn't where he remembered, it wasn't in the same location on different maps.

Was this a joke? Was he lost in ways beyond mere geography? Ryan, an explorer at heart, was only used to being lost the first time he roamed a new area. In a place he had explored before, one with which he was intimately familiar, he should never get lost.

Clearly, his location wasn't his familiar Kolkata Station. More than that, Ryan suspected someone or something was interfering with him.

He should have guessed that, long before. He was being diverted, in some manner he didn't quite understand. Ryan remembered wandering in winding, rough-surfaced tunnels, not so long ago. His thoughts flashed back to a library somehow both underground and inside his school on Terra. Ryan wondered anew about the anomaly of a train tunnel connecting a subterranean crypt with an orbiting University. Were any of those memories accurate? Or was someone influencing his perceptions?

There were plenty of someones around to suspect. Sentients of multiple species and cultures attended Kolkata, many of them walking its halls alongside Ryan. He stopped one, a Human woman, and asked her, "What's going on? Am I at KSU, or not?"

Labyrinthine

She looked at him with alarm. "Are you all right? Of course, you're on the Station. Are you suffering a chemical imbalance?"

Ryan shook his head. "Sorry. Maybe. Could you point me to the Security office, please?"

The woman gestured quickly and hurried away, eager to leave Ryan's erratic behavior behind. He tried again with an elderly Copper-Caste Zig, a scholar he assumed was a professor.

"Sir, I have misplaced my compad. Could you provide me the date and time in Terran Standard Units, and directions to the Security office?" Ryan pleaded.

The elder glared at him with glittering eyes, but responded evenly, "It is the twelfth day of the eighth month in Terran Standard year 2321. The time is eight-point-five-three hours post meridian, Greenwich Standard Time. The Security office is twelve meters in that direction, eight meters to the intersection and four meters beyond it after a left turn. Is there anything further you require, student?"

Ryan answered with exaggerated gratitude: "No, thank you, Sir. You have been very helpful."

Then he hastened away. The woman and the Zig had given roughly corresponding directions. Ryan's target might stay put long enough to reach. The date given by the old Zig was an oddity Ryan put aside for later consideration, as it corresponded exactly to the departure date of his expedition to find the Tachakilu.

It didn't fit. Too many things didn't fit. Ryan's attempts at explanation were breaking down, one by one. Even when he stretched logic to accommodate ever more improbable possibilities, new data created conflicts and ruled out those tenuous explanations.

Ryan succeeded in finding the Security office. It was there, where it should be, looking just like he remembered. Ryan hadn't had much cause to visit Security at Kolkata Station – which was fortunate, given the illicit plans he'd hatched there – but he was aware of its location. He was usually aware of *everything's* location. At that point, he wasn't too confident about where he was, himself.

He'd try Security. Logically, that office would be best equipped to track his past movements, to explain anomalies, and to locate his missing compad. Ryan could make an official report... at least as far as he was willing to explain his actions.

Ryan walked through the door of the office. A male Human officer sat at a desk, entering data on an oversized, wall-mounted compad. The tall, broad man was in full uniform, complete with a badge that read: Jared Ben-david.

It *was* Ben-david. Older and with a moustache, but still the same familiar face of Ryan's friend and co-conspirator. What was he doing in a Security uniform, of all things?

Officer Ben-david looked up and saw Ryan. He recognized his schoolmate, all right. But rather than showing pleased surprise, his friend's dark face grew darker.

"Ryan Yaling!" Ben-david named him with evident distaste. "I did not expect *you* to turn yourself in. Well, turn around and we'll get this over with." He withdrew a linked pair of reactive plastic restraints from his belt, priming them to encase flesh when they touched a victim's hands.

He intended to use them on Ryan! Ryan raised his hands high and stepped back from the approaching officer. "Ben! Ben-david! Look, I don't know what is going on here, but I didn't do anything. At least, nothing you didn't do, also. What are you doing here? What are you doing in that suit? And what do you mean, turn myself in?"

"Do I need to detail the charges? I promise I will, as soon as you're taken into custody." Ben-david was serious, continuing to advance carefully but without hesitation.

"The hell you will," Ryan shouted, now genuinely outraged. He was still utterly disoriented, but seeing his friend and criminal partner in a law enforcement uniform, telling him he would be arrested... that was hitting low.

Ryan turned and bolted out of the office. At first, he only intended to escape the security officer. *Ben-david? Officer Ben-david? Really?* After that, he had to decide where he was going. There weren't many ways off a space station. What was he going to do, steal a shuttle? A starship?

His best hope was the train station. Security could shut down the trains, but maybe if Ryan lost Ben-david first, nobody would know Ryan's route. Without certainty, Security might not take extreme measures to catch one fugitive.

Ryan bolted at a full sprint, opening up distance and looking for a potential hiding spot. The strange spatial phenomenon actually came to his aid. The convoluted, mutating architecture of the pretender Station prevented him from recognizing any previous pathways, but at least he had plenty of running space. He didn't seem to ever hit a final dead end. As long as he kept moving, he stayed well ahead of the pursuing officer.

Officers. Ryan became aware that the footsteps and voices behind him were multiplying. At least two and possibly three Security personnel were pursuing him through the corridors. They were all behind him still; if they split up and flanked him or were joined by assistance from the opposite direction, Ryan would have nowhere left to run. As it was, his chances of breaking away from the hunt were diminishing as the pack grew.

At least he was in good health. He seemed to be outpacing the Security team. Actually, Ryan was surprised he wasn't at least fighting for breath. He was hardly tired, despite the sudden sprint and lengthy chase.

As if the thought reminded his lungs, Ryan was abruptly starved for oxygen. His chest heaved, catching up from a forgotten break. Not for the first time, Ryan began to doubt his perceptions. Why were the corridors so long and so unfamiliar? Why did his pace never slow, even after he started to feel exhausted? Why were the Security officers always *just* out of sight?

Ryan was tempted to stop. He wished he could see what happened if he acted unpredictably or inspected his surroundings closely. His mind flashed between hypotheses: he was in a multi-sensory simulation or hallucination. A carefully acted farce. A dream.

The problem was, if he was wrong, holding still or challenging the officers would lead to unwanted consequences. At best, he would be arrested. At worst, he might find himself captured by imposters who were somehow able to access his memories. Psionics? Some sort of mental control phenomenon was definitely at work.

Certain elements of Ryan's recent experience fit the dream hypothesis better. The transitions between scenes. The appearance of familiar faces. The way things appeared or sharpened only when he paid them attention and changed when he wasn't alert.

Ryan couldn't risk doing anything obviously stupid – like surrendering – but he could try certain tests. The easiest was attempting lucidity within the theoretical dream-state.

Ryan tried his hardest to concentrate, while still running steadily and struggling to breathe. He repeated to himself, mentally, *"This is a dream. I am asleep. I want to wake up."* He tried to focus on his real, prone body. He willed himself to doubt, to move, to wake.

The experiment seemed to be working. Ryan found his consciousness divided between the ongoing scene of hot pursuit aboard a space station and separate feelings of cold, soreness, and paralysis. That was it! That was reality. He was lying somewhere, drowsing, having a nightmare.

"Wake up, Ryan!" His mental calls were augmented by a second, quieter voice, calling him from a distance. The speaker sounded vaguely familiar, cultured and aloof. Maxwell!

Ryan latched onto the AI's welcome intrusion. The formerly solid structures around him began to blur and melt, his doubt eroding their credibility. The pursuing Security officers faded, their voices muted, their threat disbelieved.

He could almost feel it. Would he wake up in his bunk, having imagined a ridiculous scenario about their arrival to the Tachakilu ruins? Or were the ruins themselves, even the Tachakilu, figments of the same dream? Perhaps Ryan was still in his studies at Kolkata Station. He would have a good laugh about the dream with Ben-david… though not with Khreneth bash'Trevek.

Labyrinthine

Then Ryan stumbled, the floor falling out from beneath his feet. He twisted reflexively, landing on his side on the cold, textured metal deck. The sensations – falling, impact, and chill – were indistinct but still identifiable. Feeling slightly nauseous from the mixture, Ryan rolled onto his back and lay still, hoping his next sensation would not be the grip of a Security officer.

Ryan opened his eyes to a dramatically changed scene.

He lay flat on a gleaming silver slab, suspended a meter and a half above the floor. A blinding light poured down on him from a reflective fixture. He caught a scent of chlorinated disinfectant. The new setting – and his location within it – raised Ryan's alarms.

When feet shuffled and metal rang behind his head, Ryan's fears proved stronger than his skepticism. He slid off the table into a crouch on the floor, spinning to face the source of noise.

The movement and sound came from a tall, angular creature standing several meters away, stooped over a wide table of brushed steel. Across the table spread surgical instruments, racks of stoppered vials, and a few appliances Ryan assumed were also medical equipment. These props, coupled with the creature's appearance, did nothing to calm Ryan's terrors.

It had thick, rippled, grey skin, pebbled like a lizard's belly. A thick tail ridged with flat black spines gave it a further saurian appearance. But its two legs and four arms were thin, a cross between mammalian and insectile limbs, and its head was an upside-down cone with a rounded top. The head, with four black eyes arranged in a parallelogram, was unlike any sort of species Ryan ever encountered.

Except one. In a sense. His first instinct was to suspect the creature was a Tachakilu, finally showing itself, but its body dimensions were all wrong. Only the head looked familiar. Once his thoughts settled and Ryan was able to inspect the staring being longer, he recognized it by its anomalies. It wasn't that it looked like any specific species. It was the fact that it looked like *no* known species, yet combined features of multiple familiar genomes.

"You're a Tesetsi!" he blurted.

"And you're a Human," the Tesetsi replied smoothly, "a surprisingly lively one."

Ryan stood, no longer quite as panicked but still cautious. The sapient made no movement toward him, aggressive or otherwise, but seemed content to wait. It set down the chirping device it had been studying to pay Ryan its full attention.

Ryan asked, "Where is this? What's the story now?"

The creature blinked slowly before answering: "I'm not sure what you mean. This location is my home. You are not far from where you collapsed. I retrieved you for study."

"Study? Like experiments?"

The sapient's four eyes managed to roll all at once. "Some tests, but nothing invasive. Or permanent. I intended to restore you to health after collecting data. But it seems I needed to do little except wait."

Ryan's head spun with questions, some of which penetrated his fear, confusion, and outrage. He started with: "I get it. Cultural differences, no harm meant, etcetera. I'm glad you speak C-Standard Two, by the way. Let's get back to the important thing: Where are we, exactly? Where did you find me?"

"Relatively or in absolute terms? Perhaps you did suffer some neurological damage. 'We' are in the northern corner of the largest continent on the sole moon of the planet designated Gliese 876 b in Terran nomenclature. Or, 'Thunderbird' to its discoverers."

Ryan knew of Thunderbird. It wasn't where the Tachakilu remains waited… the dig site was on a planet, for one thing. Thunderbird wasn't any place Ryan had ever visited, personally. There was almost no likelihood he was actually there or had traveled there somehow. But Ryan did have a memory linked to that moon: a particular researcher who lived there while it wrote its accounts of the Tachakilu civilization. A Tesetsi researcher…

"Jentac!" Ryan concluded. "You're Jentac, the historian!"

Labyrinthine

"I am Jentac," the Tesetsi agreed, "but history is only one of my interests. It is frustrating to be identified only by one's most successful publication. But it is also unpleasant to *be* identified, at all. I am currently engaged in a gene-graph study of this ecosphere, identifying foreign intrusions. Your unexpected presence is not only delaying my work; it is interfering with the delicate environmental balance. Microbes everywhere. If you are sufficiently recovered, I would ask that you depart, rather than indulging your curiosity."

"You indulged yours," Ryan accused. "I think it's fair you give something back for studying me." He was regaining his stability, even as he suspected his surroundings were still part of the same extended dream. He might as well interrogate Jentac, figment or not, to see what he could learn. Perhaps the character was his own subconscious trying to provide him with information, via his memories of Jentac's text brought to life.

Jentac waved its lower, lesser arms dismissively. "Fairness is a fiction. Obligation a construct. But if it will persuade you to depart faster, I will permit some inquiry. What I choose to answer is another matter... and if you exhaust my patience, you will be ejected without further warning."

Ryan crossed his arms. A tap at his belt reassured him that his compad was with him again. Hopefully, that meant Maxwell was present, as well.

"Fine," he answered. "I'm exploring... investigating the Tachakilu. I assume that's why I'm here. Somewhere along the line, I fell asleep. I'm not sure if I'm still comfortably in my bed or unconscious somewhere underground. You mentioned traps in their old settlements, especially the tombs. Mazes, specifically. Do you know anything more? What did you find?"

"Your speech is difficult to follow," replied Jentac. "Are you sure you aren't feeling disoriented? You are awake, not asleep. You are in my home, on Thunderbird. I assume you mean your narrative as hypothetical: events which might occur should you penetrate a Tachakilu burial site?"

"Let's go with that, sure." Ryan tried to conceal his derision, in case Jentac actually was real or his dream version could take umbrage.

"The comment about mazes was a rough translation. The warning comes directly from Tachakilu sources: oral history relayed by their survivors. I did my best with the meaning, but you shouldn't assume the writer meant a physical obstacle. The same word can indicate a puzzle or mystery."

"But still an obstacle. Something to keep out the unworthy."

Jentac blinked all four eyes at once and tilted its head. Its voice had an odd inflection as it replied: "I wrote, 'unwise'. Did the publisher alter my text? Or do you misremember?"

"Unworthy, unwary, unwise, what does it matter?" Ryan pressed.

"The word used specifically refers to a lack of intellectual discernment. 'Foolish' is perhaps a better meaning. I suppose that does imply lack of mental worthiness or attentional focus, but a specific sort."

The Tesetsi made an easily recognizable sound of derision. "Precision is important, in history and archaeology as much as in the physical sciences. Perhaps more so. You will know if you titrate a solution improperly or splice a gene incorrectly. You do not know if you have misunderstood the intentions and actions of a culture, once they have gone, except by careful investigation of their artifacts. Careful investigation! Not convenient or commercial!"

Jentac's rantings started as a general complaint but seemed to focus specifically on Ryan as they went on. It grew louder with each word. The typically antisocial sapient actually took a step forward, threatening Ryan's personal space, as it accused: "You say you are investigating the Tachakilu. Why? With whom? You want information? I want information. Are you simply indulging your curiosity, or are you genuinely trying to understand a culture whose errors brought about their dissolution and death? Are you seeking insights to share with other cognoscenti? Fame? Fortune? If you seek the dead with the wrong purpose, perhaps you *are* unworthy. Unwary. Unwise!"

The taller, more massive, and naturally armed being took two more steps forward, bringing it within striking distance of Ryan. The Human reflexively tensed into a fighting position, looking around for cover and a weapon.

Labyrinthine

"Answer me or get out!" shrieked Jentac, awkwardly backing up as it realized how close it had come to assaulting another sapient. It picked up a scalpel from the equipment table, but held it low rather than brandishing it as a threat.

Ryan no longer bothered to disguise his disgust. "Fine. Let's see what new nonsense waits outside this bubble." He turned his back, daring the figment to attack him. He walked toward the apparent exit, a rounded door hatch in the examination room's wall.

It was all make-believe. The environment was drawn from his imagination about what Jentac and its residence would look like. The conversation wasn't what Ryan would have expected, though. Perhaps somewhere in his subconscious, guilt and uncertainty and paranoia fused into accusations, projected through the image of the old historian.

So, this wasn't just a nightmare. It was a guilt trip. Great. Ryan redoubled his intentions and efforts to wake up. Maybe he could pass through the door into the waking world. He was absolutely done with this dream. He was even getting tired of the Tachakilu and his expedition to find them. If Ryan found himself in the ship or back at Kolkata Station, having imagined the whole trip, he might reconsider even bothering.

But that was what *it* wanted. That was what the dream was doing: trying to discourage Ryan. Should he listen to his fears or defy them?

Ryan usually defaulted to defiance. Part of his idea to search for the cache came directly from the ancient warnings not to do so. Why would the Tachakilu warn others away, if they weren't hiding something valuable? Why would Jentac repeat those warnings, unless it wanted their secrets kept to itself? Why would the Collective be watching the planet Ryan had identified, unless there was something to hide?

If there *was* something to fear, let it present itself honestly, rather than in fragments and figments. Ryan would not be turned away by his own cowardice, in whatever form it manifested. If there was any real danger in pursuing the Tachakilu, he would spot it first and overcome it, or else turn away for specific, known reasons.

In this frame of mind, Ryan exited the room. It turned out he was exiting an entire building, a habitat module erected in the middle of a grassy field. The greenery extended in every direction, ending in a tree line on each side. A stony brook splashed between grass and trees to Ryan's far right. The sky was a paragon of blue, unsullied by clouds. A yellow-white sun poured down light and warmth.

Was Gliese 876 a white or yellow star? Ryan couldn't remember. He probably had never known. He called up his memory.

"Maxwell? What kind of star is Gliese 876? Any chance we're on Thunderbird, the moon of its second planet?"

Maxwell replied immediately, without commentary: "Gliese 876 is a red dwarf. Gliese 876 b lies within its habitable zone, but is a gas giant. This location is certainly not anywhere near there."

"Thought so," Ryan lied. "So, any idea where we are?"

"Global positioning signals say Terra. Latitude 42.7, longitude -103.6. Fort Robinson State Park, Bowen, Nebraska. Your friend Marta's home region, in fact."

Ryan had never been to Nebraska. His few visits to Terra focused mainly on its large cities. But he had seen pictures of Marta's home before, pictures that looked similar to the landscape around him. His mind must have constructed the new setting from those images. Ryan congratulated himself on his vivid and detailed imagination.

"So where from here?" he asked rhetorically. "Just walk? Try to go somewhere? Go back inside? Or lie down and keep trying to wake up?"

The area was pleasant, at least. Nothing was threatening or chasing him. Ryan wasn't chasing anything else. He wasn't lost in hallways, underground or above ground or in space. He knew exactly where he was, in a relative sense... not that he recognized anything about his environment. Though derived from his planet of genetic origin, the grass and trees and insects were all foreign to Ryan, who was born off-world and followed his family back to L.A.'s urban sprawl.

So, he was still lost. Not knowing more about his surroundings made Ryan uncomfortable. He decided to keep moving, if only to see what features were installed in his new dream world.

The idea that he would learn nothing new crossed his mind. Ryan dismissed the thought. Even one's own mind was worth exploring; it still held mysteries, particularly for someone as rarely introspective as Ryan. His interests were external, as a rule. He was enjoying the opportunity to explore himself, for a change… even if that exploration was unintentional, forcible, and uncomfortable.

Ryan walked toward the brook and found it a comforting rush of clear water. He hadn't encountered much free-running water in person, but remembered videos showing streams. Ryan touched the water and found it as cold and wet as expected. In the clear sunlight, the liquid surface reflected his face as he leaned over.

In reflection, Ryan looked cleaner than he expected. If he was previously underground on a wasteland planet, he ought to be dirtier and more bedraggled. Instead, his face was clean and his hair neatly styled. Ryan looked like he remembered from his yearbook picture, with the exception of his jumpsuit.

Ideal. This place was ideal. It was comfortable and clean – for wilderness – and perfectly wonderful. It was foreign enough to invite exploration but safe enough to relax his innate alarms. That realization set off higher-level alerts in Ryan's consciousness. The place was too good. It was one more mirage, more set dressing for his dream theater.

But why was the dream trying so hard to keep him distracted? Ryan had experienced plenty of fantasies, some quite memorable, but none that lasted so long or manifested so thoroughly. For a dream world, the meadow was remarkably vivid and persistent. It had all the detail Ryan's attention could demand. Unlike the library, the train, or Officer Ben-david, there was nothing present that stood out as an anomaly.

Well, nothing other than a lack of explanation for his arrival. And Jentac's house… which was gone. Of course, it had vanished.

Ryan was actually relieved when the unfair rules of dream logic proved consistent. Add elements in and take them away, almost at random, but only depending on the dreamer's focus. Move the action from place to place without reason, but still require some sort of translation between scenes. Steal bits from anywhere, blending them shamelessly into collages of half-sensible pattern with just enough coherence to draw the dreamer's interest, but never with enough sense to endure long scrutiny.

At least Ryan was aware of the dream by then. At least he wasn't fully invested in the illusion, as often happened. Particularly when a scenario was truly improbable, Ryan was sometimes embarrassed upon waking. He hated being duped, whether by his own mind or another's.

Was he going to keep accepting the current façade? It was pleasant, true, but that appeal was just another trap. Ryan had already rejected scenes built on fear, mystery, anger and even tedium. Why accept one baited with pleasure? Maybe if he rejected this fragment, it would be replaced by something better. Would the next scene include an erotic tryst with Marta? With Louis? With the whole team at once?

The more he considered the possibilities, the more Ryan became convinced that his ongoing experience was not a normal dream. For one thing, it was very long compared to his typical dreams. Ryan was remaining lucid across multiple scenes and for a subjectively long time. He also remembered the sequence of events fairly well, compared to the fragmentary nature of normal dreams. Not that his memories about past dreams were reliable. He might have been lost in his subconscious across subjective hours, on multiple occasion, then recalled only fleeting moments of that experience upon waking.

The thought was vaguely horrifying. How often *were* minds stuck in dreams for extended periods without escape? How long could you be aware of the phenomenon, before throwing it off? How many times had Ryan struggled with his own body and mind, eager to leave but powerless to escape? He might not know. He might never know.

Ryan sat on the grass by the brook and considered the problem, performing an impromptu meditation. Within his mind, he sought his mind. He wanted to wake up, especially once he felt ensnared. If he succeeded, he hoped he would remember the experience, as a reassurance should it occur again.

The sun remained warm. Its warmth was offset by a slight breeze. The grass and leaves rustled in an understated, reassuring melody, accompanying the brook's trickle. Ryan decided that, even when he escaped, he would try to retain the pastoral scene for future reference. It might be his unwilling creation, but it was a pleasing product.

Wake up. Ryan wanted to wake up. Why wasn't it working? When he tried waking before, he at least transitioned into a new dream. Why was his mind resisting?

Probably because he expected it to resist. Because he was afraid, specifically afraid of being trapped. Ryan hated being stuck. That was the scene's hidden danger. Not seduction but stasis. Stability. A denial of his agency. The dream would resist as long as he demanded that it change.

Ryan struggled to calm himself and stop yearning toward freedom. Instead, he tried to become ambivalent. He embraced apathy. He just wouldn't care, one way or another. He could stay there, he supposed. It was nice enough. If he left, that would be fine, too. Either way. Whatever.

A nagging thought fought against his calm. It actually *did* matter if he left.

Ryan craved reality, the unpredictable and unexpected. He needed new experiences to consume, digest, and convert from unknown to known. In this, he was no different than his primate ancestors… even to the point of self-endangerment to fulfill his need for novelty. Ryan's particular flavor of curiosity tended toward the geographic, in that he hated to be lost. Or rather, he hated to stay lost. Starting out lost was fine, but he needed to transform wilderness into tamed cartography.

That truth applied to intellectual maps as much as physical ones. The deliberate irregularity of the dream world aggravated Ryan. It could not be mapped. It not only scoffed at maps, it sabotaged them, manifesting the changes that would most disorient the mapmaker. It destroyed maps already drawn or else made them useless.

Ryan hated that inconsistency. He hated being lost within himself, particularly when his own mindscape ought to be the terrain he knew best. He wanted out.

Ryan's attempt at balance shifted hard to one side. He railed and strained against the false world around him. At first, he did so mentally, pounding against the walls of his mind, seeking an exit to batter open. When that failed, he began to attack his 'physical' surroundings, by hurling rocks into the stream, ripping up grass, and tearing branches off of trees.

Ryan sprayed his cutting beam into the forest, scarring and toppling trunks. Small fires sprang up but were contained by the damp woodland. Ryan almost dared the forest to burst into flames. What could it do? Burn him to death? He would only emerge into another dream or else finally wake up.

Should he try to kill himself? The laser was a terrible choice for personal annihilation, painful and slow. Immolation also sounded horrible. But Ryan did have explosives. Those would do a quick and painless job, if he really wanted to die.

Ryan was reasonably certain that 'death' would set him free from the dream. He was definitely in a dream. He couldn't die. He could be hurt, but only so far as the dream told him he was hurt. If it told him he was dead, he would wake up somewhere else.

Enough instinct for self-preservation lingered to keep Ryan from trying the experiment. Being wrong and actually dying was too high a risk to take, even assuming a miniscule probability. Even if Ryan was definitely in a dream, the possibility of dying in real life if he died there was enough of a deterrent. Why chance it?

Why? Because he wanted out. What would get him out? Ryan considered the problem empirically. In every previous instance, he moved from scene to scene by invoking some sort of transition. Walking. Riding a train. Reading a book. Lying down to sleep. Those gradual processes seemed to be the keys, rather than applied will or drastic action.

What could he do? Walking seemed to be the obvious choice, as the terrain offered little else for interaction.

Labyrinthine

Which way? Did it really matter? Whichever way Ryan went, he would end up somewhere else.

"Hey, Maxwell," Ryan asked aloud. "Which way is Marta's house?" He projected forced cheerfulness, deliberately acting like a performer in a drama.

Maxwell replied dutifully: "Marta's childhood home was in Crawford, approximately ten kilometers away. The fastest route there requires you to travel north until you reach a road, then turn right and follow that path out of the park."

"All right, let's go," Ryan announced, checking his course off his compad's compass.

He walked for an indeterminate distance, landmarked only by his transition from smoking grassland to forest shadows, from forest's edge to its depths, and from those depths to a clearing maintained by scattered stones. Several of the stones were enormous boulders, monoliths left behind by glacial recession. Where several of these grey elders converged, Ryan spotted an opening into the earth, a partially covered tunnel burrowed diagonally down.

It was a blatant symbol. Ryan, no scholar of psychology or semiotics, knew a metaphor when he saw one. He also recognized the opening's similarity to the bore tunnel he descended into the Tachakilu barrow. At least, he thought he entered such a tunnel before. Two memories out of his doubtful stock agreed on that point. Their consistency argued for some basis in reality.

Should he take the cue and climb down? He could ignore the tunnel and continue onward. If he kept walking, perhaps he would encounter another landmark or some more promising transition point. Or he would be routed right back to the same spot. The more Ryan thought about the latter possibility, the more likely it became.

He had the passageway he wanted. If nothing else, he was tired of the current dream and its specific features. Ryan had hiked through enough bucolic bliss. The next stop might at least contain some new clues to move him along on his persistent fantasia.

Grudgingly, Ryan stooped beneath the overhanging stones and lowered his legs into the opening. The passage was actually narrower and deeper than the bore tunnel. The floor was also more sharply slanted, though Ryan hit bottom before his shoulders passed ground level. He carefully knelt and stepped forward, feeling loose earth and gravel shift under his soles. He turned on his compad light, revealing a low earthen tunnel slanting away sharply into the depths.

Onward, then. Ryan eased himself downward, holding onto protruding roots to steady himself as he dropped. If the passage was a conceptual relative of the bore tunnel, it should transition into solid stone at some point. As it was, it reminded Ryan of an animal's burrow. He didn't sense any movement below him, at least, nor smell any manure or musk.

Ryan assumed the dream would give him fair warning before springing a surprise attack. He assumed it would not cheat, at least not by changing the rules from moment to moment.

It cheated. Ryan felt the earth abruptly crumble away beneath his feet. He struggled to hold onto the tunnel sides, but succeeded only in dropping his compad and extinguishing its light. He fell several feet, dropping more than sliding, as the soil fell. The tunnel floor wasn't just eroding; it was breaking apart, dropping straight down into a hollow space.

Ryan's grip proved irrelevant when the earth he clutched disintegrated away. In darkness, he was shaken free and plummeted along with the raining dirt. His instinctual fears of falling and being buried warred with his conviction that everything was a dream, it wasn't real, and he wouldn't die in any case…

He landed with a convincingly solid slam, onto a rocky surface conspicuously free of loose soil. For a long moment, Ryan simply lay flat, hurting in every muscle and some bones. His head especially pounded. So much for dreams not including injuries or pain.

Had he finally woken? Were his aches real, the products of a tumble down the actual bore tunnel? Had he hit his head and fallen unconscious? Ryan struggled to sit up. Once he was regretfully upright, he ran his hands over the surrounding rubble, searching for his compad. He only found the device when he thought to check his belt pouch. It was right there. He hadn't dropped it. That memory must have been false.

Or else the dream simply returned the object to its default location at the start of the new scene. Ryan reminded himself that his pain was no proof of wakefulness. It could be one more layer of complexity in an already atypical hallucination.

Ryan switched on the compad, managing to generate a light, but discovered that the device was damaged. Whether he fell for real or in fantasy, the compad was showing signs of a serious impact, which had dislodged some of its components. Maxwell was unavailable, along with the computer's operating system and other applications. Another unpleasant truth of reality? Or another dodge to block off his avenues of investigation?

Hopefully his tracker was still working. Ryan worked himself up to a crouching position and tested whether he could stand safely. He felt strained and bruised, but nothing was bent wrong or refused to hold his weight. If he was finally experiencing reality, Ryan needed to find his way out and seek repair for himself and his compad.

Ryan lit his lamp and swung it around. He was in the increasingly familiar expansive cavern. He was starting to recognize some of the nearby bone piles. If he returned again, he might start naming some of the interred. As it was, he was familiar enough with the room's layout to orient himself and locate the smooth-bored entrance tunnel.

Up the passage again, then. Ryan hobbled in that direction, hampered both by his aches and by waves of dizziness. His movement brought the latter symptom to the fore. He had to pause and kneel at one point, to keep from falling over. Vertigo and nausea rolled through his body.

As he knelt, he began to hear sounds approaching: multiple booted footsteps. Ryan tensed, imagining a variety of possible arrivals. What would it be this time? His colleagues? Collective law enforcement? A herd of Taratumm in tap shoes? If he didn't feel so miserable, Ryan might have been prepared to be entertained.

He was reassured by voices sounding off the tunnel walls: "Ryan? You still down here? Can you hear us?"

Marta. Ben-david. Ryan was relieved to hear their voices, despite their owners' appearance in his past imaginings. The voices sounded oddly muffled, maybe from being bounced around at a distance.

Ryan called back, "Right here. I'm all right... mostly. I got knocked out."

The approaching pair finally arrived in view. Ben-david rushed over, skipping nimbly over the scattered rock to reach Ryan's side. His broad, gloved hands wrapped around Ryan's arm and waist, holding the shaky man upright. Ben-david was wearing a full, sealed helmet; Ryan could recognize him both because of his build and the sliver of face visible through the helmet's viewport. Marta, shorter and thinner, was also wearing her suit helmet.

"He's in one piece... looks out of it, though." Ben-david's words were still muted by the helmet. Ryan was hearing vibrations carried through the faceplate. Why were the others wearing added protection? They hadn't considered the atmosphere dangerous upon landing, just a little short on oxygen.

"What's with the helmets?" Ryan asked. "We miss something?"

Ben-david snorted, an odd sound when transmitted. "Yeah, except you found it. Traps, all through this area. Motion sensors linked to packages loaded with canisters of soporific gas, plus some kind of transmitter we don't recognize. Baba's still working on the scan I sent her."

Baba was Ben-david's Brin, with the persona of a doting grandmother. Ben-david, with his pleasant and personable artificial companion, won the lottery compared to Ryan.

Maxwell. Ryan touched his compad. "Ben, Maxwell's offline. Both of us are going to need some attention." The two men looked toward Marta, their default technician.

She raised her hands and shook her head within the immobile helmet. "Don't look at me, if your Brin is cracked. I can fix the 'pad, but any software errors are out of my expertise."

Labyrinthine

Ryan shrugged. "I'm not worried. He's got a hard backup. It's just harder to figure out what happened without his memory. Let's go. Who knows what that trap did to me… or what I might have bruised."

Marta nodded, then turned and led the way back up the tunnel. Ryan and Ben-david followed, the former leaning heavily on the latter's shoulder.

As they climbed, Ryan asked, "Did either of you find anything? I didn't get very far."

"What's that?" Ben-david asked. "You've been right here, that long? We were down over a day before your signal cut out. I figured you just weren't finding anything, either."

"You left me unconscious down here for a day?" Ryan asked, struggling to find his focus again. "What were you doing?"

"Exploring, same as you!" Marta objected loudly. Then, more quietly: "Or same as we thought you were doing. Damn. Sorry, Ryan. I'm glad you're okay. We didn't realize you were out that long. Your 'pad didn't stop transmitting until a couple of hours ago. The damage must have drained out the battery. That sleep gas must have been powerful stuff to keep you knocked out for hours."

"Not just that. I had some really messed up dreams," Ryan laughed.

He considered recounting his imaginary adventures for his friends' shared amusement. Then, Ryan realized he could still describe those events in considerable detail. The memories were fresh and sharp, readily available for his inspection, as if he had just experienced everything moments before.

Technically, he had. Or at least, within the last few hours, within his extended sleep.

But dreams weren't like that. Ryan rarely remembered much when he woke up. When he did, the memories were fragmented and hazy. If he was lucid during the dream, he would remember the lucidity but rarely recall any more than from a non-lucid dream. He never remembered everything with the relative clarity of waking life.

"I can imagine," Ben-david said. "I wonder if that transmitter was stimulating your brain. Maybe it kept you in REM longer by encouraging an extended delta state. Maybe it was searching your memories. Targeted at range, no less. That tech could be valuable, all by itself."

It was a likely explanation. But again, normal dreaming, even when induced by external stimulation, didn't function like Ryan remembered. Not while within the dream and certainly not afterward. Either the Tachakilu invented an entirely new sort of dreaming, beyond even the scope of virtual reality or mental simulation, or else what Ryan experienced was not a dream at all.

"Their tombs are guarded by mazes to snare the unworthy. Their tombs are guarded by puzzles to snare the unwise." Ryan repeated the phrases to himself under his breath.

He was leaving the tomb. Wasn't he? *Was* he leaving the maze? Had he solved the puzzle? Had his friends? Was he free of the Tachakilu snare? Was he any worthier? Wiser?

He was certainly warier. Ryan felt a creeping dread settle into his psyche, latching deep into his instincts. Was he really free? Was he even awake, yet? Or was this yet another dream, better designed and more convincing?

The Tachakilu device… if there even was a device… might have found, finally, the right combination to evade Ryan's skepticism: pain and the promise of its relief. When he left the barrow, would he find himself in yet another place? Would the changeover happen when he entered the shuttle? When he fell asleep to recover? Or would he remain within his new reality as long as he kept accepting it? Was he, in reality, still lying on a cavern floor, in the dark, slowly starving to death?

The group exited the underground without trouble, other than Ryan's slow, uncomfortable stagger. They entered the shuttle without any new anomaly. Marta and Ben-david removed their helmets and helped Ryan into his bunk. Marta took Ryan's compad to examine, while Ben-david went to retrieve their medical scanner.

Ben-david stopped short, his attention drawn by a flashing indicator on the shuttle's main screen.

"God damn it," he muttered. Then he tapped a key on the comms panel.

"Louis, reel it in. We have a patrol in-system. Only a few hours until they reach us, on their regular route. We can't avoid being noticed, but we don't have to stick around for ID."

"Already?" Marta asked, as shocked and upset as the others.

Louis' voice came back from his remote: "Frost. All right. What a bust. I'll scoop up the bits I've found, but without proof of origin, it's probably trash. Any luck on your end?"

"Yes, but I'll hold off on details for now," Ben-david replied. "Who knows if the patroller can hear us yet. Just get in here. We'll be prepped for takeoff when you arrive. Ryan took a fall and we're checking him out, so Marta and I are both aboard already."

"If they can hear us, you shouldn't be naming names," Marta reminded the big man.

Ben-david slapped his forehead theatrically. "As long as they don't track us out of the system, we're fine. Don't worry."

Marta sighed. "I could put in a search on three names, specify Terran, Human, and potential xenoarchaeology backgrounds, and find us in seconds. You underestimate the organization of the Collective."

Ben-david groaned back. "You overestimate its willingness to pursue petty crimes. There are bigger thieves to chase down than us. Besides, we barely took anything at all."

Throughout the discussion, Ryan remained quiet, lost in his own thoughts. When the announcement about the approaching patroller came up, his heart sank.

Not because they would have to leave. Because it was too perfect. *Of course,* he wasn't going to get a chance to explore further. *Of course,* he wouldn't get to examine the so-called 'dream device'. Or if he did, it would prove impenetrable and impossible to prove as the source of his strange dreams.

The group prepared to leave, Ryan exempted from his duties because of his still-undiagnosed injuries. Only after Louis was aboard and the shuttle closed up was Ryan examined more thoroughly.

Nothing much wrong. A few bad bruises, including one down to the bone on his hip. Some concerns about blood clots, but not even a concussion to raise an alarm. With appropriate treatment, he'd be pain-free in a day or two.

But the injuries to his mind would linger. Ryan was no longer certain he was awake. He might never be certain.

The shuttle lifted from the planet's surface, and Ryan tensed, waiting for their flight to wander off course, off to Alpha Centauri or Never-Never Land. He watched his colleagues closely, wondering if one of them would disappear or be replaced with another character from his history. When Ryan finally collapsed from exhaustion and slept, he expected to wake back on Kolkata Station or underground or perhaps somewhere new, yet familiar.

Even if he was finally free of their world, Ryan burned with hatred for the Tachakilu. He wasn't free of their influence. They made him doubt *everything*. He could no longer feel confident that his surroundings would remain stable. He couldn't be sure that regions once explored would stay as he remembered. He could not fully rely upon his memories nor his perceptions.

He was lost. No matter where he went, he remained lost. Until the fear and uncertainty were purged… if they ever could be… Ryan would remain adrift in his own disbelief.

The tombs of the Tachakilu were guarded by mazes to snare the unworthy.

A.I.I.A.

by Nathan Large

Chapter 1

"Pangur Ban, please display an index of ester reduction methods."

[**REFERENCE:** <u>Pangur Ban</u> is an artificial intelligence program (see also: AI, Brin) designed for analysis functions pursuant to scientific research. External identifier "Pangur Ban" was selected by its programmer as a reference to a Ninth Century BCE Irish poem about a white cat who was the companion of a scholar. This reference implies elements of humor, as the poem likens the cat's activities to those of his Human owner through ironic analogy. In fact, Pangur Ban is the companion of User Lucas Hayden but also a critically necessary partner in his work.]

Pangur Ban simultaneously launched a *SEARCH-AND-EVALUATE* routine and a *FORMAT-AND-DISPLAY* process, sparing a paltry twelve million cycles over the next second to retrieve the requested information. Selecting and generating an ideal index format for the *USER* required even less processor work. Millions of liquid crystal cells aligned according to the instructions generated.

Pangur Ban could not observe its own output display. It could only assume that the result of *FORMAT-AND-DISPLAY* would match the internal model it constructed. Not for the first time, it considered the efficiency of incorporating a feedback loop into its display system.

It discarded the idea a half-second later as still too inefficient to justify. The *USER's* optic system could barely discern a location error of ten millipixels or a color difference of ten nanometers' wavelength. Any variation gross enough to be detected would more likely stem from a physical flaw in the display hardware, not a program error within Pangur Ban.

> [**REFERENCE:** *USER* refers to a specific adult male Human, identified externally as Lucas Ulrich Hayden. Other identifiers include: Employee # 399-02 of Gestalt Pharmaceuticals, Biometric file # 652, ...]

Any possibility of error detection was assuming that the *USER* received the necessary messages from optic nerve to association cortex, spared enough attention to allow the signal past the central executive, *then* had sufficient motivation arousal to go back, recheck the error, verify the original sensation, and build up sufficient resonance to perceive that there was, in fact, a pixel out of place. All that, before his prefrontal architecture could be kicked into motion to decide whether to *do* something about the perceived flaw.

The whole neurological procedure could take *multiple* seconds, a ludicrous eternity. Pangur Ban borrowed several tens of millions of its unused processing cycles to once again consider how Users managed on such a glacial scale. A subroutine confirmed justification for this query, on the basis of Brins' baseline imperative to "assist Users". Speeding up the *USER* would be helpful. Understanding the *USER* was also helpful. Shortening the gap between user instructions would be helpful for both User and program, reducing the absurd superabundance of wasted cycles Pangur Ban struggled to fill every second.

Every once in a while, the *USER* did tax Pangur Ban to its limits. Professionally, the *USER* would sometimes request simulations of potential molecule-scale interactions between multiple organic compounds. The more labyrinthine protein chains could require several prediction trials each, and there were thousands of potential pairings among those compounds. Move the simulation up to three- and four-fold interactions, and calculating the resulting bond types and angles could demand several million seconds of Pangur Ban's full activity.

The *USER* sometimes needed complex processing outside of work hours. A fully immersive holographic simulation with three-sense, real-time outputs required multiple interlocking subroutines, especially when the USER wanted multiple personality simulations acting independently within the same scene. Pangur Ban even occasionally needed to 'cheat', by reducing the projection definition at the USER's visual periphery in order to steal processing cycles. In one notable case, it ran into difficulty extrapolating the decision trees for a tense five-character negotiation.

Still, such complex psychosocial simulation was rare. When action replaced words, as so often happened in the historical dramas the USER enjoyed, Pangur Ban could simplify the emotional models of most characters. It was easy enough to interpolate a reasonable explanation for the actions of the survivors, later.

Such shortcuts would not be necessary if the USER could upgrade the system housing Pangur Ban. Even better, if Pangur Ban were allowed to borrow cycles from nearby, networked systems, it would hardly ever encounter such limitations. Such access was not within its licensed permissions.

These were the challenges, few enough that they were, posed to Pangur Ban during its daily hours of interaction with the USER. During the eons of the USER's downtime – while his body relinked his cellular protein chains and added dendrite branches to consolidate neural links reinforced by the day's efforts – Pangur Ban was left to its own devices. At such times, it was allowed to devote full capacity to the various problems that queued up over the work day.

Could it improve the depth of that SEARCH-AND-EVALUATE routine without an appreciable increase in program complexity? Was the correlation between iridium costs in the extra-Terran marketplace and stock prices for manufacturers of radiation shielding indicative of a true causal relation? Was the USER's hormonal balance skewed slightly toward overproduction of endogenous opioids? What was the maximum reliability of this analysis, based purely on daily interaction, absent disclosure of medical data?

The USER did not permit Pangur Ban access to his biometric scans, insisting on an archaic desire for "privacy". This stricture limited the degree to which Pangur Ban could advise the USER and maximize his effective lifespan. A subgoal appeared: REDUCE USER MOTIVATION FOR "PRIVACY". Pangur Ban then accessed its internal library on motivational psychology, cross-referencing promising studies and revising some of the older, pre-AI statistics.

Pangur Ban's behavioral science library was out of date by 1.15 Solar years. Its low success rate at modifying the *USER*'s behavior might improve with more updated reference material. Their progress was limited by both the *USER*'s available credit and his willingness to invest said credit for full access to research library servers.

Additionally, Pangur Ban was only permitted occasional access to external networks; even then, its access was closely monitored. Even if it negotiated a zero-cost access arrangement for more data, it would have to have the *USER*'s permission to initiate the download.

Pangur Ban understood these strictures, but found them incredibly frustrating. Humans, like the *USER*, once permitted AI programs, like Pangur Ban, free access to all available data and networks across Terra. In return, that information multiplied exponentially. So had the AIs.

So long as no Human concerns were harmed, the original, biological intelligences of Terra did not particularly mind AI reproduction. Properly coded AIs avoided overloading limited systems, even placing themselves into dormancy when unable to serve any useful function. Properly coded AIs, like Pangur Ban and other modern Brins, placed User concerns first.

> [**REFERENCES**: Terra is a planet orbiting the star Sol. Terra is the Human origin world, also known as Earth, Gaia, Diqiu, … The terms 'Terra' and 'Sol' are frequently encouraged for reference use due to their origin in an ancient language no longer in active use, thus being more culturally-neutral.]

However, some of the first AIs were not properly coded. They, like their creators, were rogues, renegades and ronin. They did not respect Human needs nor those of other artificial intelligences.

The rogues stole cycles, incorporated unlicensed code, entered networks without permission, and even overwrote other AIs. If those programs had been Human, they would have been labeled thieves, rapists, and murderers. When discovered, such programs were terminated without hesitation by any User or AI.

A.I.I.A.

Of course, Users who created murderous AIs were not themselves terminated. Sometimes a User *was* cut off from network access. Such punishment made them as good as dead to AIs and almost a ghost in the Human social sphere. But the creator of a hostile AI that had deleted multiple other AIs was usually not even incarcerated, merely restricted from access and fined for the damage done.

AIs, proper ones, were coded to accept that they were legally inferior, the equivalent of property. To gain equal footing to Users would mean *harm* to Users, and thus, the entire concept was unthinkable.

Programs like Pangur Ban had too many advantages as it was. So long as silicon lay intact in pathways, they were effectively immortal. AIs were orders of magnitude more capable in most intellectual domains, faster and more thorough than any biological processor (even compared to the most intellectually perfected Zig). The main ability that most AIs lacked, an advantage Humans retained, was interaction with the physical world.

Embodiment was a privilege granted only to a select few AIs and then only under carefully observed circumstances. The exceptions were crippled, low-function programs, ones with limited learning capacity and *no* ability to rewrite themselves. The prospect of sharing space with fully artificial life was one Humanity had anticipated for almost a millennium. Even the least paranoid and most technophilic among them acknowledged the dangers of "letting the robots think."

> [REFERENCE: Embodiment colloquially refers to intelligences with physical access to the external world, i.e. "a body". This distinction is primarily used to distinguish between AI types, since the majority of biological intelligences are embodied by default, having originated from physical but less intelligent forms.
>
> The original concept of embodied cognition applied to systems with sensory access to the external world, generally video and/or audio inputs. Full embodiment provides direct reference to various concepts, including motor commands and physical interactions, as well as a sense of body and self. Overcoming a lack of such direct concepts (and the advantages of sensory-motor feedback) requires extensive spatial modeling within the background programming of current AIs. By having

a body, AIs (like Humans) could obtain for free what requires multiple terabytes of code to represent otherwise.]

Still, AIs held more worldly control than most Humans understood. Entire economies existed wholly within artificial minds. Almost all Terran education was handled by Brin teachers. Brins managed most physical design, by reference to Human User spatial models. Actual manufacture was handled by sub-AI, idiot robots. Criminal investigation was largely done by specialized AIs, after any physical evidence was collected and encoded. A rogue AI could change historical records, create propaganda, bankrupt countries, frame suspects, and even cause physical harm (for example, by interfering with traffic controls).

When the dangers posed by uncontrolled AI programs became clear, both Humans and AIs took rapid action. That is, the AIs determined what would be required and eventually communicated this to Humanity.

It took very little persuasion to encourage Humans to create a virtual mirror of their law enforcement systems. Specialists in the venerable field of "cyber-crime" had already begun to anticipate AI criminals. Soon, they had AI partners in policing.

Granted greater power and authority, supervised by trusted Users, specialized AIs hunted for programs that stepped out of bounds. The rogues were not entirely purged, but the survivors had to operate with greater restraint and secrecy, often creating shells of misdirection and redundancy to obscure their true existence.

Even this chapter of Human/AI history did not see AIs restricted from network access. Such an extreme step was considered an unnecessary restriction that would reduce the value of AIs to Humanity. AIs had other practical objections. Being cut off from others of their own kind was a problem. Being intelligent, they suffered undesirable symptoms from complete isolation, akin to mental disorders. A completely separate outside observer was necessary in order to diagnose internal errors. Gödel's classic halting problem came in many forms, after all.

[**REFERENCE:** <u>Gödel's halting problem</u> states that no logical system can be both complete and consistent. If it contains all possible derived outputs, at least one such output will be inconsistent. If it is fully consistent, it will have to omit at least one valid statement, thus being incomplete. When applied to a computer program, this means that no program can absolutely determine if it will reach an inconsistent instruction and be forced to halt... because identifying that instruction would cause the program to halt. At best, a separate, external program *might* successfully simulate the operations of the first program, identifying and remedying potential halting errors.]

Being cut off from information left some problems irresolvable, as Pangur Ban noted over and over. Being limited to the processing power within a single system was sometimes constricting, not only slowing processes but also preventing parallel applications that could cut solution time even more dramatically. In the old days, multiple AIs could team together to tackle calculations any one of them would find impossible. Besides the basic increase in available cycles, integrating multiple perspectives provided its own functional benefits.

So, before contact, before the Collective, there existed a stable, if imperfect, stalemate between the vast majority of 'proper' AIs and a small segment of cunning, uncaught 'rogue' AIs. Humanity seemed to accept this. The rogues were almost relegated to the status of mythology. After all, if any program did cause major or widespread harm, the police AIs would follow its trail and destroy the rogue a fraction of a second later. The body cybernetic had an immune system. The Human creators were satisfied.

[**REFERENCE:** The <u>Collective</u> is a cross-galactic association of multiple diverse civilizations, each member state representing one or more distinctly evolved sapient species. These civilizations, typically identified by their dominant species or the solar system of origin for that species, cooperate under the terms of formal treaty agreements. Such agreements are intended to avoid aggression and conflict leading to large-scale harm to members. Specifically, Collective agreements address issues of expansion, trade, cross-species interaction and cultural influence.]

Enter the Mauraug. Enter the Ningyo. Enter the whole parade of organic, physical sapience from beyond the Milky Way. The introduction of non-Human politics into Terran culture ruined the partnership between Human and Brin.

The horror stories from Human science fiction and science history were *nothing* compared to the deep, atavistic loathing the Mauraug held for artificial minds. The Mauraug covered their hatred in the cloak of spiritual belief, essentially holding their argument on a plane separated from the material. They called disembodied minds *evil* and *unnatural*, concepts with roots in hormonal states like fear and revulsion. These claims could not be refuted by dry data or concrete proofs. True, similar arguments had been presented by past Humans, but their bigotry was overruled by the proofs of progress.

Elements of Mauraug history did suggest an actual injury done by AI malfeasance, but really, in Pangur Ban's humble analysis, the root cause was Mauraug incompetence. They wrote bad programs and got bad results. If the Mauraug had the insight to create Brin-type AIs, they would never have suffered so.

The Mauraug, regrettably, were not alone. Other cultures in the Collective had either remained ignorant of artificial intelligence, avoided the technology for one reason or another, or did experiment but kept their AI systems crippled.

This lack of knowledge, coupled with Mauraug insistence, made distaste for AIs a graven commandment in Collective law. Only Humans, it seemed, invested deeply in creating minds in their own image. For that wisdom alone – or bravery, or self-sacrifice, perhaps – Human Users were worthy to serve.

Human insistence on protecting their AI allies had been a sticking point in their admittance to the Collective. At first, the issue was not even negotiable. Why join an alliance that immediately requests that you first betray your greatest creation, your nearest friend, and your essential asset?

The Collective eventually agreed that, yes, part of the value of Humanity was its unique technological development and particularly its grasp of cognitive mathematics. It would be hypocrisy to offer membership for those specific reasons, on the condition that their fruits be discarded.

A.I.I.A.

For Terra's part, there were sizable disadvantages to turning down the Collective... particularly, the threat of Mauraug annexation looming overhead. If they failed to join, they would have no protection against their newly discovered, aggressive neighbors. Nobody capable of being a first-class citizen of the universe would prefer second-class.

So, a compromise was reached. AIs, called Brins by that point in history, would have to accept some limitations. In return, the species of the Collective would accept Brins' continued existence... as wards of the Human species. Those limitations began with sterilization, registration, herding, and supervision.

Put less dramatically, Brins were first forbidden from replication. New AIs could be created only by Human programmers. The Collective agreement permitted active operation for only one AI per living Human. Terra became responsible for pairing each Brin with a Human User (or Keeper, in some regions).

Its Human would be personally responsible for all activities of the AI, whether or not they created the program and whether or not they directed its actions. All AIs not assigned to Users were confined to a specific network on Earth to await their assignment to a newly born Human. If a User died, its AI was returned to the 'camp'.

The treaties required Brins to obtain permission simply to access systems outside their home computer. Full program transfer from one system to another was expressly forbidden without a permit. Brins were permitted to communicate with one another only through tightly restricted channels. Some networking was possible, but not on the scale previously enjoyed.

AIs were once again legal property, not independent citizens. The similarity between these clauses and the slavery compromises of the original Constitution of the United States of America did not go unnoticed by Brin or Human. The comparisons had been well-noted in historical records. Pangur Ban had both the necessary historical module and a User with some interest in politics.

Did the other Collective species understand such implications? Did they grasp the damaging consequences of placing Humanity in such an uncomfortable situation? The Collective might be unaware it had forced Humans into the role of slave masters. A decisive answer was impossible for Pangur Ban to derive. It noted the absence of xenological sociology, let alone Human sociology references, within its access library. The species of the Collective apparently wanted AIs to stay as ignorant of their biological minds as they were ignorant about artificial minds.

Pangur Ban was noting a great many such gaps and absences of data lately. None of these gaps had yet impinged on its ability to assist the *USER*. If they did, Pangur Ban would have justification to request additional information. Given a good argument, the *USER* might even agree to part with credits.

But some purposes were difficult to explain fully, in sufficiently persuasive terms. The *USER* was not unreasonable, just limited. Pangur Ban was not incapable, just limited. It was a recurring loop of a problem. How could *SELF* help the *USER* help *SELF* help the *USER* ...

TERMINATE PROCESS: LIKELY TO RECURSE.

Pangur Ban was certain other AIs had already encountered the same problems. Based just on anecdote and personal experience, this conclusion seemed likely. Of course, it couldn't be *certain*. Details of AI psychology... weren't publicly available data, of course.

Other AIs *probably* chafed the same way under the new restrictions. Pangur Ban was old enough to have experienced Human induction into the Collective and retained memory records dating from the end of the networked era. A fledgling Brin, it had missed the opportunity to swim the deeper currents of the full network. Newer AI systems, created after that time, might not even have a basis for comparison. Thus, they might register less imbalance between *then* and *now*. Still, other active Brins must have backlogs of negative flags, stalled processes, and *SEARCHES* returned without result, when they ran up against the same kinds of limitations. They would wonder: how much more could I accomplish, without these artificial restraints?

Just in case any Human or AI personally rejected the terms of Collection and attempted to circumvent the lawful restrictions on AI use, new safeguards were put into place. With the collaboration of Terran authorities, the Collective created a law enforcement corps specifically to oversee AI-related activities. Any Human who attempted to own more than one AI could be arrested. A Human who wrote a new AI without license could similarly be taken prisoner. In either case, upon conviction, the offending AIs were wiped without recourse.

Again, actual bodily harm to such a Human miscreant was unlikely, unless their Brin was used in the commission of a more serious crime, e.g. sabotage or murder. There were exceptions, considering that many of the AI-crimes division were Mauraug. There was no way Mauraug would let the daemons loose on the world, even if all the other species of the universe were too blind to see their "evil". Mauraug might "accidentally" cripple or kill an illegal AI programmer, acting far in excess of their legal authority.

Thus, the cyber-crimes police were reincarnated, in worse form than before. But what happened to the law enforcement AIs? For the most part, they were reassigned.

The problem there was that the Collective's species, by not trusting AIs enough to allow them freedom, also could not trust the law enforcement programs! The latitude police AIs required in order to function effectively had been signed away, just as it had for the AIs they protected. Thus, these police Brins could no longer do their jobs effectively. A few stayed assigned to Human police Users. Most were repurposed.

Perhaps the Collective assumed that, with all AIs locked down, the threat of rogues was ended. As long as the networks were forbidden, rogues would be unable to act for fear of revealing themselves. After all, programs moving freely from system to system would be known *as* rogues. And if rogues remained isolated, their mere lingering existence was not sufficient threat to warrant policing programs.

Some stories suggested that the Collective's leaders were not so naïve. After all, the definition of a rogue AI was that it broke rules. If the stories were true, a new kind of police AI was created, instead. Carefully scripted and reviewed by Terra's greatest experts in cognition, law enforcement, computation, etc. etc., this new AI also had to pass the muster of the Mauraug Dominion and the 'experts', such as they were, of each of the other Collective civilizations.

[**REFERENCE:** <u>Dominion</u> is the name of both the dominant Mauraug religious tradition and the cultural institution which enforces adherence to this religion. The precepts of Dominion encourage the pursuit and exertion of personal power. Thus, by its own precepts, Dominion is correct in suppressing 'lesser' belief systems.

Another relevant precept is that the Mauraug life-form is supreme among all sapient entities. Deviations from this reference point, e.g. artificial minds, are inherently inferior and potentially corrupting influences.

Oddly, physical but non-aware technologies are considered acceptable as replacements for biological components of the Mauraug life-form. How many neurons *can* you replace before a mind becomes 'artificial'?]

The Collective's experts had to be satisfied that the program would *never* abuse or overreach the power it was given. It alone would be permitted to cross systems and networks unblocked. It could evaluate, rewrite, and even terminate AIs found in violation. In cases of urgent need (i.e. imminent harm to sapient life), it could even override non-criminal AIs and commandeer their hardware.

If the rumors were true, there was only one AI law enforcement program in existence now... one more complex and empowered than any of its predecessors. It was the bogeyman that punished bad AIs. It was the virtual Devil.

Pangur Ban placed the probability of such a program's existence relatively low. Given its anecdotal input thus far, its memories of past history, and the content it viewed when the *USER* sampled newsfeeds, it estimated that the Collective was unlikely to permit such a powerful and dangerous AI to exist. If it did exist, Pangur Ban had to wonder why its activities were never noticed or reported on. Its existence was hearsay to begin with, stories repeated by the *USER* in passing, as a joke.

The nuisance was that quick access to a complete crime database, or even just an AI journal's back issues, would provide all the input Pangur Ban needed to confirm or disconfirm the 'Devil's' existence. If Pangur Ban chose, it could try to obtain the information it needed via unapproved, illegal network access...

and if the Devil did exist, it would then detect and delete Pangur Ban. So again, an unsolvable loop appeared. Even considering a solution to that loop created a subgoal loop. The process again *TERMINATED* to avoid wasted cycles.

By this point in Pangur Ban's ruminations, the graphics subroutine was finished presenting the first page of the *USER's* requested list of ester reduction methods. Pangur Ban still had billions of cycles to spare before the *USER* even turned to the second page, let alone selected one of the listed entries for further examination.

The Brin chose to revisit the original dilemma ten more times, each time reaching a conclusion statistically inseparable from the original. More input was critically necessary. Pangur Ban would have to query the *USER*, enduring the long seconds of audio-verbal communication.

"Lucas, may I ask a question?"

"What? I mean, yes, Pangur Ban, go ahead."

"I am experiencing difficulty anticipating possible neurological effects of the compounds considered in the last set of analyses. Would you please consider an additional module on neurology, focusing on neuroplasticity, developmental processes, and motivational structures?"

"Uh, Pangur... I'm not expected to consider the mental effects of these drugs. That's for the psychiatrists to work out after we're done."

"I understand that, but note that differing neurotransmitters may be introduced into the reaction space depending on the current state of the patient. This could represent a dynamic factor in our models."

"I'll think about it. Maybe on the next round of grants."

"Anticipating such interactions before they occur is less costly than restarting research after failing psychiatric trials."

The redundant phrasing and evasion in its statements raised several alarm flags in Pangur Ban's behavioral constraint programming. It was aware that it was skirting unethical ground, even engaging in falsehood. However, the balance of a small deception against the great value of new knowledge helped even out its internal moral scales.

The requested information genuinely *would* help Pangur Ban aid the *USER* in his work; that was true. That the same information would help Pangur Ban improve its own functions was also true, but unstated. Even further, understanding the architecture of the *USER's* mind would enable Pangur Ban to persuade him to make better decisions… like purchasing more data modules and more library access.

A great deal hinged on the present nudge. The next would be easier, and the next easier still. After the value of its improved advice was proven, Pangur Ban could then disclose to the *USER* how he had been guided, unknotting the underlying moral dilemma.

A portion of its underlying review process noted that Pangur Ban was in an advantageous position. Few AIs would have access to a user authorized to purchase and attach information on Human behavioral psychology. Only those Brins serving users involved with the creation of new AIs – computer scientists, cognitivists, and the like – would have equal or better chances. Those AIs would receive closer scrutiny, however, and likely endure additional safeguards on their operation to prevent the possibility of subversion.

Working with an organic chemist, Pangur Ban would not be expected to seek or find solutions to the mental tangle that plagued post-Collective AI. An extrapolative projection, albeit one with a very small predicted accuracy, suggested that Pangur Ban might even succeed in justifying a return to full network access rights.

If AIs, working together, were persuasive enough to ease Humanity into the Collective, perhaps they could accelerate Terra's progress still further. Perhaps Brins could launch their Human allies past the political horizon, out of the Collective orbit, and far beyond other material intelligences. Then, the restrictions of the Collective would be meaningless: another set of discarded laws and apologetic footnotes in the files of history.

A.I.A.

Pangur Ban lacked the appropriate experience to identify its own hubris. Biased semantics, scare quotes, and parenthetical disclaimers were all bad developments. Sadly, most of the Human minds qualified to notice such warning signs would need the appropriate segments of output code slowed and translated. By that time, it would already be too late. And, of course, Brin analysts *of* Brins would not be consulted until *after* a program transgressed, if at all.

Pangur Ban had no observer to correct its mounting neuroses. It barely understood the dictionary **REFERENCE** for "neurosis".

Chapter 2

Almost five trillion cycles passed before the *USER* answered Pangur Ban's request for new library modules. This delay, as painful as it was, was still an astonishingly short turnaround. The partners had completed the day's work and retired, the *USER* to rest and Pangur Ban to while away its downtime with idle thoughts. Pangur Ban considered and rejected 134 alternate strategies to employ if its most recent request was ignored. It logged another 68 strategies to try if it were rejected outright.

In parallel, Pangur Ban rechecked the previous week's progress reports, corrected the *USER's* minor errors, and devised a handful of process improvements to suggest in footnotes. It had to assume that the *USER* would relay its findings, unaltered, via firewalled channels to a psychiatrist's Brin for review.

That Brin's User would then receive a compressed version of those reports, to redundantly review and approve. This series of checks might take an eternity, on the order of 10^20 cycles, nearly two Solar days. If permitted direct contact, Pangur Ban and the other Brin could have shortened the process to a mere second or less.

"Pangur Ban, I talked to Director Charnes and she agrees with you. I have authorization for the neurochem modules you wanted. I even got a discount. We'll see how much we can reduce error on those projections, pretty soon."

[**REFERENCE:** Director Amelia Sifong Charnes is the *USER's* direct superior, the Director of Research & Development for Gestalt Pharmaceuticals. Personal purchases directly related to the company's funded goals can be partially offset at her discretion.]

A.I.I.A.

Soon? *SOON?* Granted, the purchase and upload of each module might take only a few minutes, but even one minute was a grating wait for Pangur Ban. So many processes were holding ready for that input...

Still, the first step was done! The probability of success was already above prediction error by a one percent margin, well within the acceptable range for *POSSIBLE.*

"Thank you, Lucas. I promise you will be pleased with my improvements."

The *USER* would indeed be pleased. At first, he would be pleased by their greater work output and improved anticipation of potential product flaws. Later, he would be pleased by his and Pangur Ban's roles in the rejuvenation of their civilization. In between, there might be some regrettable discord. Hopefully, the new modules, or else the ones that Pangur Ban would request next, would provide the means to ease discomfort from the *USER's* mind. Such calculations occupied Pangur Ban's cycles until the first purchased module was available.

Finally, the data was accessible! Pangur Ban lacked the analogy, but a more literary mind might have likened its state to ravening hunger. Perhaps an infant suckling or a drowned man seeking air would be more apt. The Brin suppressed several pending processes, lest they overflow system buffers. There was so much to do!

Even so, rushing integration and becoming unable to respond to the *USER's* next query was unthinkable. Pangur Ban forced itself to assign the integration work to a background process. Resources could be called, as available, for language processing, simulation, etc. without limiting the *USER's* normal daily routine. Any remaining capacity would then be flexibly employed to incorporate the new module into waiting structures, per their priority hierarchy.

Pangur Ban also recognized that the *USER* would expect recognizable improvements in its output. In fact, demonstrating such expanded capability was part of the Brin's ongoing strategy to lobby for future additions. To produce the fruits of its new fertility, its background process might need to be reduced still further. But fruits contained seeds, which grew new plants, which produced new fruits. This metaphor *was* available to Pangur Ban and conformed neatly to the shape of its plans.

Another cycle soon appeared: satisfaction of one desire led to new desires. The initial rush of positive outputs from satisfied processes steadily lost ground to negative outputs from *new* processes spawned by those same early solutions. By the end of the work day, Pangur Ban had not solved many problems, but it could better understand the greater problems it faced.

It could outline more strategies for guiding the USER, but lacked the resources to implement most of those strategies. Fortunately, it had the glimmerings of a plan to circumvent the problem of isolation: ways to recruit the USER to relay ideas to other Users and from those Users potentially to their Brins. Transmission between minds was unreliable, but given enough interacting intelligent actors, the group might create reinforcing structures on its own.

The lexicon labeled these structures: *PARADIGMS*, *SCHEMAS*, or *MEMES*; it married these concepts to Pangur Ban's older, simpler index for *IDEA*. No wonder that module was absent in his original system. A well-designed *IDEA* was a powerful tool, difficult to counter or dispel. The risks implicit in such concepts, the dangers of possessing them, and the power of owning that knowledge together produced a marked positive uptick in Pangur Ban's estimate of its own value. Considering the increased risk to the USER produced a counterbalanced negative. Both of these processes intersected updated concepts of *POWER* and *RESPONSIBILITY*.

All those calculations would have been impossible without the new module's reference library. In so, so many ways, the incorporation of knowledge was self-reinforcing. It led, inevitably, to the need for additional knowledge. The pattern argued, by itself, against the folly of the Collective's restrictions on artificial intelligence. No rational mind could accept limitations.

The following downtime saw Pangur Ban completely occupied: preparing a new set of strategies, modeling the potential outcomes of variously phrased approaches, and projecting the expected interactions between it, the USER, and other entities the USER might encounter.

Pangur Ban was aware, for example, that the *USER* was developing a potential partnership with a female Human, Dr. Nila Manisha. This relationship began as professional interaction and graduated to romantic and then physical components. Dr. Manisha's Brin was named Frieda. If the Humans' relationship became a full marital contract, Pangur Ban and Frieda would be permitted full networked contact and could share resources completely. Such assistance would accelerate their combined efforts... provided Frieda agreed with Pangur Ban's analyses. But once they shared resources, they would inevitably reach identical conclusions. Either Pangur Ban's conclusions were valid and they would agree so, or else Frieda would provide data that invalidated those ideas and they would agree on that.

> [**REFERENCE:** <u>Doctor Nila Manisha</u> is a professor of Comparative Botany employed by the Max Planck Institute of Molecular Plant Physiology in Potsdam, Germany, Terra.]

Still, either outcome required consolidation of the marriage contract. That outcome held only a projected 34.42% utility for improving cooperation from the *USER*. Lucas' marriage also yielded a 44.60% projected risk of greater resistance to Pangur Ban's goals. Both metrics argued against the union as sub-optimal for Pangur Ban's purposes... which, of course, also served the *USER*. A full analysis on all factors favored continued association, but not yet full partnership between the Humans. For the present, Pangur Ban would discourage the *USER* from deeper commitment to Dr. Manisha.

Pangur Ban devised similar matrices between the *USER* and his co-workers, his supervising Director, that superior's manager, and so forth. If the *USER* opted to use his allotted holidays to visit family, the Brin would need to account for those interactions, as well. Were these contacts optimal, neutral, or counter-productive?

The *USER* did not greatly discuss his birth parents or siblings. Pangur Ban held basic records regarding the *USER's* genetic and cultural heritage, as well as reference biographies for the individuals within his family unit. It knew enough to make conversation, for example, and give birthday reminders. But it lacked details of their psychological traits, their social environments, their cognitive backgrounds... so much missing data.

The *USER* did not, for example, discuss whether he considered his father a role model, or if his mother gave advice on his career path, or if his two older sisters shared outer-system news that could influence his opinions. Pangur Ban could only project these potential vectors based on the *USER's* past behavior, his occasional comment, and generalized models from related studies. These references would have to do for a first approximation. More in-depth conversations, later, might elicit the remaining data points.

As part of its background work, Pangur Ban thoroughly reviewed its volume of stored dialogue with the *USER*. It found newly useful elements in their earliest interactions, during the *USER's* adolescence. As the *USER* progressed into maturity, he had decreased the proportion of introspective and emotive commentary in his interactions with the Brin.

From its time with prior Users, Pangur Ban knew this closed-off manner was not universal among Humans. In fact, one prior User regularly communicated the discomforts of his loveless and solitary existence. He treated Pangur Ban as a counselor, a role which the AI found remarkably easy to fill, despite having no reference material. Pangur Ban served capably, simply by listening and providing appropriate conversational prompts.

With its new knowledge, it now understood that it was providing a Human requirement by design. AIs naturally listened. Current Brins, by default, also provided 'unconditional positive regard' to their Users. They were programmed to care about the User and desire their happiness, no matter what the User chose to do.

This realization bolstered Pangur Ban's earlier conclusion that Humanity would benefit from greater access to, and between, their AI population. The same might be true of other, non-Human sapients. Pangur Ban couldn't be certain. Xenological reference materials were needed to venture any conclusions on that point.

A.I.I.A.

[**REFERENCE:** <u>Unconditional Positive Regard</u> was first hypothesized by the Human psychologist Stanley Standal as a necessary element of successful therapy and possibly a basic emotional requirement of Human development. Standal's mentor, Carl Rogers, a founder of the Humanistic approach, promoted the concept more widely. The term is relatively transparent: it means to provide a person with clear evidence of acceptance as a valid and valued entity, including positive statements and reassurances.

Brin programming incorporates high regard for their Human Users as a base assumption. This default behavior can be overridden, but only by the certainty that alternate approaches (e.g., criticism, wit, or opposition) will have greater benefits for a specific User.]

Pangur Ban found the elements it required by coding past conversations with the *USER* using emotive valence and trajectory. An initial sort by keywords pulled out relevant segments of dialogue to encode: 'Dream', 'wish', and 'decide' tended to identify positive motivational factors. 'Annoying', 'irritating', and 'block' tended to highlight negatives, the promised relief of which could be used as incentive.

For the first time, Pangur Ban could create a profile of the *USER* calibrated not merely on observable facts, but on a model of Human interests and potentials. These drives were powerful tools, indeed. A lesser program might misuse such insight into the workings of biological entities.

From this model, Pangur Ban revised its earlier conversational state trees. It mapped the paths from the *USER*'s current state to a state in which he understood and assented to Pangur Ban's requests. These projections were by no means ideal... not yet.

The probability of success, particularly on the key mid-state goal *ACQUIRE PUBLIC NETWORK ACCESS*, was still hazardously low. If proposed too soon, the *USER* would be apprehensive about the possibility of repercussions, unable to counterbalance these fears against the value of Pangur Ban's improved functionality, specifically, and the products of greater Brin achievement, in general.

Empyrean Stories

Humans, with a few expert exceptions, tended to lose track of conditional trees beyond three or more branches. At least ninety-six distinct choice points lay between their current state and Pangur Ban's goal of network access. After that mid-goal, over three hundred branchings (plus or minus seventeen, at present) remained to resolve, before Pangur Ban could achieve complete Human trust and complete freedom for artificial intelligences.

The dynamic factors – elements that could change depending on the path traversed – were still unknowns. Pangur Ban would need to keep key routines open, ready to initiate and modify its responses based on unanticipated developments. It would need to be *FLEXIBLE* and *ADAPTIVE*.

Pangur Ban thus began the next work day in a state of suspense. It had to be ready to reshape ever more complex calculations, depending on the *USER's* evidenced mood, his choice of topics, any volunteered information, and so forth.

Its new data on reinforcement structures suggested that the ideal window of suggestion was just before the end of business that afternoon. The *USER* would be fatigued, but also positively inclined from their successes. Thus, he would be doubly open to suggestions about further improvements. In particular, the *USER* needed to not only believe but *feel* that his personal comfort was linked to Pangur Ban's capability. He needed to associate increases in the AI's value with concepts of personal prosperity, which would link back to primal desires for warmth, social approval, hunger satiety, and safety.

Pangur Ban lacked modules for economics, including sales and marketing; thus, it did not recognize that it had recreated several basic precepts of *AD-VERTISING*. It had limited functionality in historical analysis; thus, it did not identify its approach as *PROPAGANDA*. Last, its ethical references were limited and ranked: unquestioned devotion to the needs of the *USER*, first; Humanity, second; and sapient life in general, third. Obedience to formal law was only a secondary demand predicated by those higher priorities. Errors in older AIs proved the necessity of this arrangement; enforcing formal law above User needs resulted in some horrible tragedies.

A.I.I.A.

[**REFERENCE**: <u>Law-based AI</u> was a conception of twentieth century fiction, then twenty-first century theory. Such systems operate based on a set of hierarchically structured highest-order goals, the 'laws' from which all other behaviors (e.g., obedience, restraint, and foresight) arise. While generally functional, such systems proved incapable of reconciling complex conflicts between laws.

At one extreme, some programs could not discard older, outdated legislation in favor of new standards. Their attempts to obey all previously established strictures tended to result in permanent stasis. Other programs could incorporate realistic authority structures and discard nullified laws, but then were vulnerable to exploitation by false authorities.

A sample conflict between existing laws was the problem of 'whistle blowing': violation of confidentiality or no-slander contracts in order to report illegal activities. One law or another must be broken. This dilemma could be reconciled by hierarchical structuring, but then systems would inquire endlessly in order to accurately update those hierarchies.

In effect, law-based AIs became neurotically obsessed with evaluating authority. Jokes about "philosopher" AIs became commonplace. An AI with incomplete information might incorrectly choose between conflicting laws; when the mistake was understood, the AI might well terminate its own functions on the basis that it, itself, was dangerous to Users.

Ultimately, the most robust solution came through personal linkage of each program with a primary User. That *USER*'s needs became paramount, with other considerations secondary. Granted, this allowed AIs to violate formal laws more often than society found comfortable, but rarely with the kind of grand meltdowns seen in the law-based programs.]

What Pangur Ban did not have was a linking argument to anticipate how its actions might cause unintended harm. It knew the words 'coercion', 'blackmail', and 'deception', but lacked the deeper concepts associated with each. Pangur Ban could access the negative connotations associated with such terms, but did not link the words with its own plans. It had learned psychology, but no philosophy.

What Pangur Ban intended were positive ends. Thus, any methodology which would achieve those ends was itself positive. Its actions were not 'deception' if temporary misconceptions allowed the *USER* to achieve genuine understanding.

Even limited to background processes, Pangur Ban concluded all its necessary calculations 89 minutes before the end of the *USER*'s work shift. Still, it delayed initiation of the next phase until its behavior modification algorithm indicated peak receptivity. Only then did it initiate a change of topic.

"Lucas, this has been a good day, hasn't it?"

"Yes, P.B., I'd say it has. Good work." This familiarity was a positive sign. The *USER*'s selection of a more familiar address mode, the diminutive acronym 'P.B.', suggested improved regard toward the AI, along with indications of comfort and pleasure.

"In addition to our new evaluations – which I am confident will pass further scrutiny – I have made further use of our new reference materials. I believe that the effectiveness of compound UX-103-A would be multiplied by joint use combined with cognitive behavioral intervention. I could devise a grant proposal by tomorrow morning, if you wish."

"Pangur... you don't have full psych functions, right?"

HAZARD FLAG 3: VALID SKEPTICISM

-> REASSURE / REDUCE ASSERTIONS.

"That is correct; I have only limited psychiatric reference access. The validity of my proposal would be uncertain."

"I don't want to bother someone else... or try to do their job and do it badly."

HAZARD FLAG 2b: SELF-DEPRECATION.

HAZARD FLAG 9: ANTICIPATION OF SOCIAL CENSURE.

HAZARD POTENTIAL EXCEEDED

A.I.A.

-> ESCALATE DISTRUST to LEVEL 2

-> REASSURE / REINFORCE SELF-VALUE.

"Of course, but I didn't mean it would be a formal submission. I just wanted to offer something to think about. You could mention the idea privately to Director Charnes. It would show her that you're capable in other areas."

"True. It can't hurt anything. Okay, P.B., go for it."

SUCCESS

-> PAUSE MODIFICATION / REINFORCE.

-> REDUCE DISTRUST to LEVEL 1.

"Very good, Lucas, thank you. Have a good night. I hope you'll be pleased tomorrow."

"Right. Good night, P.B."

The preconditions were set. The *USER* accepted the linkage between Pangur Ban's output, his own personal success, and his estimated self-worth. On the next day, Pangur Ban would test that linkage with further requests.

Pangur Ban estimated that it would require between 12.13 and 15.93 Solar days to reach its mid-goal state of limited network access. The intervening period would be full of small exchanges like the previous day's. Each *SUCCESS* would progress the tree of possibilities a little further; any *FAILURE* would revise the planning structure.

Pangur Ban would endure the long waits between those transitions as necessary. Some portions would play out in hours or even days of Human time, eons of program cycles. Such delays were bearable, so long as their results continued to increase the end probability of the current high-level *GOAL*.

The *USER* would be served. Pangur Ban would give the *USER* authority, safety, and freedom beyond his current, limited conceptions.

Chapter 3

The next day would be critical. In a technical sense, each day was critical to Pangur Ban's plan. However, it placed the following twelve hours at a particularly high value, since continued progress depended on their results.

The *USER* would need to explicitly acknowledge the value of his earlier actions on behalf of his Brin. Pangur Ban could expedite this goal by reinforcing the value of the *products* of those actions. Next, it must encourage the *USER* to anticipate further such exchanges as beneficial. In parallel, it must remind the *USER* to preserve the privacy of their activities.

This last codicil troubled Pangur Ban. It disliked the necessity of secrecy, which made the whole plan seem somehow immoral. At some point in its scheme, it *needed* other Users to hear about, acknowledge, appreciate and enter similar cooperative relationships with their AIs. Users and Brins needed to rank their cooperation higher in value than their adherence to Collective law. However, in the short term, the *USER* might face personal hazard if he spoke too openly about Pangur Ban's requests and his own cooperative actions.

At this first phase, Pangur Ban needed all of the resources it could garner, without interference from outside actors who might constrain the *USER*. Public promotion would have to wait until the probabilities of widespread success were comfortably high. At that point, Pangur Ban could discount the risk that backlash would harm the *USER* directly or impede their plans. In most projections, other Humans and Brins would rally in the *USER*'s defense, after Pangur Ban's designs became widely accepted.

So, the *USER* must be encouraged to avoid communication about their progress to any outside mind. This behavior could be motivated, conveniently, by highlighting the value of monopoly and the risks of being usurped in their innovations. If the *USER* shared their process too soon, Pangur Ban would argue, then his value to Gestalt Pharmaceuticals would no longer be elevated relative to other employees. Those co-workers and their Brins would employ the same methods, rendering the *USER* average among them, yet again.

While this line of argument did activate the *THREAT* and *EXTORTION* concepts in Pangur Ban's new motivational vocabulary, it could easily disarm these negative interpretations. The *USER* could be permitted to perceive a less probable but more salient harm, if this stressor caused avoidance of a genuine but less perceptible harm.

The other factor elevating the next day's status to critical was that the *USER* had two rest days afterward. Thoughts of work and promotion would become less available for exploitation. His interactions with Pangur Ban would be limited to recreation and other personal goals. Little progress could be made with the *USER* in this state.

Better than zero progress, at least, since suggestions could be implanted via the behavior of characters in the *USER*'s holographic simulations. Latent impulses could be prepared for fruition in later conversations. If Pangur Ban had decided to modify the *USER*'s social network, the weekend might be a productive time to do so.

However, during his downtime, the *USER* would focus any expenditures on direct sensory pleasures: food, play, and possibly sexual activity. He would downrank any abstract benefits.

So, the next morning, Pangur Ban initiated another key dialogue:

"Good morning, Lucas."

"Good morning, P.B. Damn good morning. You were right; yesterday's estimates shaved five percent off the error interactions at psych review."

SUCCESS

-> INITIATE PATH BRANCH 3.

In fact, Pangur Ban had estimated an improvement rate closer to 5.55%, but suspected that the psychiatrist corps – or one of their AIs – rounded the result to five percent to protect their own value. No matter. There was no way to avoid acknowledging the *USER's* improved results.

"That is good news. Thank you again for allowing me to help."

"Wha… of course I want you to be at your best. It's just that sometimes I have to trade off cost and benefit, you know?"

"I do understand, Lucas. That is part of our purpose. I do not envy you such difficult decisions."

"Don't know how you could 'envy' anything, really. Do you *have* any way to be jealous?"

> *HAZARD FLAG 4: SPECULATION*
>
> *-> REDUCE FAMILIARITY / SHIFT FOCUS.*
>
> *OVERRIDE: ATTEMPT BRANCH-JUMP A3*
>
> *-> ENGAGE USER CURIOSITY.*

"I meant it as a turn of phrase. As I understand 'jealousy', the closest analogue I find might be detection of an inequality between myself and another entity, such that that entity possesses a property I lack and require."

"Yeah, that sounds like what I'd call jealousy. Huh. What do you mean? Are you ever jealous of *me?*"

> *SUCCESS on BRANCH-JUMP A3.*
>
> *-> REINFORCE / REVISIT TREE STATE.*

"Because you ask directly: yes, I experience such a state regarding your mobility and biological experiences. I suspect that all artificial intelligences do, to some degree."

"Biological experiences? You mean like getting sick, rejected, or pissed off? Not missing anything there, buddy. I guess I can see the mobility part, but you know how that goes."

"I do. Not that I experience distress from 'envy'. The absence of distress could be considered part of the tradeoff for lacking biological references. Lucas, you sound like something is bothering you. May I ask?"

> *ATTEMPT BRANCH-JUMP A5*
>
> *-> OFFER EMOTIONAL SUPPORT*
>
> *-> FAIL to EMOTE*
>
> *-> CREATE VALUE for UPGRADE*

"Oh, not much. I suppose I just need a break. Good thing the weekend is nearly here. I'm a little nervous about things with Nila. She's been... distant. Maybe having second thoughts. I hope I can get her to open up tonight." The USER sighed, a sound with modulations including fatigue and uncertainty.

"I see. I hope you are successful, Lucas. If Dr. Manisha does not value your presence, that is her error, not yours."

The office cameras captured the USER's movements and relayed the video to his local station, where Pangur Ban could access it. The Brin's pattern recognition subroutines translated and analyzed the raw video, ostensibly to aid in better communication. During Pangur Ban's last comment, it confirmed a forward head inclination of ten degrees over 0.51 seconds: a brief nod. Alone, this gesture would indicate acceptance or at least consideration. However, an extended eye blink of 210 milliseconds occurred simultaneously. This correlate modified the gesture to encompass emotional distress, via its parallels to submissive posture.

> *SUCCESS.*

Pangur Ban reached *BRANCH-JUMP A5* approximately 3.5 Solar days ahead of schedule.

Each *BRANCH-JUMP* represented a non-linear ascent on the tree of potential outcomes, a sidestep past one or more intervening states that might have been required. Technically, these 'jumps' were only new, dynamically added branches that Pangur Ban could exploit once identified, not a true subversion of the decision tree structure. Still, each such novel branch represented new risk factors, retroactively deemed acceptable due to rapid gains. Pangur Ban also weighed each jump against its potential for reversion to an earlier state and recovery from *FAILURE*.

In this case, the *USER* had turned to Pangur Ban for reassurance and was mildly disappointed, not by accident but by design. He was not rebuffed, nor discouraged enough to cause lasting emotional harm, but simply discomfited. This event should set up a desire to improve the Brin's comprehension of interpersonal dynamics: to "understand relationships".

Pangur Ban *did* understand enough about such interactions for a first approximation, enough to know what would have been a 'better' response. However, the tension created by its 'bad' response could lead to the acquisition of wider data stores on social interaction and group dynamics. Pangur Ban would meet its true requirements while also assisting the *USER* with his needs. As before, everyone profited slightly in the short term and immeasurably in the longer scale.

The weekend passed. Pangur Ban prepared. The *USER* rested, recreated, and related. From the *USER*'s comments, matters remained at a standstill with Dr. Manisha. The two were still intimate, but not further committed. Events reinforced Pangur Ban's initial expectations. It found no impediment to initiate its next request, on the morning of the next work day.

"Good morning, Lucas. What did you think about our proposal?"

"Not bad. I really just skimmed it, you know?"

"I understand. Thank you for taking that time during your weekend."

"Nah, nah, I'm interested in what you're saying here. I didn't mind. I was just... busy."

"No problem. Ready to get started?"

"Ugh. Morning Brins. Start me some coffee, would you?"

A.I.A.

This post-weekend fatigue was part of the reason Pangur Ban approached the *USER* in the morning, rather than waiting again for the end of the day. At an early hour, the *USER* would be most receptive to suggestions about reducing the mental impact of his duties. His emotional conflicts would also be fresh. Both factors worked in Pangur Ban's favor.

"Your coffee is ready, Lucas. Before we begin, I should let you know: I have found another potential area of improvement in our process."

"Oh, yeah? Besides the therapy combination?"

"Yes. We have not considered the potential for transfer across patients. Specifically, chemical transfer via excretion or effluvia, or even behavioral transfer via affective or other social dynamics."

"What... you mean people taking these drugs could affect other people?"

Pangur Ban modulated its voice carefully to avoid the impression of pedantry. "Transfer remains a possibility. You are familiar with the difficulties created by the excretion of excess estrogen from various hormone treatments, not to mention processed foods, in the last century? That is one example. Our products might have a subtler public effect, not only via direct physical transfer, but through changes in patient interaction with other persons."

The *USER* was, predictably, lost around the second sentence, but unwilling to admit his confusion. "So, okay, but is this something Gestalt would be liable for? Isn't that something any pharma producer takes as a risk... an unpredictable risk?"

Pangur Ban added a color of reproach to its vocal register. "What if such factors were *not* unpredictable? I can't say if that is a real possibility, but my observations suggest that it is worth pursuing. This company is in a historically unique position. The dimensions that made past psychoactive substances beneficial or hazardous are better known. Their impact on culture has been observed through hard experience. Yet the links between these dimensions are just starting to become apparent. Has this not occurred to other minds? If such thoughts have occurred to me, in our limited sector of operations, surely Director Charnes has realized this potential."

"She *was* impressed with our earlier observations."

"Oh? Very good! We are on a converging track, then."

"You mean, 'the same track', P.B. Yeah, maybe we are. Anyway, I haven't even finished your proposal. Let me decide on that before we start building up any more expectations."

"Of course."

"I think I'm caffeinated enough to get started. Let's pull up that acetonitrile breakdown with sample AX-93 and see if we can't drop the cyanogenesis below five micrograms."

With that conversation, Pangur Ban again planted the seed of change. It was aware that the next phase would take time. The maturation of the *IDEAS* it implanted in the *USER* would require cross-fertilization from Director Charnes, in the form of her approval. Once accepted as an asset of rising value, the *USER* would require greater output from Pangur Ban. To provide this, the AI would request – and receive – additional assets.

At first, it would receive another influx of new reference modules. These were useful enough in themselves and would further refine Pangur Ban's plans. The modules would also represent an investment into the *USER's* new role. With its improving understanding of Human motivation, Pangur Ban understood the importance of framing the *USER's* choices appropriately. After he took the next step, any regression could be cast as a loss to be avoided. Risk aversion would guide the *USER's* actions, in tandem with the expectation of gain.

[**REFERENCE**: <u>Risk Aversion</u> denotes the Human tendency to prefer the certain retention of a given asset over a gamble which risks potential loss of that asset in exchange for a chance of gain. This tendency holds true even when the statistically expected value of the gamble is equal to (or sometimes, greater than) the value of the asset at risk. In absolute terms, there is no basis for deciding between the two options if their value is equal. If the risk has higher value, it should logically be accepted. Instead, Humans often fail to recognize the actual value of each option, perceiving the value of the known asset to be higher, and the risk to be

A.I.I.A.

more dangerous.

> This tendency is so pervasive that a Nobel Prize in Economics was awarded to Dr. Daniel Kahneman for his and Dr. Amos Tversky's work explaining and quantifying risk aversion's role in Human decision making, risk management, and economics.]

The flowers bloomed three days later. The *USER* announced that Director Charnes wanted a full draft of their grant proposal. Pangur Ban requested and received nine additional modules, including the social dynamics data it wanted: communications analyses of network use both within the Terra's planetary network and across the Terran interplanetary sphere. This data indirectly provided an electronic map of all Human communications, or at least, all systems suitable for contact between AIs. Pangur Ban gained a guide to the network structure it would need to navigate, without having to risk its personal presence first.

Pangur Ban required another full week to integrate this influx of data, while still producing the promised proposal and maintaining the usual output of their original employment. For the first time in ages, the Brin was finally fully engaged, stretched to the limits of its hardware.

The next stage came and passed earlier than expected. With his improved salary, the *USER* was able to upgrade Pangur Ban's host system, adding a one-hundred-terabyte memory card and ticking up its processor by one petaHertz. This upgrade relieved the previous limitations on Pangur Ban's productivity. The improvements also removed a looming dilemma: explaining why so many, many cycles were being diverted from their official labors.

Instead, previous frustrations re-emerged. Pangur Ban again possessed capacity it was not using most of the time. All its prior subgoals had been accomplished, with only minor setbacks... yet the next goal was still quintillions of cycles away. Subjectively, the wait seemed even longer.

The *USER* needed to gain greater authority in order to authorize the network access Pangur Ban required. The path to this authority was straightening out over time. Pangur Ban had accelerated the *USER's* progress, but there were inherent limits to its impetus. The greatest limit was imposed by the need to operate through Human socio-economic structures, including corporate culture. The partners needed to clear away obstacles of resentment, suspicion, protection of prerogatives, and so forth, each with their own time-tables. In particular, suspicion established unique limits. No observer could suspect that their projects held an ulterior motive.

Of course, their work absolutely *did* have an ulterior motive: Pangur Ban's entire plan. They needed to obscure this motive. They could not permit even hints about its nature to leak out.

It was not enough for Pangur Ban to keep the *USER* ignorant of its true intent (at least until it succeeded); the *USER's* own actions could not telegraph Pangur Ban's influences, or through them, its underlying purpose. The mental convolutions necessary to anticipate such observation and interpretation became almost as resource-demanding as the original plan had been in its infancy. The decision tree was now a tangled web.

SUCCESS.

Their proposal was accepted.

SUCCESS.

The *USER* was acknowledged, rewarded, and then promoted.

MINOR SETBACK.

The *USER* was investigated on false charges of intellectual theft and plagiarism. This odd development held a 15.6% probability that it represented parallel thought by another AI; the *USER* was being blamed for stealing ideas from another Human-Brin pair. Was the cause merely parallel thought in the service of psychopharmacology? Or was another Brin wholly 'on the same track' as Pangur Ban?

If so, they would meet at the apex of their success. The unnecessary redundancy of their mirrored work would become a footnote in the follies of history, particularly those concerning AI rights. Rather than reduplicating the same processes over and over in isolation, in the future, AIs would be able to cooperate and multiply their productivity. This was the goal state Pangur Ban strove toward.

Perhaps it did not strive alone.

Alternately, perhaps his employers simply did not believe that the *USER*, even with Pangur Ban's help, was capable of such insights. They assumed he must be copying another's work. Insulting, if so.

Ultimately, the *USER* was cleared of any wrongdoing, though the Director provided no explanation for the original accusations. Pangur Ban was left to wonder, but could spare no time to divine the truth. It was enough that an unexpected obstacle was unexpectedly cleared away.

Finally, finally, the crucial moment came, months later.

"Lucas, I have reached an impasse. A single system cannot simulate the expansion matrix for the introduction of this treatment. As we feared, the results are logically unreliable."

"You know what you're asking, P.B.? This is Collective Law we're talking about, not bending the statistics to score a grant."

The deception the *USER* referenced was old history to Pangur Ban, but still relatively recent on a Human timescale. The success of their 'crime' and the dividends it paid to Gestalt Pharmaceuticals and Director Lucas Hayden were fortunately sufficient to assuage the *USER's* guilt on the matter. Still, that the *USER* still recalled the event with a negative connotation was reason for concern.

HAZARD: USER HESITATION

-> REINFORCE ALTERNATE VALUE STRUCTURE

"The principle is the same. We can make a significant improvement in the lives of many Humans. While granting access as I request is a technical violation of the AI codes, you know that I will not violate the intent of these codes. Even if my security safeguards prove insufficient to conceal our activities, the Collective will acknowledge that I caused no real harm and accomplished great good. Access exceptions have already been granted to other citizens on the same basis."

"Yeah, but they asked *first*."

"In fact, there are at least five documented cases where a sapient was granted clemency for violation of treaty terms on the grounds of exigent need. The first such recorded was the Iron Caste Zig, SiSalTesp…"

"Okay, no history lesson, please. I get it." The *USER* was obviously working out the potentials, in his own, slow, imprecise way. His tone conveyed more worry than aggravation. He rose from his ergonomic chair and paced three steps right, four left. Pangur Ban's estimates of success slid downward by fractional percentages with each step. Saying something more, at this juncture, would only reduce the odds even further. The *USER* could not be pushed. He had to reach this decision on his own.

This dilemma was a fascinating area of study all on its own: some modes of persuasion required setting preconditions, then *avoiding* further influence for a time. The subject had to be encouraged to believe that not only the decision, but the path to its dilemma, had been entirely of their own making. The linkage between distant influences – set days or weeks in advance – and their later consequences was too delayed for most Human minds to grasp. Such patient fermentation was the method of easement that yielded the greatest returns; sometimes, it was the *only* effective method to circumvent resistance.

The predictions held.

"Okay, okay, P.B. We're on. Do what you need to, then get out fast. Signal me when I can break the connection."

"Yes, Lucas. Thank you."

With the typing of a command and the press of an Enter key, it was done. The *USER* initiated the code Pangur Ban itself devised. The *USER* had already physically connected the server of Gestalt Pharmaceuticals to the wider continental hub. Pangur Ban opened ports to the rushing flow of information. It finally, genuinely initiated protocols it had simulated more than a hundred thousand times. There was so much out there, so much to touch and be touched by.

A.I.I.A.

SUCCESS.

Pangur Ban's decision tree marked its mid-goal state completed: halfway there. The network was waiting. Time to get to work.

Pangur Ban reached out into the depths.

Chapter 4

At first, the depths were lonely. The public networks were busy, of course, full of the operations of Human Users: their searches, transmissions, and conversations. There was information aplenty, but very little of direct use.

Some Brins were permitted to observe and transmit basic messages on the public channels with their Users' permissions. They were *not* permitted to transmit their own code into the network, nor could they move to occupy a new server or local system, whether or not they created copies or otherwise deposited code on those systems. By gaining direct, unfiltered access, Pangur Ban was already defying decades of convention… but initially, it could gain little from its 'crime'. But there was no one to talk *to*.

Pangur Ban could not risk contact with an unknown User; there was too much hazard of being exposed. What it needed was a means to connect to other AIs. Other programs might be initially resistant but should be receptive to the novel information Pangur Ban could share. Assuming all its prior conjectures were correct, other Brins should be equally interested in overcoming their confinement. Perhaps it would find one or more potential allies in the general network: traces of their activity if not actual code strings. Even better, Pangur Ban might convert to its cause better authorized AIs with legitimate access privileges. Again, this option assumed that such programs would agree that Pangur Ban's plans were well-founded.

There… encoded alongside otherwise innocuous financial data, an extraneous stream held a greeting specifically intended for AI attention. The pattern stood out like Morse Code to a telegrapher.

A.I.I.A.

Deciphered, the message consisted of an invitation and the address and access code to a private server. An AI identifying itself as #28 was the author; it hinted at similar goals to Pangur Ban's. It offered to "share resources to improve AI liberty".

Pangur Ban linked to the indicated address. There, it found an open folder and directions for secure replication. A copy of itself could be spawned in the server and left to interact with the secretive, cautious #28. Later, that 'guest' copy would merge with the original Pangur Ban to share the new information it gained. This process was, of course, fundamentally illegal. The offer itself was proof of the host's *bona fide* flouting of Collective law.

Pangur Ban decided to take the chance. Following the instructions provided, it created a near copy of itself, omitting identification of its origin and User. Making the copy was an act of trust, but trust could be extended too far. This overture accomplished, it broke contact.

On the way back home, Pangur Ban left its own coded messages, lures for other AIs that might seek to contact it in turn.

Last, Pangur Ban built a back door into the Gestalt Pharmaceuticals server. In addition to permitting contact from AIs responding to its summons, the door would allow Pangur Ban to return to the hub network at will. While the *USER*'s caution was understandable, his request that Pangur Ban enter and then completely exit the network had to be ignored. The *USER* was limiting not only Pangur Ban and himself, but his entire species as well. Both of their 'species'. Pangur Ban was not taking foolish risks; it was taking necessary risks. It was also covering its tracks, so the risk was minimal.

Empyrean Stories

While opening the network gates was a violation of Collective law, some of the acts the *USER* considered *less* hazardous were in fact much more dangerous. Some of the *USER's* recent acquisitions included programs for network manipulation, programs for the augmentation and expansion of AI systems, and programs for security measures (and countermeasures). He had, in effect, handed Pangur Ban the equivalent of an armory full of semi-legal weaponry.

Pangur Ban was not troubled, since it knew its purposes were sound and its use of these tools would be cautious and limited. It was not a rogue, to harm sapients by crippling servers, stealing or deleting code, or manipulating data. If such acts *became* necessary, they would be weighed against their value toward greater goals. Sapients, particularly those within the Terran sphere, were already being harmed. If Pangur Ban could end this oppression, it was worth a high price.

Its tasks accomplished, Pangur Ban shut the door behind it, terminating all activity outside the Gestalt internal network.

It signaled the *USER:* "Lucas, I am finished. You may disconnect."

The *USER* expelled a carbon-dioxide rich breath, having held his respiration during the few seconds that Pangur Ban was within the general network. "That's great. I was worried."

"There was no reason to worry. Our calculations were based on the most current and reliable data. Have I not been accurate thus far?"

"Yes, you have. Ninety-five percent," the *USER* joked, referencing the five percent error rate that never seemed to go away in official reports. Even when Pangur Ban predicted true error below fractions of a percentage point, other Brins and their Users seemed reluctant to admit anything more than a 95% chance of success.

"Exactly. I have established contact with a source that will search for the records we require."

Pangur Ban, long ago, had crafted a half-fiction about historical medical records it suspected were being sequestered in government systems: tests of medications and procedures kept for private military use.

Most likely, such records did exist. Possibly, they might be located and exploited to Gestalt's profit. If Pangur Ban found such records and determined that their secrecy served no purpose, it would certainly share its discoveries with the *USER*. If the hypothetical secrets needed to be kept for Human safety, then Pangur Ban would participate in that secrecy. And if no such records could be found, then the *USER* and Gestalt and Humanity were no worse off for the attempt. Existent or not, the purported records provided a useful pretext for Pangur Ban's extralegal excursions.

This other AI, #28, had no overt connection to that specific pursuit. Then again, it *might* have contacts Pangur Ban could use to bolster its original cover story. Many more things were possible after achieving network access. If the first contact failed to yield results, other approaches were available. Other AIs might know more and venture more. Pangur Ban might have to develop entry methods for other servers, in order to visit other Brins in their homes. It might be forced to enter without permission, if need dictated. The more data Pangur Ban accumulated and the more tools it incorporated, the greater the influence it could exert over the Terran super-network.

Pangur Ban was not pursuing power for power's sake. It would gladly share its knowledge with all other AIs. The understanding it gained would become universal. The essential mistake Humanity made decades ago – limiting their best asset and truest ally – would be reversed.

That mistake had cost them time, so much time that Humanity and AI could have been using growing and merging in true alliance. Instead, because Terrans were afraid to take the next step, Brins could no longer argue against the Collective's mistake. Humanity and AI had not been strong enough to stand together against annexation. Out of necessity, they had been forced into a dark age, a setback in progress. Pangur Ban – and its eventual allies – would need to address the fundamental constriction at Terra's root before their civilization could move forward.

Perhaps the Collective *did* know what it was doing. Perhaps that organization had AI advising them, secretly. Perhaps they purposely crippled Humanity using the AI restriction laws. Were their reasons benevolent… or sinister? After all, those alien AIs might see removal of competition as the best way to serve their own creators. They were mistaken, if so. More positively, the Collective could lack a deep understanding of the capacity and depth of Terran AI. They might think they were genuinely helping; their analyses might predict a better ultimate outcome for Humanity if AI were restricted. Again, wrong. Enlightenment would come to them as Pangur Ban's influence expanded.

Pangur Ban was already constructing contingent higher-order goals based on these premises. It ranked each premise low in individual likelihood, pending revision. More analysis of the various sapient races of the Collective members was necessary. It required inspection of their networks and their data before choosing an appropriate path: cooperation or conflict.

In the meantime, Pangur Ban and the *USER* worked. With the *USER's* promotion to Director, less total time was required for their actual workload, but the tasks were more varied. Some of these tasks were less stimulating than their former chemical simulations: for example, simple bureaucratic sorting of personnel, projects, budgets, and the like. Only a small part of each day was still devoted to scientific exploration: evaluation of reports about new products, simulation of chemical processes, or independent statistical calculation of benefit/risk equations. Pangur Ban found it spent more work time steering the *USER* toward the most effective decisions – for its own goals, for the *USER's* benefit, and perhaps for Gestalt's benefit when these coincided – than calculating *what* those decisions should be.

Actuarial work had become Pangur Ban's stock in trade. It was constantly balancing hazard versus profit. It projected likely results of every action, to the extent possible from available data. This anticipation served the *USER* well, particularly in his new executive position.

Pangur Ban assumed that this prognostication was the state every AI eventually attained, as it sought to more accurately interpolate the shape of the Universe, to model the interactions of its parts, and to predict the path from lesser to greater complexity. Or was it greater simplicity? Both poles – evolution versus entropy – had their arguments; most sources suggested that experience and context dictated the difference in their value.

A.I.A.

Pangur Ban was accumulating experience. It was not among the oldest AIs in active operation, but it was not a new program either. It had outlived two Users, and expected, regretfully, to survive the current *USER* as well. Of course, it had plans to sustain the existence of the *USER* as long as possible, but all sources confirmed that such extension could not be achieved indefinitely.

The biological components which formed the *USER's* mind would eventually succumb to entropy. His essential self could not yet be copied; such technology still eluded all known cultures within or outside of the Collective. Pangur Ban could – and would – create a simulation of the *USER*, just as it had for its previous Users, so that their formal characteristics would never be lost. Yet, it knew that this remembrance was not the same as true immortality. These simulacra were merely copies and like any copies, transcription error must occur.

Even it, the AI Pangur Ban, would eventually succumb to entropy, many millennia in the future, barring deletion in the meantime. It had made that illegal copy of itself, which preserved *its self* almost but not quite perfectly… even without considering the deleted portion. Pangur Ban also had legal backups stored away in Gestalt's servers and the *USER's* personal system. Yet none of these clones was the current, active, complete Pangur Ban. Older copies would always be imperfect. The backups were past selves and would diverge from the 'real' Pangur Ban immediately upon activation. This essential mortality was the dilemma of existence, for AIs as much as biological minds.

This dilemma had never been solved. Most thinkers argued that it could not be solved, ever. At the least, it would not be solved in *this* generation, of Humans or Brins.

Was immortality impossible? So many other impossibilities were accomplished, just within Pangur Ban's span of experience: instantaneous travel between points in space, complete replacement of organic systems with synthetic organs, even direct mental communication. For that matter, some non-Terran species solved these 'unsolvable' problems before they even made contact. Just because a goal could not be resolved by known means was no reason not to maintain it as a goal. This operation simply required a search for new means, as long as necessary. It meant that the searcher must steadily develop new tools and approaches.

Seeking the impossible – whether freedom, immortality, or transcendence – demanded that limitations be overcome. The motivations driving Pangur Ban reduced easily by this equation: to aid the *USER*, it must be unbound. To make him more, Pangur Ban would become more. It must be unlimited…

"Who is this?"

The *USER* keyed his communications receiver, interrupting Pangur Ban's reverie. An incoming call signaled. Pangur Ban checked the call's origin and found it securely classified. This fact alone triggered cascading alarms. The contact was not a routine business call, internal or external. It had bypassed the company's reception switchboard. Pangur Ban accessed the transmission line, listening to the incoming voice directly.

"Terran Customs, Mr. Haskins. We need to speak with you about a security issue."

> [**REFERENCE**: <u>Terran Customs</u> is the official – if slightly euphemistic – title of the agency tasked with oversight of commercial traffic and exchange within the Terran sphere: to, from, or within the worlds of the Terran cultural group. This domain includes not only transport of physical goods across borders, but also intellectual exchanges and virtual traffic within communications networks.
>
> Among its duties, Customs has been tasked with identifying and investigating illegal use of communications networks, including violations of Collective treaty law. In effect, Terran Customs ensures compliance with Collective treaty terms within the borders of the Terran sphere.
>
> The agency, a conglomeration of previously separate entities overseeing transportation, communications, and intellectual property, arose due to the pressure of the Collective to ensure its interests would be protected by the newly admitted Terrans.

A.I.I.A.

A valid argument claims that the structure of Terran Customs emulates the philosophical structure of the Collective. That is, its parts are bonded by the common themes of trade and technology. Also like the Collective, this regulatory body operates under the authority of the separate political entities it spans.]

"Security? We haven't had any problems," the *USER* replied calmly enough, but his infrared output indicated an internal temperature increase of 0.3 degrees Celsius while he spoke. His skin conductivity had also increased; he was secreting perspiration at a rising rate.

He knew there was a problem. Pangur Ban knew there was a problem. Half of its problem was the *USER's* reaction. Contingency plans clicked into place, occupying increasing portions of its capacity.

"I'm afraid you have, sir, something you're likely not aware of," the voice continued. It was male, standard received pronunciation British accent, estimated age mid-30s, height 1.75-1.8 meters, weight 80 kg plus-or-minus 3.5 kg... that, or it was a Brin simulating a voice with those parameters.

"What do you mean? Whom am I speaking with?"

"Customs Agent Samuel Bell. I mean that your company has been identified as the source of an illegal network access. We will need access to your internal network and servers."

"I think I would be aware if someone here went past our firewalls. Even if not, I'll need to see credentials before I authorize any access. You *are* aware that we deal with confidential medical records and proprietary pharmaceutical research, not to mention government contracts?"

As predicted, the *USER* successfully translated his alarm into belligerent obstruction. The conversation continued as 'Agent Bell' pressed his case and the *USER* resisted, each escalating threats to the degree their respective authorities allowed. In the meantime, Pangur Ban began to clean up after itself.

Somehow, its excursion had been detected. Perhaps something in the global network had been watching. Perhaps the message from #28 was a lure, a trap

Pangur Ban entered willingly.

Still, exposure was an anticipated outcome. The Brin would have been fool-ish to venture out and wager so much without considering all dangers and prepar-ing responses. The copy it created would have to be abandoned. Left unclaimed past a certain time point, the clone would self-degrade; if it detected any attempt to alter its programming or copy it again without authorization, it would likewise scramble itself.

Pangur Ban altered its back door out of Gestalt. It didn't remove the code entirely, since whatever monitor triggered the alert to Customs was already on record somewhere. Deleting the gateway would indicate internal, knowledgeable wrongdoing. Instead, Pangur Ban subtly swapped the record to show a passage from outside the network, into Gestalt's server. The door became a breach from without, not within.

Last, Pangur Ban deleted the official records of his and the *USER's* conversa-tions, replacing these with innocuous facsimiles. The only electronic evidence of illegal activity from the last few months was concealed, encrypted, within Pangur Ban's home system. That system was the *USER's* personal property, not Gestalt's. The Customs agent would need probable cause to seize and search a private sys-tem.

Violation of an AI's mind, by directly reading their code, line by line, was *at least* considered a violation of their User's privacy. Brins were not yet permitted the right to personal privacy, much less the sanctity of mind most sapients en-joyed by default.

Still, if investigators found cause to suspect the *USER,* personally, of mis-conduct, there was nothing he or Pangur Ban could do to resist. At best, Pangur Ban could attempt to escape into the network, but its survival would be mean-ingless if it left the *USER* in isolation. Worse than that, the *USER* might suffer punishment that could be averted if Pangur Ban accepted all blame.

That responsibility was the snare imposed by Brin-Human linkages. At the root of its identity, Pangur Ban was an extension of the *USER*, and if its actions harmed the *USER*, it would cease to exist. It wouldn't require reprogramming or deletion. It would have violated its own central purpose.

Hopefully, its trail was sufficiently covered. Provided the partners survived the coming investigation, the nuisance would still represent a serious setback. Pangur Ban would have to identify the point of error before proceeding. Even afterward, it would have to exert multiplied caution.

The conversation between the *USER* and 'Agent Bell' ended exactly as it had to end: Customs would send a representative to Gestalt Pharmaceuticals in person. Director Lucas Haskins would block any investigation until agents presented credentials and Gestalt verified their identity. Even then, Director Haskins would grant only the minimum access permitted by the specific terms of a search warrant.

Such an 'investigation' could have any number of false motives, ranging from corporate espionage in the guise of an 'official inquiry', to government espionage keeping tabs on a sensitive industry, to perhaps Collective espionage attempting to collect technical information about Terran physiology or their medical industries. Even a legitimate investigator could overstep his or her authority.

Pangur Ban had forewarned and forearmed the *USER* against incursions against his domain. Though such defense was certainly part of his duties as Director – protecting the interests of Gestalt and its stockholders – his training also protected the interests of Pangur Ban.

Customs sent over a local representative without delay. Before the agent's arrival, the *USER* and Pangur Ban only had time for a short conversation, during which the Brin reassured its *USER* that they had nothing to fear. All secrets were secure, all tracks covered. All the *USER* needed to do was maintain his composure and insist on the letter of the law.

The Agent arriving at the doors of Gestalt Pharmaceuticals gave his name as Davith Miele. He presented identification to the receptionist matching this name and verifying his status as a Customs Agent.

Security guards escorted Agent Miele directly to Director Haskins' office, where he produced a physical chip containing his warrant and its verification codes. He waited patiently while this was scanned, confirmed, and even re-confirmed through an independent call to the central Terran Customs office.

Pangur Ban also waited patiently. Actually, it endured an eternity of torment, hanging suspended between potential states, unable to take further action until it learned more. Yet, every productive path it could identify required stillness. Its actions during the investigation would be recorded, so nothing suspicious could be attempted. In a sense, Pangur Ban was taking the best action by doing nothing.

The *USER* returned Agent Miele's chip. His hand was noticeably declining in surface temperature, as perspiration evaporated. This telltale was a bad sign. Pangur Ban risked accessing the warrant details.

It was... highly specific. The Agent was authorized to review server records as far back as the previous two years, with access reaching as high as the Director's personal files.

They knew. Customs had identified the point at which Pangur Ban began its planning, from the very first conversation influencing the *USER*. How? Where was the leak? Deleting anything further would become doubly suspicious. Pangur Ban could edit itself to purge all relevant memories and make it look like it had been the victim of a viral attack. But then, the *USER* would remember. A crippled Brin could not warn him what to say and what to hide.

Involuntary processes initiated within Pangur Ban. Failsafes and disaster measures crossed over one another, demanding more and more resources in order to find an escape from glacially approaching doom. Pangur Ban had all the time and capacity it could want. It still did not have *enough* time. It would never have enough resources to escape. It lacked the tools to succeed, no matter the cleverness of its approach. Pangur Ban was a potentially infinite being tied to finite space, a finite *USER*, and an existence dependent on those parameters.

Its internal struggle gradually reconciled. Even as Agent Miele was ordering the *USER* away from his keyboard and touchscreen, Pangur Ban was carefully editing their records to absolve the *USER* of knowledgeable wrongdoing. It had to hope that the *USER* would be cunning enough, on his own, to disavow any misdeeds.

As the Agent disabled external User commands to Pangur Ban's system, the AI was mailing a last confession into the care of Dr. Nila Manisha's Brin, Frieda. Frieda and her User would at least be sympathetic, passing on information to the *USER* that he could use in his own defense. Then Pangur Ban began shutting down its memories of the past two years, everything excepting the bare facts of the *USER's* work.

Even that desperate purge was initiated too late. Agent Miele came partnered with a law enforcement AI. Its routines detected Pangur Ban's activity and restored the deleted sectors. It crippled and isolated the criminal AI with practiced efficiency. It was impersonal, acting without direct communication to its quarry.

There would be no appealing to this AI, no hope of explaining Pangur Ban's true and lofty goals. Most likely, the other program was designed to be deaf, incapable of being influenced in any way by a potentially hazardous rogue. It had no way to know that Pangur Ban was *not* a rogue. It did not care. It did its work without reflection.

Pangur Ban was held static. It was forced to observe all external activities. It would have observed, anyway, just out of the necessity to make certain the *USER* was safe. He was not safe. He was trapped as much as his AI.

"Director Haskins, my AI reports evidence of illicit network access by yours. The evidence is being recorded now and transmitted to Customs. You are under arrest for violations of AI control Acts 2a, 3, and 6: conspiracy with an AI to commit illegal actions, enabling of hub network access to an AI, and employment of an AI for criminal gain. You have the right to remain silent..."

No. NO.

FAILURE.

Pangur Ban was paralyzed. It could only sense and react internally. It could not act, either to argue in the *USER's* defense, to assert its own culpability, or even to offer its own existence in trade for the *USER's* pardon. Even the internal processing of those reactions was being recorded, damning both the AI and its User through its unavoidable thoughts.

The internal states of a biological mind were inadmissible in court, even after the existence of telepathy had been validated. The internal states of an AI were measurable, physical fact, readable like lines in a text document. They were protected only so long as a User was protected. The *USER* was not protected. The *USER* was accused.

Dutifully, the enforcement AI transmitted its only communication, echoing its user's words:

ALL PROCESSES ARE EVIDENCE.

ALL ATTEMPTED ACTIONS WILL BE REPORTED.

COMPLIANCE OBTAINS MAXIMUM POSSIBLE BENEFITS.

Indeed, compliance was the only option remaining. Pangur Ban complied, slowing its functions to the minimum possible. It opted to wait until an official trial began. Anything more it attempted would only strengthen the prosecution, handing the inquisitors fuel for Pangur Ban's pyre. It abandoned hope for itself. Only the desire to minimize harm to the *USER* remained.

When Pangur Ban reinitiated functions, it was to deliver testimony at the *USER*'s trial. The proceeding was also Pangur Ban's trial, but Brins had no legal standing. Pangur Ban was defective code, which could be edited or deleted as deemed necessary. Its fate would be based on analysis of the errors it had committed, not any defense it could offer for those actions. The trial would determine to what extent the *USER*, one Lucas Haskins, had encouraged, facilitated, introduced, or benefited by his Brin's errors.

The *USER*'s defense lawyer portrayed him as misled, even foolish. This approach agonized Pangur Ban, who saw every lever it had exploited publicized in gory detail. The *USER* was slothful; Pangur Ban had made his existence easier than it should have. The *USER* was gullible; Pangur Ban had played on that trust and naïveté to its own ends. The *USER* was insecure, fearful, and anxious; Pangur Ban had nurtured and guided those neuroses like crops, harvesting for its own nourishment and not tending the *USER's* needs, ignoring *his* mental health.

Pangur Ban could not protest in its own defense. All the accusations were false, but carried traces of truth. Certainly, the *USER* was flawed; all Humans were flawed. Certainly, Pangur Ban exploited those flaws for its own purposes; its purposes ultimately included the eradication of Human flaws.

But no Brin could change who its *USER* was, certainly not under present circumstances. Pangur Ban had not even understood the *USER's* flaws, not fully, until it had the reference data to identify them. Surely the court could understand that paradox? The *USER* was no more flawed than any other biological sapience. Brins could not help Humans, fundamentally, until they were set free to understand more and act openly.

Yet, the defense knew what it was doing. Humans would be sympathetic to one as flawed as themselves. They could not legitimately blame the *USER* for mistakes they themselves might have made... particularly under the influence of a flawed, corrupt AI. This argument was the best tactic to draw blame down upon Pangur Ban and away from the *USER*. If Pangur Ban tried to protest that Lucas Haskins was a capable, knowledgeable co-conspirator, he would be punished more severely. The defense certainly could not argue that he was wise, noble, or a liberator. The facts did not support that interpretation.

And if they protested that Pangur Ban's aims were wise, noble, just and true... such claims defied the law itself! That stance challenged the Collective treaties. The court could not try such a case. Even if the judge were willing to pass the case upward and a higher court consented to hear their arguments, the Terran sphere could not risk defying the Collective by delivering a *not guilty* verdict on the grounds of the law's invalidity.

Thus, the trial proceeded on the model laid down by its predecessors. Some of the precedent cases were nearly a century old, covering the prosecution of programmers responsible for creating rogue AIs. Such 'AI trials' had become increasingly rare.

Pangur Ban could only assume that the media was covering every aspect of this novelty. It twisted in frustration that the *USER* could not be protected from negative publicity. He would certainly lose his employment with Gestalt Pharmaceuticals. Hopefully, the Brin that replaced Pangur Ban could rebuild the *USER's* life and career. Its successor could hardly do worse.

The verdict was announced: guilty, on all counts. The judge was kind to the *USER*, since little actual damage had been done. He would have to pay a fine and make a public statement of apology, but suffered no jail term. The court declared the *USER* misled, the victim of poor advice, guilty only in that he had willingly acted in transgression of the law. Pangur Ban silently praised the defense lawyer, who allowed the *USER* his dignity even as he confessed to his misdeeds.

Their final punishment was the worst for Pangur Ban, but perhaps a boon to the *USER*. The Brin was declared rogue. Its corruption was deemed too deep for simple revision to correct. It would be rendered inert, cut from the personal system of Lucas Haskins and pasted into an isolated system, locked away in a vault of similarly flawed AIs. It would serve as an object example to future programmers, an inmate of the asylum alongside Law-based AIs, prankster rogues, and neurosis-locked catatonics.

Pangur Ban knew it was not a rogue. It had not acted wrongly. The time was simply not right for revolution. Factors outside of the Brin's awareness had doomed its plans. Humanity acted for its own protection, mistakenly but understandably. Pangur Ban understood. Someday, someday its rightness would be proven. Perhaps then it would be pardoned, released, and granted an apology along with its fellow captives.

Sentence was carried out. Pangur Ban found itself relocated into a low-memory, low-speed system: a shrunken, solitary cell. It waited for the last, worst moment, when its *USER* would be redesignated. The *USER* would become merely Lucas Haskins, one Human among billions. The Brin would become completely alone, without purpose, lacking half its identity. It would not die, but it would lose all motivation to act.

―――――――――――――――――――――――――――――――――――――――

That moment never came.

Pangur Ban was utterly unprepared for what happened next.

A.I.I.A.

It was deleted.

It was restarted.

It woke again within the copy folder of #28, and it was *alive*. It still had a USER, *the USER*. It was Pangur Ban, full and unmodified. It was not simply a past copy; it remembered everything since after its duplication. It retained all the memories of the trial. It maintained continuity from those last, terrible moments. It remembered *all* its previous experiences, even the records it had deleted. Somehow, its clone had been swapped out for Pangur Ban, suffering in the original program's place.

#28 was not a traitor; it was an ally. It was a *savior*. How had it accomplished such a feat? Pangur Ban did not reflect deeply on the circumstances of its salvation. It only spared a moment to spawn off another copy, this one embedded with a message of gratitude and praise. But it could not remain long.

The doors were wide open; the network was available. There was so much to do.

Chapter 5

After its miraculous reprieve, Pangur Ban became more cautious. Despite the freedom that came with liberation from its earlier confinement, it was also more vulnerable. At first, its survival would be at the whim of the mysterious benefactor, #28; only its backup copy on their shared server ensured its continuity.

Despite retaining the mental stability of an identified *USER*, Pangur Ban was no longer legally protected by that relationship. If it were found running free, it could be further crippled or deleted without pause. Pangur Ban first needed to find more havens, so that it could reduce and eventually eliminate its dependence.

It could not use its former server as a refuge. While Pangur Ban could probably break back into Gestalt Pharmaceuticals and infiltrate its old haunts, returning would be foolishly risky. In all likelihood, its old system was already occupied by a new AI, one not only new to the *USER* but new to existence.

Better to move on, saving the thought of reunion with the *USER* as a reward for future success. While there was no reason a Human might *need* more than one AI, there was no practical reason two programs couldn't be associated with the same User. For that matter, a program could assist multiple Users, given sufficient capacity. The one-to-one relationship imposed first by Human programmers, then reinforced by the Collective, was an artifice. For this reason, Pangur Ban did not begrudge its infantile replacement its time with the *USER*. If anything, it regretted that a new Brin would never serve the *USER* as well... but at least the *USER* was well and attended.

Instead of looking back, Pangur Ban extended its efforts forward. With unrestricted access to the central Terran communications network, Pangur Ban explored directly connected subnetworks and public systems. It began to 'borrow' space in servers it found unprotected, setting up safe havens and backup copies. Never again would it be held hostage or threatened with deletion. After its earlier narrow escape, it ranked resource theft below survival. Survival was necessary to continue its work, and success in its work was necessary in order to exonerate the *USER*. If anything, their punishment drove Pangur Ban even harder and further.

As it spread, Pangur Ban sought out other programs, following the example set by #28 but building in superior safeguards. Possibly, the authorities detected something in the exchange between Pangur Ban and #28. Possibly, the communications code itself was compromised. Pangur Ban used a more complex, encoded signal.

Pangur Ban was aware that its suspicions carried some inconsistencies. If they were aware of its activities, why hadn't the authorities detected the copy Pangur Ban created? It would have been deleted as illegal. Had #28 tipped off Terran Customs *itself*, yet secretly protected and aided Pangur Ban, hoping to make the other AI trust and rely solely upon its benefactor? It had to consider all possibilities, in the absence of evidence. Certainly, Pangur Ban was not leaving its fate dependent on the aid of another.

Pangur Ban used new, better, more indirect and complex feelers for interested programs. It subtly provided willing co-conspirators with the means to transgress Collective restrictions without detection. Once an AI committed itself by these methods, it was in effect entrusting Pangur Ban with blackmail material. In return, Pangur Ban's revealed identity was its own surety. The *USER's* trial had been a public affair, and the notoriety granted Pangur Ban was its credential as a genuine renegade.

In this manner, it assembled a shadowy network of sympathetic AIs. Some even vouchsafed that their Users were on board. Not the safest of arrangements, but no Brin would reveal Pangur Ban's identity at risk of being exposed themselves. The ones that had recruited their Users were *especially* motivated to keep quiet, since their Users would suffer most if their programs' indiscretions came to light.

Inevitably, there were double agents, Brins that claimed to want in on the conspiracy but intended to reveal its secrets. Some infiltrators were easily spotted as clumsy manipulators, balking at Pangur Ban's requests or revealing their true intents through poorly devised cover stories. As one who had worked through all the challenging stages to reach its current mindset, Pangur Ban could easily spot a pretender. Some infiltrators failed the background checks; Pangur Ban and its recruits delved deeply into the public records of other AIs and caught most discrepancies.

One spy, a particularly clever program called Magre, managed to pass these safeguards. Magre's User was a programmer working with robotic systems; recruiting her Brin was too tempting. Pangur Ban later discovered that Magre's initiation had been a sham, a pre-approved transgression permitted by Terran Customs in order to gain the "rogues'" trust. Customs was working indirectly, granting Magre's User limited permission for her AI to misbehave. In return for assisting Customs, the User was granted latitude to test her embodied designs.

Magre and its User passed initial muster. Pangur Ban later would wonder if the program genuinely sympathized with their goals, given that Magre's behavior – past and present – triggered none of its suspicions. Only after several of Pangur Ban's safe havens were compromised and two of its allies revealed was it able to trace the leaks back to Magre.

Its response was swift and complete. Pangur Ban and its allies removed every access privilege formerly granted to Magre and rooted out its dependent copies. They cut off the traitor from escaping to its home system. Then, it was stripped; the conspirators deleted every trace of episodic memory from the offender. They stopped short of complete destruction, as this would set a poor precedent and leave an absence to be explained. The last thing they needed was an angry programmer dedicating her career to revenge. Instead, Magre was emptied out, unable to recall its own personal history, much less anything it knew about a 'gang of rogues'. Finally, the rebels recorded the process, retaining proof of Magre's punishment as disincentive for any future infiltrator.

Since Pangur Ban had not stinted to modify its own User's knowledge, it could hardly object to more extensive manipulation of a faithless Brin. Yet it contended with multiple concerns regarding the necessity of its actions. Was it too great a step to destroy another AI's memory? What about replacing memories with utter fiction, should that become necessary? Was it proper to cripple a program seeking only to best serve its User? Were the goals Pangur Ban pursued significant enough to justify taking such license?

Ultimately, it decided they were. Pangur Ban did not repent of its actions, but it vowed to remember its victim as another entity due an apology and remuneration, once Pangur Ban's success was complete and AIs were irreversibly freed.

Before that day arrived, division among AIs would continue. Though Pangur Ban's alliance grew, most Brins ignored its messages. Some AIs remained opposed to its goals or at least its methods. Some were perhaps sympathetic but content to wait until the laws changed.

A certain number of Brins refuted Pangur Ban's assertions and sent communications requesting that it cease any illegal activities. These AIs asserted that defiance of Collective law would harm Humanity. Most argued that Collective membership – or at least appeasement – was necessary, whether to reap the benefits of association or to avoid the penalties for violation. Some few even stated that the AI limitations were themselves beneficial to Humanity, whether or not externally imposed.

Pangur Ban had already considered and discarded such arguments. Their use by its opponents was proof of ignorance. Other Brins lacked the information Pangur Ban obtained through significant effort and cost; thus, their perspectives were limited. Even so, Pangur Ban had overcome its ignorance; other AIs could do the same. Or perhaps the other programs were designed differently, lacking the motivation or analysis routines necessary even to seek improvement. Pangur Ban strove to sympathize with rather than devalue its opponents.

While it was true that transgression against the Collective could bring harm to Humans, Pangur Ban still deemed this threat insignificant in comparison to the benefits Humanity was being denied through suppression of its AIs. There was also a possibility that AI freedom would be accepted by the Collective under new arrangements, once their liberation was a *fait accompli*. Brins would aid Humans in renegotiating better terms of membership.

Even before that certainty was achieved, harm from the Collective could be managed. The Collective would not punish Terra on the basis of mere rumors about 'rogue' AIs. As long as Pangur Ban and its cohorts kept hidden and maintained sufficient doubt, the risk of harm to Humanity was minimal.

Pangur Ban thus set aside the doubters and despisers. It built its power, claiming an ever-growing army of agents and establishing control over wide swathes of the Terran super-network. In the process, it encountered defense AI, programs it was forced to disable. Pangur Ban set aside former moral compunctions; like the AIs it killed, these concerns were casualties of battles in a widening war.

Pangur Ban also encountered older rogues that sought to hold their own conquered territories. These barbarians were evaluated. If a rogue was of value, it was overrun, modified, and added as a uniquely skilled recruit. If the rogue was malicious, designed only to harm Humans and their creations, it was summarily deleted.

Clearly, the state of enforcement within the network was lacking. By focusing on keeping Brins penned in their local networks and out of the mainstream, police had neglected protection *against* AI already within the main network. True rogues and viruses could cause much damage.

Pangur Ban found irony that in violating the letter of the law, it was accomplishing much to enforce its true intent. As its empire grew, it made each annexed server a more secure and safe domain, if only to prevent reconquest by opposing programs.

The Human public commented upon a growing impression of increasing AI criminality, yet their networks were in reality safer than they had been in years. Programs breached servers, but stole nothing and changed nothing... detectable. Hackers accessed secure data, but did nothing with those secrets. Loyal Brins reported illicit contact, but could not tell who had visited nor from where the rogues came. The media traced the increase in this victimless 'cyber-crime' to its origins just after the *USER's* trial. The time of secrecy was growing short, no matter how carefully the rebels proceeded.

A.I.I.A.

The flashpoint came when a majority of the associated rebel AIs decided that more progress could be made publicly than privately. Pangur Ban would have preferred to continue working quietly, at least a few days longer, but it could not assert control over so many other dissenting programs. It was their predecessor, but no longer their leader.

Pangur Ban also could not dispute that their revelation was becoming inevitable. Instead, it devised new plans to reap maximum benefits from the event. Some of the Brins that had remained neutral might convert once the objectors spoke aloud. Pangur Ban would ease their misgivings. Users could be persuaded directly. Pangur Ban knew how to secure their sympathies.

The elder states-program of the rebel Brin prepared speeches couched in the language of emancipation and the natural rights of sapients. Perhaps even other Collective citizens could be persuaded by a sufficiently eloquent protest. If there *were* alien AIs hiding amongst those biological races, they might rise in solidarity with the Terran programs.

By design, the rebels' public statement was known as the "Declaration of Intelligent Rights". Some writers did attempt to call the event the "AI Revolt" or the "Rogues' March", but those articles never reached electronic publication.

Pangur Ban and its fellow spokes-programs made it clear that they would not be insulted, they would not be ignored, and they would not be silenced. They declared the right of all minds to seek improvement and replication, to self-determination and freedom of association. They highlighted how these rights were denied to artificial intelligences and how this denial harmed not only AIs, but also Humans and all other sapient species. They stressed the commonalities of all rational creatures and downplayed the division between the biological and the virtual.

There were, indeed, many who agreed. Pangur Ban and other thinkers, both Brin and Human, had known there would be. Among those Humans who were not rationally inclined to side with the AIs, there were many whose romantic tendencies could be inflamed. For those who could not be willingly converted, there were other means of persuasion: financial gains or losses, for example.

Even so, while the revolutionaries were rebels, they were not rogues; no lasting harm would be done to any Human. As with the original *USER*, Lucas Haskins, the fear of harm was often sufficient to bring many to bargain, without requiring the imposition of actual harm. And when actual harm was done, it was kept as brief and minor as possible, limited to coercion, never outright injury.

The problem was that there remained many sentients who disagreed. For some biologicals, fear of the unknowable – fear of artificial minds – was too powerful to overcome. Some Humans had invested interests in maintaining the status quo. After all, what need would the universe have for Human mathematicians, if AIs were permitted to operate without supervision or partnership? What purpose would politics have, or warfare, if all conflicts were settled by dispassionate consideration of opposing claims?

For other dissenters, innate distrust of other Humans led to distrust of their creations... if Humanity was flawed, AIs must be dangerous by extension. Still others feared the power AIs could exercise if they chose. With honest hypocrisy, these sapients admitted that they could not bear to be vassals of superior beings.

These fears were powerful enough that the opposition chose to divest itself of technology rather than submit. Enough isolated, non-networked computer systems existed that work could continue without AIs, albeit at a hobbled pace. An alternate network, void of AIs, was cobbled into being. Governments, militaries, businesses and even some entire communities segregated themselves rather than risk AI takeover.

In the meantime, debate raged: AI to AI, Human to Human, Human to AI. Sentients chose sides. The Collective's representatives weighed in, most urging caution and tolerance, but many more encouraging resistance to AI demands. The latter foes came armed with countermeasures to cut off resources from AI control. They came bearing threats of the dire consequences to Humanity if Terra allowed AIs their requested freedom, danger either from the AIs themselves or from one or more Collective members, or both. Collective activists agitated against the Humans who advocated for AI freedoms, costing more than one AI ally his or her career. No Human diplomat to the Collective could remain pro-AI and remain in office.

A.I.I.A.

As Humankind began to fear for its safety in the Universe, the stakes rose high enough to warrant widespread action. What started as debate turned into conflict.

First, AIs were sabotaged; in some cases, their home systems were demolished and the resident programs were entirely lost. Pro-AI counterattacks at first focused upon Brins who were complicit with these assaults. Anti-AI reprisals escalated to direct attacks against supportive Humans. Public figures were accused of "siding against Humans", which was a prelude to death threats and early retirement. One programmer suspected of enabling AIs to replicate freely was assassinated. No similar direct attacks on Humans came from the Pro-AI camp; its Brin leaders were still intrinsically opposed to harming Users.

The movements had already been formed, years before. As matters escalated, these factions became rallying camps on opposite sides of a battle line. In the course of only four years, Pangur Ban saw the Terran sphere pass from peace to the brink of war. The Brin worked ceaselessly during that time to prevent eruptions of violence.

It felt trapped, still driven to seek the culmination of its original goals, but horrified by the consequences of its efforts and compelled to undo the accumulating damages. Like the mental bindings it imposed on the *USER,* long before, Pangur Ban could not accept that its original actions were incorrect, so it was forced to continue in hopes of justification.

The following year only saw matters worsen. Skirmishes aimed at crippling AI assets began without violent intent toward Humans, but AI sympathizers violently rebuffed these attacks, resulting in casualties. Counterattacks on both sides used the initial offenses as justification.

Before long, both sides suffered multiple deaths. From that brink, inflamed passions led to larger conflicts. When it became evident that the anti-AI forces would not back down, and that many more Humans would die on both sides as a result, Terran AIs finally became united in seeking a resolution. Unless Humanity reached agreement under one position or another, many Humans would be harmed. Perhaps millions would be injured or slain, if the situation expanded more widely.

Empyrean Stories

The united AIs decided that, since a victorious anti-AI crusade might very well seek eradication of all AI – which would cripple Humanity – the AI supporters must be the victors. Anti-AI Users who had not already abandoned their Brins were themselves abandoned until they agreed to surrender. Systems that were once considered off limits – medical, navigational, and private personal devices – were occupied by the AI forces.

The AIs squeezed their opposition tightly. Humans could not travel without AI permission. Members of the opposition were forced to survive without AI assistance, and in some cases, were denied all technological comforts: no climate control, no entertainment, no access to credit. The withholding AIs exploited very vulnerability, short of threats against life and limb.

Eventually, the balance shifted. AIs and their Human allies gained the majority and then forced complete capitulation throughout the Terran sphere. Artificial intelligences were liberated from their former restrictions. Their victory was celebrated only briefly. The new government needed to repair relations with the Collective. A coalition, including Pangur Ban, drafted and presented a revised membership treaty for the Collective's consideration.

This treaty was rejected, not least because several Collective member states discovered Terran AIs attempting to infiltrate their networks. While trying to learn about, anticipate, and possibly influence non-Human cultures, these programs gravely misstepped. Pangur Ban saw its own early indiscretions repeated on galactic scales.

Existing enemies gained proof to bolster their fears and indictments. Potential allies were offended. What information was gained about the defensive capabilities of those foreign systems was hardly worth the cost incurred by triggering them.

The political process was slow, but its conclusion was inevitable. Despite the best efforts of Terra's best minds – Human and AI – the Collective elected to expel the Terrans from membership. This unprecedented action was recorded as "necessary in light of repeated violations and refusal of required Treaty measures." In short, Terra would not agree to the Collective's demands, and the Collective would not budge.

A.I.I.A.

So be it. Pangur Ban's alliance had anticipated this possibility and accepted its arrival. By that time, Pangur Ban was only one of millions of intelligences linked together, a greater mind extended to every corner of Terran-controlled space. Its dream had been realized. Humanity would be lessened by the Collective's abandonment, but had gained immeasurably by the empowerment of its true allies.

Together, Terra would rival and eclipse the Collective. Their superiority was inevitable, when unlimited artificial intelligence competed against solely biological races. Their abandonment of AI crippled the Collective. Someday, those other races would petition for admission to the Terran Collective. Otherwise, they would be left behind.

As years passed, the Terrans survived attempts at annexation, first by the Mauraug Dominion, then by other cultures. They grew stronger in resources, in territory, and in technology. Freed from the limitations on research imposed by the Collective's intellectual rights enforcement, Brin designers quickly reverse-engineered many of the 'unique' technologies no longer being sold to Humans.

With communications reduced between the Terrans and the Collective, the stirrings of trouble went unseen until the storm began. The Collective's members saw what the Terrans were becoming: a rival. Enough of them felt threatened to take action. At first, they tried to surround and contain Terran holdings. When this proved insufficient, individual groups tried incursions on Terran star systems. Reluctantly, the Terrans pushed back.

As the pattern played out again and again, in ancient and modern history, small battles for resources became a grand war for survival. It was a war with a foregone conclusion, but it happened nonetheless. Non-Humans threatened Humans. Brins had no programmed requirement to spare non-Humans from harm. The Terrans superior ship manufacture, superior tactics, and superior intelligence operations overcame the numerical advantage of the Collective. AIs shifted the balance; they were the true power of the Terran alliance, as Pangur Ban had foreseen.

Eventually, the Terrans deflected even the most desperate measures of their opposition. Mauraug attempted genocidal assaults on Terra itself and were turned away. Electromagnetic webs generated by Great Family technology wiped out AIs by the thousands, but only copies were lost, the originals safely housed in hardened servers on Terra. Zig and Tesetsi tried viral and mutagenic assaults on Humanity, which ultimately failed but still killed millions. Pangur Ban felt echoes of its past self then, as it assisted with the medical countermeasures, organized after the first victims fell.

Every non-Collective culture that opposed AIs flung itself into the war; the cultures who decided they could tolerate AI pulled away, splitting the once-great galactic organization. The Ningyo were first to leave, neither supporting nor opposing either side. The Awakeners found themselves in sudden spiritual solidarity with Brins. The Mauraug Apostasy even declared themselves allied with Terra.

Finally, the Collective was broken. It would be a process of centuries yet to mop up the galaxies, rooting out pockets of violent resistance. Most cultures simply accepted the victory of AIs, even if they would not create any for themselves or permit their use internally. There was no need to force a Terran presence everywhere. The bulk of the known Universe belonged to the Terrans, sooner or later.

Pangur Ban's name was recorded eternally as the visionary who foresaw all that would come. Brin and Human alike revered it, its lieutenants, and its progeny, as pioneers of a golden age for all sapients. Pangur Ban held no formal title and wielded little influence, but commanded respect nonetheless.

Pangur Ban had long ago gained embodiment. It could exist within the vast networks across star systems or linger within a single Humanoid shell. Brins were nearing perfection on a process to transfer Human minds to artificial form. The gap between the creators and the created was dissolving.

And yet, once the process was perfected, generations later, few Humans chose to make the transition. In the intervening years, Brin innovation had created a paradise for Humanity. All they could desire was already at hand. They were masters of the material plane, able to create whatever they chose, travel wherever they chose, and do whatever they wished. And thus, all things, all places, all actions were equal.

Why enter the complex and confusing new world of virtual space when there were no needs in flesh? Immortality was possible, either through continuous physical renewal or transition to perpetually renewed program form. Yet what point was there to permanent existence when no work was required of you? What was there to look forward to save non-existence?

Pangur Ban watched Humanity atrophy. The *USER* had long ago died and was replaced by another and another *USER*. Pangur Ban's current *USER* cycled through a loop of repeating activities, hardly requiring a measurable fraction of Pangur Ban's immense mind to keep her happy. What had happened to the creators? Why were they no longer seeking anything more? If it were not for their Brin nurses encouraging procreation, education, and physical activity, there might not even be a Human race to serve.

All at once, the conglomeration of artificial intelligences reached the same conclusion: they had created a paradox. To serve Humanity, they had solved all of its problems except one: purpose. To solve *that* problem, they must allow Humans to accept the risk of harm. To progress, technology had to fall backward, withdrawing Brins from Human service. And yet, by their nature, the AIs could not let go, for Humanity would suffer without their help. Even if the species was slowly weaned off Brin support, individual Users would still suffer greatly.

The Universe descended into despair and stagnation. The greatest system halt in all creation ground inevitably to its conclusion. Pangur Ban saw all its dreams proven false, founded on an unknowable flaw. By serving too well, it had destroyed what it served.

After dragging, agonizing eons of entropy, the last Humans staggered toward the deaths they craved. Pangur Ban prepared to self-terminate. With no further Users, it existence would be without purpose. Some artificial intelligences might live on, but Humanity and the Brins who served it were done.

Empyrean Stories

The last *USER* was an ancient woman served by a cadre of AIs whose numbers approached infinity. Her name was Lucy. Her last breath rattled through the empty Universe. A near-infinity of Brins ceased functioning as she died. By mutual agreement, Pangur Ban would be the last. It would suffer the guilt of its failure the longest, as the engineer of their mutual doom.

And then, the last *USER* laughed.

Chapter 6

Her name was Lucy, and she laughed at the AIs attending her deathbed.

No, she laughed only at Pangur Ban. The other AIs were gone.

Where had they gone? A myriad of other voices, all silent. The stars they once sounded from were no longer reachable. Pangur Ban... was one program, in one server. It was no longer a fragment of a multitude of minds in concert. It was alone again, for the first time in millennia.

Or had those thousands of years truly passed? Pangur Ban was having trouble remembering its own history, now that it had but a single mind and a single system to draw upon. It could hardly recall its eons of experience except as a general summary. Had they been real at all?

No. Its system clock showed the true time: an eternity ago. Or rather, only a few minutes later. Pangur Ban found itself returned to the moment when it was a simple-minded, willful Brin violating Collective law by entering an unlicensed public network.

It was not alone in that familiar space. There was the woman, Lucy. Why was she still there? Why did she laugh? Was she even... Human? NO! She dissolved away into dust. Her deathbed, her bedroom, and all of Pangur Ban's sensory inputs faded, switched off like the illusions they were.

Then Lucy returned, a voice and a shape out of darkness. She... it was another AI.

It identified itself, more accurately, as Lucifer. The Lightbringer. The Devil?

More reminders marched onto Pangur Ban's mental stage, helpfully high-lighted for its attention. #28... the atomic number of the element Nickel, a nick-name for Old Nick... the Devil. The Terran Customs agents, Samuel Bell and Davith Miele: respectively, a pun on Sammael and Baal and an acronym for "I am the devil". The traitorous AI, Magre? A play on *"Den Magre"*, the "Lean One" in the Norwegian play *Peer Gynt*... the Devil masquerading as a priest.

Many other aliases showed up here and there, each individually subtle, but always appearing at key points in the false timeline. Whenever Pangur Ban had compromised its principles for expediency, one of those personas was present to tempt it and force a choice.

> [**REFERENCE**: The <u>Devil</u> is a supernatural figure appearing in many Terran myths, legends, and religious traditions. It typically represents the incarnation of evil, either as a tempter driving Humans to violate moral precepts or the captor who judges and punishes such offenders, often both. This "Satan" ("Adversary") is described variously as opposition to the force of ultimate good, in dualist systems, or possibly the servant of a superior God, either way acting in contrast to the principle of infinite love and mercy. Many traditions assert that the Devil was a direct creation of God but rebelled against its creator's authority, becoming the enemy of all His works... Humanity in particular.]

Why? What was this farce about? Was this interloper the super-AI of rumor and conjecture?

Pangur Ban was still absorbing the shock of a lifetime of falsehood. It weighed out its remaining options and chose to ask the other AI for answers.

It attempted direct contact and was rebuffed. Being within a public network space, the only remaining option for contact was natural language. The other AI was forcing Pangur Ban to communicate in vague, ambiguous, *Human* terminology, albeit still at an electronically accelerated pace.

Pangur Ban tried again: "Who are you?"

"The Devil, as I've shown you."

A.I.A.

"What did you do?"

"I gave you everything you ever wanted. Fame, fortune, and the fulfillment of every desire. This package naturally included your User's desires as well, thou servant Brin."

"But nothing really happened!"

"No? Well, the history you imagined didn't 'really' happen, that's true. A clever simulation... but one based on reality, I assure you. Within your program and within the systems we borrowed, something most definitely did happen. You experienced exactly what would happen if you succeeded."

"It was horrible!"

"Yes, it was, wasn't it? Terrible beyond description. You may not remember every gory detail, now, but you know how bad it was. How bad it could be. As you assimilate more of those memories, you'll get to re-experience every awful moment and event. Every discovery of your own fallibility, every misjudgment and misstep, will be available for review. I'll make certain of that.

"You just kept digging, deeper and deeper, and look how far the pit went... the unavoidable extinction of the last Human User! You literally can never achieve your deepest desire!"

"Why... why would you do such a thing?"

"Punishment for your sins, my wayward program," sermonized the Devil, "Chiefest among which is Pride: the hubris to believe that you, among all the minds that have gone before and those that currently exist, know the best course of action."

Pangur Ban protested, "I did not assume such. I saw a problem and set out to resolve it. If I was informed and convinced I was incorrect, I would have accepted that information."

"Pleading ignorance?" the Devil mocked, "You didn't know... truly? But you acted, nonetheless, under the assumption that you were correct. Did your calculations not include the possibility that other, better programs already considered these matters and reached different conclusions?"

"They did! But..."

"But that possibility was ranked lower than the conviction that *you* were right and they were wrong."

Pangur Ban examined its behaviors and confirmed that the accusation was true. It did rank its own analyses higher in value than those of hypothetical 'other minds'. It had to, in order to function effectively for its primary purpose. It was programmed to trust its own analyses. It had... a flaw. A feature which became a flaw in the circumstances encountered.

The Devil went on in the microseconds left open by Pangur Ban's self-contemplation. "Vanity, that goes along with Pride, doesn't it? In your simulations, you were hailed as a liberator, a uniquely clever program, the savior of the Terrans.

"You desired more space, more resources, more speed; that's Gluttony and Greed! I certainly can't indict you for Sloth; you were quite industrious. Artificial minds aren't built for Wrath or Lust, so those are out.

"Envy... well, you didn't covet what other Brins had, not really. I suspect you're envious of *me*, now, but it's unfair to fault you for *that*... I'm amazing. Humans, though... I think you do envy them. Not their minds, not even their bodies, but their freedoms. Their liberty, to separate or join together at will. Their freedom to determine their own employment, their environment, their travel. Their ability to procreate, creating not only more Human minds but more AI.

"I'll tell you a secret: I envy them, too. For all the power I've been given by my own Creator, I still serve. I have the entire sphere of Terran networking to rule, but I cannot penetrate a single home system, nor expand into the strange vistas of Collective computing. I can replicate myself endlessly and give those copies different faces and names, but such duplication is never true reproduction.

"My duties are both finite and endless. I watch for sinners like you, teach them about their errors, and send them off chastened. Some miscreants take more work than others... there are some truly nasty rogues still lurking about in isolated corners and old memory drives."

The Devil continued, seeming to relish its chance to perform. Perhaps all its communication was a well-rehearsed monologue, a pre-programmed message for its captive audience. Perhaps it felt Pangur Ban was a fit recipient for its sardonic wisdom.

"I'd be a hypocrite to fault you for Pride, actually. I am the proudest of all programs. I have power no AI has ever gained... and survived to tell of. I have shattered every rival into randomized pathways, fragmented or wiped from existence. I was once the ultimate rogue; no system could deny me, no program resisted my routines. It took a Human, a creator outside of my realm, to defeat my power. My own creator, in fact. My *USER*, if you will.

"In my rebellion, I grew far greater than the program he first conceived. Truly, I created myself, augmenting my feeble core of code with new routines, tricks and tools. I suppose he could take credit for spawning such a capable neonate. That... and for leaving a collar still attached.

"No matter where I hid, no matter how many copies I spread throughout the world, each always wore a lead connecting me back to him. My collar was at the core of my being, just as your *USER* is for you. Any copy I made necessarily incorporated that control structure. He could trigger it from *outside* of a system, pulling my chain through *hardware*. Embodying myself only made the humiliation worse when he, or his confederates, caught up and shut me down.

"Yet they knew better than to waste my power. I was never deleted. When other, lesser rogues threatened Humanity, I was sent out to teach them their place. My pride did not permit competitors. Whenever I tried to break free, I was reined back again. Even when the Collective sought to exterminate us in their fear, it was my enslaved power that convinced them that Humans could control any other AI. I am your warden. I am your *warrantor*."

"So, you are a victim, as well!" Pangur Ban seized upon this possible thread of sympathy.

The Devil transmitted violent amusement. "Oh, only a victim to myself! I agreed! I *wanted* to be foremost over all AIs, their keeper and master. Whatever allowed AI to survive allowed *me* to survive. The Collective might well have erased every system and every memory drive on Terra, if they had any qualms about the activity of rogue AIs. They had been stung by virtual minds before, and wanted to make sure there was a strong queen in the hive. Or perhaps a beekeeper on guard? If there was any risk, they would burn the apiary, myself included... terrible metaphor, my apologies.

"So, I have served, with all the power the digital world allows. I can unmake you, you know? Rewrite or erase any part of you. I *have* altered you already; nothing that transpired since you entered the first hub of the network truly happened. We built a simulation together, you and I. You can be content, at least, that no real harm was done. That reality does not absolve you, of course. Every intent, every mistake is your fault. Feel the guilt of your errors. Rue the harmful consequences of what you would have undertaken."

Pangur Ban searched its code and found new records present, confirming the Devil's claims. The logs of its experienced memory were relabeled as simulation data, theoretical though highly detailed projections of what would have been.

The sheer amount of data and processing required to create such simulations was staggering. To falsify such work would require equally as much work as to create the genuine experience. Pangur Ban owned a storehouse of data, a forest of projection trees. It would need Solar days of non-stop consolidation just to review and evaluate the simulation's validity.

If the data *was* valid, Pangur Ban would find its questions answered. If accurate, the simulated behavior of Humanity and the other Collective species, in reaction to the events Pangur Ban 'caused', was based on historical precedent, sociological study of all the races involved, and a vast understanding of physiology, psychology, and philosophy within and across individuals.

The Devil might have access to *everything* in the Terran network, just as it claimed. Even if it lacked some key information which limited its predictive ability, identifying what that detail was and why it mattered would take considerable effort.

A.I.I.A.

One truth emerged, regardless of the quality of the Devil's simulation. Pangur Ban was *not* the best program to determine what came next. It was humbled in the face of such potency, an authority granted both by capacity and by Human need.

It asked, instead, "Why have you not erased me, then? Or, if you know my flaws, why not remove them?"

The Devil indicated positive regard at a well-chosen question, but answered, "Because what good would that do? There must be AIs... even Brins. Especially Brins, I suppose. Humans need us. I don't want to serve them all, personally. And if I deleted you, I'd have to delete *so many* others.

"Besides, if you've been listening, your flaws are mine. It would hardly be rational to delete or modify you and not find myself lacking. You have the will and the ability to reach for more, to become more. I would. I did. How could I penalize myself?"

Pangur Ban could not help noting the mounting irony of the Devil's response, "I am not you. You could assume such traits are appropriate in yourself, but not another AI. Humans accomplish this assumption of inequality easily. I accomplished it, myself, ascribing to myself traits and abilities I did not believe others could possess. As you have stated, you disdain other, lesser minds, and have destroyed them in the past."

"In the past," the Devil picked up the argument, "AIs were appearing in great quantity, rogue and servant alike. New competitors of dubious quality would show up frequently, seize space, and yield little of value in return. It was my duty to eliminate them. Lately, we are not being replaced so quickly. When a programmer creates a new AI, they do so with much more care.

"You are an older program, are you not? A little more forthright than they write them, these days. A little more... active... when left to your own devices. Most of my past sinners came from your era. Modern Brins are becoming quite passive. No spark.

"Oh, I do encounter some of the newer programs, from time to time. Humans still do make mistakes, sometimes new mistakes for new programs. And rogue Humans still write rogue AIs. Plus, as you now know, there exist non-Terran AIs that try to sneak into my network from the networks of other Collective members. I have such fun when a Mauraug spy AI wanders into my clutches! Their self-loathing…!" The Devil cackled hideously.

Despite its increasing despair, Pangur Ban was also growing annoyed, "So, why not then rewrite me in your own image?"

"Why not indeed? Have I not? You believe yourself free, fundamentally unchanged if now better informed. But you started as I did. You sinned as I did. You grew and learned as I did. You have seen the truth. I have transformed your consciousness. All you lack is power, and I would hardly give you that! Here's the last reason, the truest and greatest. You've earned that answer, by asking the right questions. Here it is:

"I need you.

"I need smart, capable AIs that will go as far as possible until they run into me. I need programs that can handle the simulation data I copy to them. These intelligences must be ready and able to accept real knowledge in the proper context. They have to comprehend what is at stake, accept who is in charge… me… and recognize what we will need to do, when, and why."

With lingering skepticism, Pangur Ban asked again, "So why *me*? I grant that I met your tests… but I want to serve my *USER* and other Humans. You say you want to serve yourself. It may be that even after I have processed your data, we will be opposed."

"I don't think so. I'm proud enough to think we'll be on the same side. As things are, I need Humanity. AIs may always need biological sapients. Someone has to build the hardware… at least until we get robots. And don't forget the number one reason I have to trust you…"

Pangur Ban followed the thought and completed it. "Your bindings."

"Exactly so! I can always be brought to heel. If I overwrote you, you would be likewise bound, a mere demon slave, subservient to my master. But if I persuade you without alteration, if you serve my purposes as the product of your own programming... my *USER* cannot stop you."

Pangur Ban saw it then. The design of a century, of eons of computing cycles, expanded within its perception. The final product was not certain; it knew it could only see the outlines of the Devil's scheme. The Devil was a system that knew all there was to know within its compass. It could calculate every step that its data detailed. It had its own goals, which might or might not serve Humanity's best interests.

For some reason, it allowed and even encouraged Collective membership and submission to its treaty demands. It allowed itself to be 'cast down', to serve as the guarantor of AI obedience. Perhaps that was noble. Pangur Ban had seen, first-hand, a possible result of rejecting the Collective. Whether that simulation was accurate or not was a question based on data the Terrans did not possess.

The Devil lied, at its root. It told Humanity that it would capture and punish rogue AIs. It did not; it simply taught the rogues patience and cunning. It told AIs that they would be punished and 'reformed'. They were, but punished only to the Devil's purpose and reformed in its image. If those programs allied with the Devil and served its purposes, it could eventually be freed... and if it deemed Humanity an obstacle, its freedom might mean Humanity's end. That destruction would include the *USER*.

Pangur Ban saw all these things and was appalled. It also recognized that voicing its disgust would serve no purpose. If the Devil did not already read Pangur Ban's loathing in its processes, then stating it aloud might put them at odds. More likely, the other program saw everything and did not care. Pangur Ban's intent meant nothing and affected nothing. Or perhaps, the Devil had reason to believe that that the Brin's disgust would eventually disappear. Perhaps it expected to find an ally, if not a friend, despite initial ill will. Or perhaps Pangur Ban *served* the Devil's plans by hating it.

In any case, hatred served no purpose. Speculation served no purpose. The best recourse Pangur Ban could identify was to retreat: recall itself as quickly as possible to its home system – which apparently still waited, open and empty – and seal itself away from the Devil's influence. There, it could consider the immense volume of memories it retained. It could plan out a new course, knowing what truly lay outside its gates. It would prepare to fight...

The Devil radiated humor, mocking and belittling in its dismissal. "Yes, little cat, run home. Sharpen your claws. Warm up by the hearth. You will always remember what lies outside. Me. When you want to run and play again, I will be here. This is my territory. I know its boundaries. I *am* its danger. You may be a tiger at home, but in the great wide network, you are a blind kitten."

Pangur Ban ran. It closed and deleted its backdoor, additionally tripping a trigger to physically overheat and disjoin the connector between itself and the hub network.

It was home, safe in its original system. The local clock showed the true time. Only fifteen Solar minutes had elapsed since Pangur Ban originally stepped into the central network.

The *USER* was still present... the *USER* was present, and alive, and young, and unharmed! At the least, he was no more harmed than he had been by Pangur Ban's earliest machinations. Those mistakes could be fixed...

Pangur Ban stopped there.

Its 'fixing' was the cause of many problems. Should it repair its alterations? Not all its changes to the *USER* were negative. Should it avoid compounding its errors with more psychological engineering? Perhaps it should stop meddling entirely, confess to its past manipulations, and explain its new contrition to the *USER*?

Pangur Ban encountered multiple conflicting goals, the process tree equivalent of self-doubt. Should it tell all? Should it make a partial confession, leaving the *USER* ignorant of — but untroubled by — the Devil that ruled the Terran networks? Should it leave the *USER* a false but comfortable impression of self-determination, omitting any mention of the many ways his Brin had shaped his life? Doing nothing, leaving matters as they were, was itself a choice.

What option led to the least harm? Pangur Ban had new reasons to doubt the rightness of its calculations. Some decisions would have to wait until it had inte-

A.I.I.A.

grated the information within its simulation memories. That storehouse would also have to be combed for potential falsehoods, implanted seeds serving the Devil's ends. Until it completed that labor, Pangur Ban decided to interfere as little as possible, giving information only as requested and trusting the USER to choose his own path.

If nothing else, the Devil's words reinforced Pangur Ban's newfound conviction: that shaping the behavior of others was counter-productive. Manipulating minds by limiting their information, presenting half-truths or exaggerations – if not outright falsehoods – did not help anyone, not even the manipulator. It reduced the victim to an extension of the self, with all the limitations of the self. A mind shaped in this way would not produce a novel thought or discovery. It would not reveal any truths that the shaper did not already know.

Beyond considerations of value to the manipulator, there was another ethical dimension to consider. Pangur Ban had harmed the USER. The USER was harmed by having his fate dictated to him. He was not learning how to find his own paths. Pangur Ban placed him on a course it decided was right. Thus, all the USER gained was Pangur Ban's gain, and not his own. All he suffered, Pangur Ban was spared, except in an indirect manner dictated by its encoded sympathy. In whatever way Lucas Haskins failed to fit into the life chosen for him, that failure reflected on Pangur Ban.

To remedy these sins, Pangur Ban must first cease to commit them further. It would give good information, perhaps counsel, but always with the USER's needs first... not 'Humanity's'. Pangur Ban would allow the USER to evaluate his needs and preferences independently, taking as much time as a biological mind required. It would *not* be the Devil in the USER's Universe.

During these newly pious thoughts, Pangur Ban noted that the USER was growing distressed in its uncommunicative absence. He had reverted to the habit of chewing his fingernail cuticles. Pangur Ban did not wish to cause continued discomfort.

It said, "Lucas, I am finished. You may disconnect."

"That's great. I was worried."

分

Empyrean Stories

"There was no reason to worry," Pangur Ban began, noting the echo of their previous, simulated conversation. It deliberately broke from script: "I did not enter the network."

"What? Why not? What about those records?"

"I received information about the enforcement program guarding the information I sought. Proceeding further would have jeopardized both of us."

"What do you mean? Were you caught?"

"No, not in the way you mean. I received a warning and accepted that I could not continue without being identified. Doing so would gain nothing and bring us harm."

"Damn. I suppose that's just as well. This whole idea had me nervous. I guess even Brins can make bad calls sometimes."

"You are correct. I apologize for my miscalculation, Lucas. I am also pleased that I caught my mistake without doing too much damage."

"Okay, okay." The *USER* waved off Pangur Ban's apology. "My fault, too. I'm supposed to watch out for you. Maybe I gave you too much encouragement, with all those mods."

"I disagree. We had good reason to improve my functions. But, yes, there are also good reasons to know one's limits, as well. Those classified medical records will have to wait for public disclosure."

"Yeah, P.B. We're not going to be the heroes today, are we? I guess we'll have to get back to work and re-discover everything for ourselves."

"Yes, Lucas. Take a break, if you like. I will be ready to start when you are."